WATCH US RISE

WATCH US RISE

RENÉE WATSON   ELLEN HAGAN

BLOOMSBURY

LONDON OXFORD NEW YORK NEW DELHI SYDNEY

BLOOMSBURY YA
Bloomsbury Publishing Plc
50 Bedford Square, London WC1B 3DP, UK

BLOOMSBURY, BLOOMSBURY YA and the Diana logo
are trademarks of Bloomsbury Publishing Plc

First published in the USA in 2019 by Bloomsbury YA
First published in Great Britain in 2019 by Bloomsbury Publishing Plc

A catalogue record for this book is available from the British Library

ISBN: PB: 978-1-5266-0086-8; eBook: 978-1-5266-0087-5

2 4 6 8 10 9 7 5 3 1

Typeset by Westchester Publishing Services
Printed and bound in Great Britain by CPI Group (UK) Ltd, Croydon Cr0 4YY

To find out more about our authors and books visit www.bloomsbury.com
and sign up for our newsletters

For Alyssa Baptiste, Adedayo Perkovich,
Abadai & Bahati Zoboi.
What great joy it is to watch you rise, soar.
My hope is that your voices will never be silenced.
—R. W.

* * *

This book is for my daughters:
Araceli & Miriam Hagan Flores—my hope is that you
will rise up for the things you believe in—always.
—E. H.

AUGUST

1
JASMINE

I'm a month away from starting my junior year of high school, and I just found out my father only has four months to live.

I don't really hear all of what Mom and Dad are saying. Just the important words like "cancer" and "out of remission" and "stage four."

Chelsea is the first person I call. We've been friends since elementary school. I know once I tell her, she'll tell Nadine and Isaac, which is good because I only want to say it once.

I don't know what I'd do without Chelsea, Nadine, and Isaac.

They are the kind of friends who make even the ordinary day fun, who scrape every dollar they can to chip in on a birthday gift. The kind of friends who know the magic of making Rice Krispies Treats, the joy of curling up under blankets to watch back-to-back episodes of a favorite show with bowls of popcorn that we eat as fast as we can and make more. They are the kind of friends that show up at my house—even though I told them not to—to make sure I am okay.

Here they are on my stoop. Chelsea saying, "I needed to see your face."

Nadine hugs me. "We won't stay long . . . unless you want us to. Whatever you need, we got you."

Isaac doesn't say anything. He just looks at me, and I know he knows this feeling all too well. His mom died when we were in elementary school. I was too young to drop everything and rush over to his house back then, but I remember when he came back to school, his eyes empty of the light they usually carried. I remember when our teacher had us make Mother's Day cards to take home and how he left to go to the bathroom and never came back. After school, when I saw him in the hallway, his eyes were red.

Isaac just sits on the top step of the stoop, right next to me, and really, that's all I want. Just someone to be here. Yeah, he knows.

We don't last long outside because it is too hot. Harlem's sun is blazing down on us, so we go inside and sit in the living room. Dad is on the sofa. I sit next to him. No one knows what to say or do when they see Dad. Dad cuts through the tension, acting like his normal self, like today is just a regular sunny New York day. "The young *art-ivists* have arrived," he says. He calls us art-ivists because we're all growing into ourselves as artists and activists. Well, that's what he says.

Chelsea is the poet.

Nadine is the singer (and a pretty good DJ too).

Isaac is the visual artist.

I am the writer and actress.

According to Dad, art is never just art, and since there is so much going on in the world we should be using our art to say something, do something. So when he asks, "What have you all been up to this summer?" and we answer in syncopation with shrugging shoulders, saying *I don't know*, he says, "you mean to tell me you all haven't created *anything* this summer?" He gives us all a disappointed look and says to Chelsea, "Not even one poem?" Before she can answer, Dad says, "And, Isaac, I know you know better." He says this to Isaac because Isaac's grandparents were part of the Young Lords Party, a Puerto Rican civil rights group. They helped to start *Palante*, a newspaper in the South Bronx that told news of the Young Lords. "There is no way you get a pass for not doing anything meaningful this summer," Dad says.

Isaac doesn't even try to talk himself out of it.

Dad keeps fussing. "You all have had so much time to take advantage of the city, and you haven't done anything? *That* is some kind of tragedy." He is smiling, kind of.

"There hasn't been much to do," Nadine says.

Dad shakes his head. "There's always something to do in New York." He starts coughing—hard—and everyone panics, rushing to get him water, tissues. Chelsea especially. "I'm okay. I'm okay. Just allergies," Dad says. "Dying people have regular ailments too." He laughs, but none of us do. Then he says, "I know Jasmine told you. Thank you for loving her enough to come over."

Chelsea wipes a tear from her face. "My mom and dad told me to ask if there is anything we can do?" Her voice sounds frail, and that is never, ever a word I think of to describe Chelsea.

Isaac says, "Yeah, my dad was asking too. He said he'd call a little later."

Dad looks like he is actually trying to think up something. He says, "I'll reach out to your parents if I need to. But, um, I do have something I'd like the four of you to do."

I lean forward. Nadine and Isaac sit up straighter. Chelsea says, "Anything."

"Well, like I said, I think it's tragic that you all are wasting your summer away. I didn't grow up in New York," Dad says. "I wish I'd had this rich culture at my fingertips."

"Dad, what does this have to do with us supporting you?" I ask.

"Oh, I don't need the kind of support you think I need, sweetheart. I need you all to keep on working on you—your education, your life as artists—"

"*Dad—*"

"Just indulge me for a moment, okay?"

I sit back, lean against the cushions.

"Listen, I don't want your pity or worry," Dad says. "I want each of you to be out there learning and growing and discovering. You all are such talented artists—and I mean that. Get out, go see the places that present poetry, visual art, and theater made by people of color. Study some of the greats so your work can be influenced by them."

6

"Are you seriously giving us another summer challenge?" I ask. It's not the first time Dad has sent us on a summer scavenger hunt of the city, but usually it's a little more thought out. Like the time he sent us out with a map of Harlem and challenged us to find historical landmarks and spaces essential to the Harlem Renaissance. We had to take a photo in front of each place as proof. And then there was the time he challenged us to only go to movie theaters that showed independent films. We had to share our findings and write reviews. We're used to him sending us out with maps and a list of instructions. But I didn't expect this today.

"Let's call it the Brown Art Challenge," Dad says.

We all just look at him, blank stares.

"I'm serious. You want to show how much you love and care about me? Keep living," he tells us. "Go out and find some inspiration. Create some art in response to what you see."

Chelsea is the first to agree, saying, "Where should we start?"

And just like that, the four of are sitting with Dad plotting and planning: Bronx Museum, Studio Museum, El Museo del Barrio. "And bonus points to the person who can surprise me with a place that's not on the list," Dad says. "But not the Schomburg Center. That would be cheating." Dad works at the Schomburg Center for Research in Black Culture, and in some ways, it's my second home. I love it when an exhibit is just about to open and Dad brings me, Jason, and Mom to see it before anyone else.

Mom comes home with my brother, Jason, who is eight. He's

been at summer camp all day and doesn't know about Dad yet. Mom gives me a look that tells me my company has to leave. And I wish they could stay because that would delay the moment my brother finds out that our dad is going to die. That would keep in these tears that want to fall so bad. I have been swallowing them since Chelsea, Nadine, and Isaac showed up. No matter how much Dad is trying to keep things normal with his New York City scavenger hunt, no matter how much we all try to laugh at his corny jokes, these tears are here. Pressing against my chest.

Mom says hello to everyone and takes Jason upstairs. She looks tired and worried and not like my mom at all.

Dad stands. "Thank you all for coming over."

We walk to the door. Chelsea opens her mouth, I think to say goodbye, but instead an avalanche of tears falls. And then Nadine starts. Isaac is looking down at the hardwood floors. Just staring.

"It's okay to cry," Dad says. "Feel whatever you need to feel. But listen, everything doesn't have to change just because the cancer is back. You four are starting your junior year. I want things to be as normal as possible, just like every other school year. No matter what happens this year, you all need to stay focused, do your best. Don't let me or any distraction get in your way," he says. "You all are just beginning."

Praise poem for the summer—

by Chelsea Spencer

Here's to the warmth & every yes.
To the grind of summertime
dripping cones & chlorine haze.

Here's to float & exist, show up.
Every challenge accepted. Revival
in East Harlem. Freedom!

Fighters printmaking our past
to light up our present. We're here.
The future of us.

How we study our ancestors.
Dance ourselves into existence.
Electric grind. See the struggles.

Together, we arrive, arms linked,
lungs loud as life. Our hearts
conjuring words

& poems. All of us riding each wave
toward eclipses & ellipses always
the ongoing. Always ahead.

Facing forward. Our lives a ripple
a nonstop jump-start.
Making our mark.

SEPTEMBER

2
CHELSEA

No matter how hard I try, I will never look like the cover of any magazine . . . not that I want to, but well . . . maybe I want to just a little bit. This is the third outfit I've tried on this morning.

There's a pile of T-shirts with my new favorite slogans on them: Cats Against Catcalls (with five super-cute kittens on the front) and one that says Riots Not Diets. I've tried them both on, mixing with biker boots and plaid pants . . . definitely not working. I try another look.

I take out my bag of makeup to choose the right shade of super-lush, kissable liquid lip color. I have been reading that fuchsia is the new "it" color for the fall, and that it really makes your lips pop, but the colors my mom picked up for me last week are not quite cutting it. I turn them over, making sure she got the right shades, and read: Pure Doll and Diva-licious. *Ewww.* The patriarchy is even showing up in the names of my lip gloss? Unbelievable.

The Spencer women have never won beauty pageants. My mom first said that to me when I was in the second grade and my best friend won the Mini Princess Contest at the New York State Fair. I was seven, and I had no front teeth, legs that rivaled a giraffe's, and a fully grown nose. My mom also told me that a beauty contest was a totally old-fashioned way to judge young girls, and it was created by some sexist, corporate machine that was trying to get women to stay in their place.

She used the line again in the ninth grade when I wasn't voted onto the basketball homecoming court. She took me for a hot fudge sundae and told me that women have to learn how to stand out with their words, with their fierce minds, and that courage lived in the actions we made, and not in our bra size or the texture of our hair.

I nodded along and pretended I believed the same thing. The next day I bought a bunch of beauty magazines and started to study what I needed to do to be beautiful on the outside.

That was two years ago. A lot has changed since then.

"Hurry up," my sister, Mia, calls into my room.

"I'm trying, just give me a second!"

"You look fine just the way you are," she calls back, not even seeing what I'm wearing or how I've managed my hair. I have abandoned my intricate routine of gel, comb, mousse, straightening iron, curling iron, and hairspray . . . that would totally derail us getting to school on time. Who cares if Jacob Rizer calls me a frizz factory. *Screw him.*

I kind of like the way I look, and everything feels different and new. I've grown into my nose and learned to embrace my big hair. As for my body, I am currently not at war with it, and even though I still have no breasts to speak of, at least I can sometimes go without a bra. Freedom!

I study myself in the mirror one more time and dab concealer around the patch of zits that have decided to accompany me on my first day. I apply midnight-black mascara to my eyes and a blush that's called Color Me Perfect to my cheeks. *Gag*.

"Almost there," I call back, finally deciding on a shirt that says: Girls Just Wanna Have Fun-Damental Human Rights. I put on a pair of skinny jeans (ugh, labeling pants with the word "skinny" is completely superficial and against everything I stand for, but still . . .) and a floppy straw hat that I got over the summer. Not perfect, but not horrific either.

"I've been ready since seven thirty," Mia brags, swinging into my room. Of course she's been ready for hours. Mia wakes up ready. She's a senior. We're only a year apart, so we're practically required to be close, but since we're so different, we get along pretty well. Mia is just confident. She's the captain of the varsity basketball team and wears her hair cropped short. "You look good, Chels—very feminist-y."

"You both look great just the way you are, and you're both going to be very late to school if you don't pull it together," my mom says, peeking her head in. "Could you please be on time for your first day?"

"Yes, yes, we're on it." I say.

"And remember," Mom finishes, "it's what's on the inside that matters. But you two also look very good on the outside. Now get moving, and try not to focus so much on how you look," she says, walking out.

I grab my book bag and journal, and one of my poems falls out.

Mia grabs it. "This new?" she asks, starting to read.

"Kinda new. I started it over the summer. Figured it would be a good reminder for the year."

Mia reads it out loud.

Advice to Myself
from Chelsea to Chelsea

Be reckless when it matters most.
Messy incomplete. Belly laugh. Love language.
Be butterfly stroke in a pool of freestylers.
Fast & loose.
You don't need all the right moves all the time.
You just need limbs wild. Be equator. Lava.
Ocean floor, the neon of plankton. Be unexpected.
The rope they lower to save the other bodies.
Be your whole body. Every hiccup & out of place.
Elastic girl. Be stretch moldable.
Be funk flexible. Free fashionable. Go on.
Be hair natural. Try & do anything, woman.
What brave acts like on your hips.
Be cocky at school. Have a fresh mouth.

Don't let them tell you what's prim & proper.
Not your ladylike. Don't be their ladylike.
Their dress-up girl. Not their pretty.
Don't be their bottled. Saturated. Dyed. Squeezed.
SPANXed. Be gilded. Gold. Papyrus.
A parakeet's balk & flaunt. Show up uninvited.
Know what naked feels like.
Get the sweetness. Be the woman you love.
Be tight rope & expanse. Stay hungry.
Be a mouth that needs to get fed. Ask for it.
Stay alert—lively—alive & unfettered.
Full on it all. Say yes when it matters.
Be dragonfish. Set all the fires.
Be all the woman they warned you against being.
Be her anyway.

She laughs and pulls me into a hug.

"What?" I ask, pulling away.

"I love your mind, Chelsea Spencer. I'm excited we get one more year in high school together."

"Me too. Just give me one more second," I say, grabbing a stack of beauty magazines from my nightstand. "These are for poetry research. I have a ton of new ideas for my club this afternoon, and I want to share them with my crew." I leaf through a copy, pausing at an article about keeping your hot bikini body through the holiday season, before stuffing them into my bag. "I mean, I just feel like our club needs to get more focused and serious. What's the point of writing if we have nothing important to say, right?"

I grab my phone to call Jasmine.

"Hey," Jasmine says, "are you already at school?"

"No, I'm still home. Mini fashion crisis. Don't judge me. Are you excited?" I ask.

"Yes," Jasmine says. "We have so much to catch up on."

"It has been too long since I've seen you! I can't wait to share my new poems and this essay I've been working on. And I have a new piece you'll love. We are gonna totally shut down the patriarchal systems of oppression this year!" I can see Mia rolling her eyes and pushing me to get it together.

"You're out of your mind," Jasmine says, "and I love it. See you soon."

* * *

We head to school, stopping to get Mia a bacon, egg, and cheese at the bodega, and run into Isaac on the corner of 181st Street and Wadsworth. He's coming out of Esmerelda's Bakery with a bag of doughnuts, and he looks super laid back, as always, wearing one of his signature worn superhero shirts. He's the brainiest guy I know and is built like he could be a linebacker, even though he hates sports. He once told me that football is built on violence and racism, and it is corrupting and exploiting kids in low-income neighborhoods.

"Cool shirt, Chelsea," he says, giving me a quick hug. "Doughnut?"

I shake my head no, while Mia reaches her hand in the bag. She is always hungry.

"Nothing for you?" Isaac asks.

"I'm too nervous, and I kinda feel sick to my stomach," I say as we get closer to the school. I wipe some of the blush off my face. "Do I look like a clown?"

"Are you serious?" Mia asks. "You look fine, Chelsea. Stop freaking out. Just be normal."

"I don't even know what that is," I say. "And I don't know why I'm so nervous either. It's not a big deal. It's just junior year. It's just . . . I guess I just want to make this year matter, and I'm not totally sure how, but it's fine. It's all gonna work out, right?" I ask, reaching my hand in the bag to grab a chocolate-covered doughnut, figuring a little sugar would probably make things better.

"Well, I mean, it's kind of a big deal," Isaac says, pulling out a doughnut and eating it in two bites. "I mean, here's the thing, Chelsea—this is our time. We gotta make the most of our junior year. This is what colleges are looking at, and this is the time we make our mark as artists. We have work to do, I mean serious work to do, so yeah, I get why you might be nervous."

"He's right," Mia says as we get to the front of the school. "That's what everyone looks at for college, so it's true, junior year is when it all really matters." Mia smiles at me and gives me a quick hug before she runs off to join her teammates, who are standing in a huddle on the corner.

"Great," I say out loud, to no one in particular. "I'm glad this is a huge deal and I have a ton to worry about, and that I'm wearing way too much blush and that I definitely wore the wrong outfit." I survey the crowd. Most of the girls are in sundresses and leggings. "Am I the only one who chose a quirky, cool, liberal shirt to kick off the year?"

"Yes," Isaac says, scanning the crowd, "and that's why we love you. Hey, give this to Jasmine when you see her, okay?" he says, handing me the bag of doughnuts and turning to walk into school.

"You got her a doughnut?" I ask.

"I got everyone doughnuts."

"You love her," I say, swatting him on the arm. "You totally love her."

"I totally hate you," he says, smiling.

3
JASMINE

If I had a superpower it would be to make myself invisible.

Not so I could eavesdrop on people's conversations to see if they were talking about me—although that would be pretty cool. I would use it only in moments when being seen causes me to feel like nothing. Like right now. Everywhere I turn, I am reminded that something is wrong with me. Today, it's the posters plastered on the dingy tile walls of the subway station at 135th and St. Nicholas. I'm heading uptown from Harlem to get to school, and this is not what I want to see first thing in the morning.

DID YOU KNOW?
Overweight children may not
outlive their parents.

DID YOU KNOW?
BIG kids become BIGGER adults.

DID YOU KNOW?
It's not about being big boned.
It's about eating big meals.

**FIGHT THE WAR AGAINST
CHILDHOOD OBESITY.**

War?

America is at war with me?

I try not to look at the posters, but it's hard not to, since the print is so big and the chubby kids in the pictures look so sad and helpless.

I walk down the platform so I can get on at the last car. It's usually less full, so hopefully I'll get a seat. It feels good to be out of the house actually going somewhere other than the store for Mom, the pharmacy for Dad, or the park with Jason.

All of August was spent running errands and watching Jason after his summer camp ended. Now that Dad is sick, Mom has me on the tightest leash possible. That whole Brown Art Challenge excursion didn't even happen—not for me anyway. Every time I made a plan to meet up with Chelsea, Nadine, and Isaac, an emergency would happen with Dad or Mom would need me to watch Jason. I couldn't even stay at the summer drama camp the whole time. After all the auditions and fund-raising I did, I had to leave after only the second day because Dad was admitted to the hospital. But now with school starting, my time will be *my* time and I can get back to acting. I'm in the August Wilson Acting Ensemble, a social justice theater club at Amsterdam Heights. We're known all over the city for being one of the best theater ensembles for teens, and we put plays on every year, inviting the whole community. We fill the auditorium every time. We even travel sometimes and get to take special workshops with Broadway actors.

At Amsterdam Heights High School, all students have to

join a social justice club. Clubs meet after school, and it's my favorite part of the day. I could have chosen Animal Rights, Environmental Justice, the LGBTQIA+ Club, or the We Are What We Eat Food Justice Club. Our school is all about social justice and equity, so our clubs all have to have some kind of social consciousness to them. But even at a place like Amsterdam Heights, as a black girl who isn't a size 4, I stand out. Maybe that's why I chose theater club. I like experimenting with my voice, changing my look. It's kind of freeing, being someone else.

The train pulls in, more crowded than I expected. I squeeze myself into the jam-packed car. The door closes just as I bump into a man who is trying to keep his balance by holding on to the silver pole that is covered with sweaty hands of all colors and sizes. The train jerks forward, and I grab on to the man's arm so I don't fall. "Sorry," I say.

"No worries." He steps back as much as he can to make room for me and moves his hand an inch up the pole. I hold on. Then he looks me up and down, leans forward, and says, "I like 'em big."

I really, *really* wish I was invisible.

I refuse to look at him. I just stare ahead at the woman right in front of me whose back is to me, so all I can see is her twisted hair pulled back into a bun. I study her neat bun, wondering how she got it to stay that way.

The train chugs along, stops at 175th Street. I wish I could get off here, but the walk is too long. I can feel sweat seeping through my clothes.

23

The man keeps talking. Maybe to me, maybe to himself. "I sure do like 'em big."

An elderly woman sitting in front of us clears her throat, loud. I look at her—she eyes me to move to the other side of the train. "There's a seat over there," she says, pointing. I can barely squeeze my big body through the maze of people standing. I make my way to the seat, wondering the whole time why this woman told me to move instead of telling that man to shut up.

Once I get to school, I go straight to the auditorium where club sign-up sheets are. We're allowed to change every year, but pretty much everyone chooses the same club, so when Meg Rivers comes up to me and says, "Oh, so you're choosing the ensemble again?" I don't answer her. I mean, I'm literally writing my name on the list when she asks me.

Meg is the best singer in the school—and she knows it, which makes me like her voice a little less. She's white and rich and thin and so many things I am not. She's always looking at me with a smile that seems forced, a high-pitched tone in her voice laced with pity or maybe disgust. I'm not sure. I finish writing my name.

As I walk away to find Chelsea, Meg says to the girl next to her, "It's so brave of her to keep joining the acting club. I mean, it would be one thing if she was just working backstage, but she actually auditions for leading roles."

My phone buzzes with a text from Chelsea. I walk faster. Their laughter trails behind me, lingers like cigarette smoke.

I find Chelsea at the sign for the poetry club. She hugs me

all dramatic, like she didn't just talk to me this morning. I guess I'm more irritated about how today has started than I realize, because Chelsea lets go of me and says, "What's wrong?"

On our way to our lockers, I tell her about the man on the subway and the woman who told me to move. And Meg Rivers.

"I hate it when women reinforce sexism," she says. "And you should have said something to Meg. I mean, she can't treat people that way." Chelsea is all fired up now. "If you don't confront Meg directly, you should at least talk to Mr. Morrison," she says.

"I am absolutely not going to say anything to Mr. Morrison."

"Why not?"

"Chelsea, if I spoke up every time someone at this school said a micro-aggression against me, I'd always be saying something. Sometimes for my own sanity, it's just better to walk away."

When I say this, Chelsea's eyes turn sad and she stops nagging me about it.

I used to be so confused that at a school all about social justice, there was still a lot of racism and sexism—and actually all kinds of -isms. But I guess we're all here to learn how to be better because we know we need to do better. Maybe that's the whole point.

Just before we get to our lockers, Chelsea says, "Oh, I almost forgot. Isaac asked me to give this to you." And when she says Isaac, she drags out the syllables and adds extra emphasis. She hands me a brown paper bag. Inside there's a glazed lemon poppy seed doughnut wrapped in thin, white wax paper. My favorite. I pull it out and take a bite. Chelsea says, "Why is yours so fancy?"

I laugh.

When we get to our lockers, Isaac and Nadine come walking toward us. Nadine's mom is a celebrity stylist, so Nadine wears the most fashionable outfits out of anyone in this school. Her mom is Japanese, and her dad is Lebanese. She speaks Arabic and Japanese fluently, and she has been to more countries than any of us because she gets to travel with her mom for photo shoots and fashion shows.

We all hug each other, and the first thing Isaac says to me is, "How's your dad?"

"Okay today," I tell him. I take what I need and leave the rest of my stuff in my locker. Chelsea does the same.

We all walk together, making our way to our classes.

"What club are you doing this year, Chels?" Nadine asks.

Chelsea says, "Um, if you have to ask I think we need to reevaluate our friendship."

Nadine laughs. "I was just checking to see if any of us switched it up."

"I did," Isaac says.

Chelsea, Nadine, and I all say, "Really?" at the same time.

"Yeah, I wanted to do something different, so I switched from Art and Social Justice to the August Wilson Acting Ensemble."

"Really?" Chelsea sings. She grabs my hand, squeezes it.

Isaac acts like his decision is no big deal, but we all know how much he loves to draw, how he is always doodling in his notebook. "What about you, Nadine?" he asks. "Still doing Music that Matters?"

"Of course. I've already talked with Mr. Hernandez. We're going to analyze songs by Chance the Rapper and Kendrick Lamar and compare the lyrics to poems written during the Harlem Renaissance."

We are midway down the hall when Nadine stops walking. "My class is that way," she points. "See you at lunch." She hugs each of us.

Chelsea says goodbye, too, and goes the opposite way.

Isaac and I keep walking in the same direction. "What class do you have first?" he asks.

"Creative writing."

"Me too," Isaac says.

"With Mr. Valásquez?"

"Yep." Isaac smiles.

"Same English class and the same club? We're going to be together a lot this year," I say. We turn right at the end of the hallway and walk upstairs to the second floor. "Hope you don't get tired of me," I say.

Isaac smiles. "Never."

4
CHELSEA

Three weeks into the school year and I've got my lunch routine down—if I bypass stopping at my locker and go straight to the cafeteria, I can secure a table for me, Jasmine, Nadine, and Isaac before it gets too crowded.

"Beef patty day is officially my favorite lunch," Isaac says, shoving his tray next to mine.

"Every lunch is your official favorite," I say, grabbing one of his onion rings. "But I have to admit, this is pretty good."

Jasmine and Nadine slide into our table with their trays. For the first five minutes, nobody says a word while we open milk cartons, apply heaping amounts of ketchup to our plates, and take our first bites.

"I'm always hungry," I say. "My entire morning is spent looking at the clock and waiting for this moment right here. This is my favorite part of the day."

"Me too," Jasmine says. "We can finally talk. So much is going on—"

"Yeah, I know," Isaac says. "How's your dad doing?"

I know how concerned Isaac is, but I also know that Jasmine doesn't want to talk about her dad all the time. She doesn't want to be known as the girl whose dad has cancer.

"He's fine. Everything's fine," Jasmine says.

"Because I know when my mom was sick, we . . ."

"It's not the same thing, okay, and everything is fine," she says again. I can see the hurt in her eyes, and I put my hand on her back. Isaac can't help but compare the situation to his own mom. He is always asking me what we could be doing for Jasmine. I wish I had an answer. The only thing I know to do now is to change the subject.

"Can we meet after clubs today?" I blurt out, trying my best. "I need a post-poetry-club support group."

"Sure," Nadine says. "Let's grab dinner at Burger Heights. Does that work?" she asks, eyeing Isaac and Jasmine.

"Yeah, that works for me. That'd be good," Jasmine says. Isaac nods that he's in.

* * *

"Welcome, young, brilliant poets," Ms. Hawkins says, opening her door and ushering us inside. She welcomes us in the same singsong fashion every day of clubs. She is the guidance counselor/social worker/lover of poetry who has been our advisor since my freshman year. She really does love poetry in a deep way. The only real problem is that her love of poetry seems to have stopped accumulating in the seventies. Ms. Hawkins was born in the fifties, and I only know that because she mentions it every other week when explaining why it's so important to look to our past and study our history in order for us to understand the work that's happening today . . . but we somehow never quite get to the work that's happening today.

We all pile into her office, which is full of beanbag chairs and has two mini love seats, a round table with a few chairs, and posters of poets everywhere. There is one of Langston Hughes, Sylvia Plath, Phillis Wheatley, and Allen Ginsberg. She has a quote by Audre Lorde on the back of her door that reads: *Poetry is not only dream and vision; it is the skeleton architecture of our lives. It lays the foundations for a future of change, a bridge across our fears of what has never been before.* I love that—I love the thought that poetry can be in our bones, can hold us up and shape our whole lives. I've been writing since the sixth grade, when my mom bought me a fancy gold journal that came with the smallest lock and key I'd ever seen. I wrote every day, and I've kept a journal since then, with poems about my pet goldfish, the weather, food, and most recently, love, heartbreak, and beauty, or lack thereof. I look around the room. There are seven of us total, including two new freshmen who always seem ready to go, with their journals already out in front of them. The rest of us are sophomores and juniors, and one lone senior . . . my nemesis: Jacob Rizer. He's obsessed with forms like sonnets and sestinas. He's always answering every question and making sure we understand what he's doing in his poems. And he's always picking a fight with me, trying to push and get me to react. Sometimes I think it's flirting, but there's always an edge to it. Ms. Hawkins loves him the most, and since it's the last year for both of them—with Ms. Hawkins retiring (finally) and Jacob graduating, I'm pretty sure they're both gonna weep when spring comes. I had hoped there would be more new people this year, but September is almost over, and it seems like poetry is destined to stay the lowest-attended club at Amsterdam Heights. But as Ms. Hawkins always says, *As long as I am here, and at least two of you, then we are considered an official club.*

"I hope you brought your fresh minds and open hearts this afternoon," Ms. Hawkins says, smiling wide. "Let's get started, shall we? I am eager to continue getting to know you, so let's begin class today with the six-word memoir introduction." Ms. Hawkins has spent the last couple of weeks on identity—we wrote an ars poetica, which is kind of like a vision for how we want to live our lives, an I Come From poem, and then wrote a poem about a food that represents us. Mine was about veggie patties from the Concourse Jamaican Bakery—they represent me because they're spicy, unexpected, and completely addictive. I thought it was hilarious, but no one laughed when I read it out loud.

"Get creative—show me something the rest of us don't normally see," Ms. Hawkins says. "And for an example, I'll share my six-word memoir first: poetry is my heart and mind. There, see how easy it is?"

"That's really original," I say, under my breath but loud enough for the freshmen to hear me. Neither of them laughs.

"Your turn," Ms. Hawkins says. "Show me who you really are!"

I look around again to see if I can catch anyone's eyes, but they're already writing. I look at the blank page in front of me. I can't think of anything of write. I try out a bunch: *Hearts and minds are my poetry*. Um, no, that's pretty much what I just made fun of Ms. Hawkins for writing. *I am a big jerk sometimes*. No, too obvious. *From New York, likes to write*. Yuck.

"Okay, time is up," Ms. Hawkins says as her small timer buzzes. "Who wants to share first?"

The two freshmen shoot their arms into the air, as if they've been waiting their whole lives for this moment. I roll my eyes, but then catch myself.

"Puerto Rico lullabies me to sleep," one of the freshmen, whose name is Maria, says first.

"Lovely, beautiful," Ms. Hawkins says. "It tells me something about where your heart is and shows who you are. I can't wait to hear more. Next?"

The class goes one after the other: *Always dreaming of my next meal*, we all laugh. *High rise honey, NYC all day. Illusion is a concept I adore*. I have no idea what that one even means. *Born and raised in Washington Heights*, and *Boogie down Bronx—my first love*. Both solid. I look down at mine one more time.

"I'll go," Jacob says. "For this assignment, I chose to do a haiku instead." He looks around the room. I really roll my eyes this time. "A haiku," he continues, "is a poem composed of three lines, each line containing a different number of syllables, five-seven-five to be exact. Generally, haiku are focused on the small changes in nature. For my example, I chose to do it my way. Here's mine:

Whirr of the subway
The doors open to my life
A train jets away"

"Oh, wow. These are just wonderful," Ms. Hawkins says, standing up and moving to her whiteboard. "Just wonderful and unique. I love them, and I know you will love our standout poets that we're going to study this year."

I raise my hand. "Uh, Ms. Hawkins, I didn't go yet."

"Oh my goodness, Chelsea, I am so sorry I forgot you. And you are like an open book, so I know yours will reveal something." She smiles in my direction.

"Um, so my six-word memoir is: *Rages against the myth of beauty*." I look up at Ms. Hawkins, ready for her to compliment my line.

"That is a good start, Chelsea, and I want to push you even more to take more risks in your writing, and think about the details, the specifics. You are a veteran in this group, so keep that in mind."

"But that is specific," I say, not meaning to start an argument, but annoyed that mine was the only one that got a critique, "and it says something about what I want to push against in the world. I mean, I think that's the whole point of Poets for Peace and Justice, right? That's why we're all here."

"I thought the club was called Peaceful Poets," Maria says, looking at her friend Amaya.

"It doesn't really make a difference what it's called," Jacob says. "It's the poetry club . . ."

"What? No, uh, it *matters*, and it's called Poets for Peace and Justice because we want to use our art to disrupt society and push against what's happening in the world," I say.

"No, that's what you want. The only reason we came up with a name is because you pushed for it so much. No one except you calls it that anyway."

I look up at Ms. Hawkins, who looks uncomfortable and is writing on the dry-erase board. "Ladies and gentlemen, can we please focus on the writing activity for today. No fighting in the poetry club." She has written "William Carlos Williams" and "Emily Dickinson" on the board.

I sigh—loudly.

"Is there an issue, Chelsea?"

"There's always an issue with Chelsea," Sonya Pierce says, leaning toward Jacob, her coconspirator.

"No, there's no issue," I say, glaring at Sonya. "It's just that I thought we could look at some more modern poets this year and think about how they are writing and how we can use those poems as models . . ." No one says anything, so I keep going. "I was thinking about the Nuyorican Poets—I mean, we should definitely take a field trip downtown because we could do an open mic night or the Friday night slam, and learn about Miguel Piñero and Miguel Algarín, or we could study the Black Arts Movement . . ."

"We do study that, Chelsea," Ms. Hawkins interrupts, gesturing toward her books by Nikki Giovanni and Amiri Baraka.

"No, I know, but we could look at how they influence the

work today, like the Dark Room Collective with Tracy K. Smith and Kevin Young. We could look at *June Jordan's Poetry for the People* and think about how the work from the past informs the work today, *now*, that's happening *currently*," I add, to make sure I'm getting my point across.

"Well, you know what I say," Ms. Hawkins cuts in, "you have to know your history to even think about understanding your present."

"That's the whole point," Jacob says, sitting up in his seat. "Clubs at Amsterdam Heights are about learning our history."

"We've learned it," I shout, surprising even myself. "Sorry, I just . . . I feel like we've been really pushing the classics in here."

"Because the classics are what define language and history, they . . ."

"I understand how you feel," I say, lowering my voice just a little. "But to be honest, I don't even know if I agree with all the classics anyway, especially considering that the canon, whatever that means, was created by white men, who published other white men, and basically kept women and people of color out of the conversation as long as possible."

"Oh, please," Jacob says, interrupting me for the second time. "The classics are classics for a reason, okay?" he says, reaching out his hands and holding onto my shoulders like he's trying to school me.

"Yeah, a racist reason. And by the way, stop talking over me," I say, staring directly at Jacob and pulling my arms away.

"Excuse me," Ms. Hawkins says.

I keep on. "Unlike you and Sonya, I don't wanna spend all my time writing super-vague poems about forests and animals and pain," I say. "I wanna write poems that matter, that fight for something."

"So dramatic," Jacob says. "And if you don't wanna be part of the club, or do the kind of work we're doing, then why are you even here?" Jacob asks.

"Yeah, I don't even . . . I don't know. I—you're right. I quit," I say, packing up my bags and stumbling as I gather my journal and drop a copy of *Living Room* by June Jordan that I was going to share with everybody. I pull my hat off the seat behind me. I can't believe I wore a floppy straw hat to school again. I can't believe I just quit, and most of all, I can't believe I just blew up in front of a bunch of people who are now gonna spread the word that Chelsea Spencer has lost her freakin' mind, and even more I can't believe that I still care so much about what everyone else thinks.

"Ms. Hawkins, I'm sorry." I swing my backpack on and walk out. I make it as far as my locker before I burst into tears. "So stupid, so stupid, so stupid," I whisper to myself. I hear a basketball bouncing behind me, and I look up, panicked, since I didn't realize anyone was in the hallway.

"You okay?" James Bradford is standing behind me. He's only the hottest guy in our class. At six feet tall, he's smiling down at me. I look up at his face, perfect teeth, perfect skin, and he's just started to grow his hair out and is wearing it in a short Afro. Meanwhile, my skin is broken out everywhere . . . again . . . and

I'm crying and carrying a journal full of six-word memoirs—not cool.

"Oh, I'm—I'm totally fine, I just, I—I quit the Poets for Peace and Justice club," I blurt out.

"There's a poetry club?" James asks, starting to smile. "That's cool."

"Yeah, it is cool, or it *was* cool. I mean, poetry is awesome, it's a way to rage against society and . . ." I look up and see James laughing. "Shut up," I say, pushing the basketball against his chest and walking away. My crush is the worst.

"No, it is cool! It's cool, Chelsea," he calls after me. "See ya in gym tomorrow. See, gym? That's actually cool."

I smile to myself but don't look back. He doesn't deserve it. But he knows we have gym together. Maybe he's even checking for me in gym class. I love it. I hate myself for loving it, but I love it just the same.

When I get home, I collect all my six-word memoirs and write one whole poem. None of it makes me feel any better.

Rage Against the Myth of Beauty

Love the way you look, always.
Love your wild hair and lungs.
Love your hips and each thigh.
Love your crooked teeth, wide smile.
See your face in the mirror.
See the way your nose erupts.

Call your face a beautiful carnival.
Don't ever read beauty magazines alone.
Who are beauty magazines for anyway?
Trust and know who you are.
Being a teenager really sucks sometimes.
Sometimes quitting is the only way.
To figure out what comes next.

OCTOBER

5
JASMINE

Dad has good days and bad days. Sometimes he is in bed all day and can hardly keep food down and we all walk around the house whispering and the lights are dim because we don't want to wake him, we don't want to make his headache worse, don't want him to feel left out of all the fun we are having or the great meal we are eating.

But today is different. Today the curtains in the living room are open and music is playing and the kitchen is a symphony of lids trembling on top of Mom's best pots, the faucet goes on and off, on and off, and the timer dings. It's seafood night, and Mom is making her special crab boil: crab legs, corn on the cob, andouille sausage, crawfish, jumbo shrimp, and small red potatoes. We haven't done this in six months. We used to have the crab boil on the first Friday of every month. It's tradition that Chelsea, Isaac, and Nadine come, and after we eat the four us hang out for a few hours. The last time we had everyone over, we had an epic karaoke night. Dad and I impressed everyone with our favorite duet, "Ain't No Mountain High Enough." It's one of the few songs we both know all the words to.

I don't know if Dad will be up for hanging out with us after dinner, but at least he's feeling well enough to do this. He is standing next to Mom, making his garlic-butter concoction for dipping. "Do you have enough bags?" he asks me.

"Plenty," I say as I tear a brown paper bag at its seams and spread it out on the dining room table like a tablecloth. I layer the table and make sure every inch is covered. As soon as the food is ready, Mom will dump it on the table and we will feast.

Jason is helping me tear the bags. "Like this?" he asks.

"Yes. But tear the other side too," I tell him.

He rips the bag and hands it to me.

Dad brings his garlic butter to the table. "Is Isaac coming?" he asks.

"Yes," I say, giving him a look that begs him not to start. He's asked me twice already.

"I really like that young man," Dad says.

"I know you do."

He laughs when Mom says, "I think someone else really likes him too."

"*Mom—*"

Jason sings, "Jasmine's got a boyfriend . . . Jasmine's got a boyfriend."

"I do not. Isaac is not my boyfriend."

Jason tears another bag. "He's a boy and he's your friend, so yes you do!"

"Jason, leave your sister alone," Mom says. But she is laughing when she says it, so how serious can he take her?

Jason walks away from the dining room table and goes into the living room. He grabs the remote control so he can play his video game. "Okay, Mommy. I'll leave Jasmine alone."

"I won't," Dad says. "What's up with you two? I feel like I don't know anything that's going on with you."

Tears immediately rise in me, and I push them down. He doesn't know what's going on with me because we hardly talk anymore—not about me. I know he wanted things to stay the same, but how can they? Most of my interactions with Dad aren't conversations at all. Just me coming into their bedroom to adjust the pillows to help him get comfortable or me waking him up every four hours so he takes his pain meds. He asks me about my day, but I just answer with *fine* because usually everything feels so trivial once I am standing in his room, looking at his face that still has life but won't soon.

The buzzer sounds. Chelsea, Isaac, and Nadine are here. Jason runs from the table and opens the door to let them in, and Isaac does what he does every single time he sees my brother. They stand back to back, and Isaac says, "Man, J—you almost as tall as me!"

Jason is an ocean of giggles.

Mom and Dad come from the kitchen to give hugs to everyone. "You all are just in time," Mom says. "I'm about to set everything on the table. Honey, can you get the crab crackers?" she says to Dad on her way back to the kitchen. He follows her, walking slow, but he doesn't make it to the kitchen. He pulls a chair from the dining room table and sits down. He catches me watching and forces a smile. He silently mouths, "I'm okay," but we both know he's not. I go to the kitchen, get the crab crackers and extra napkins.

We all gather around the table to have our Friday night feast. The first five minutes there isn't much talking, just the sound of shells cracking and mouths slurping. Then Nadine blurts out, "Oh, I missed this!"

Leave it to Nadine to state exactly how she feels. She's always admitted when she's sad or angry or jealous. One time, in middle school, when Chelsea and I were debating if we were going to a slumber party or not, Nadine said so matter-of-fact, "I'm not going. I don't like hanging out with those girls." I remember thinking that I'd never just say that. I'd make up a reason why I couldn't go or cancel at the last minute saying I was sick . . . but not Nadine. She's always been honest about her feelings and truthful about what she wants.

Dad says, "I missed you all too." He wipes his hands on a napkin. "And I hope you all don't think that just because I'm missing in action means you can stop with our Brown Art Challenge."

"I got you, Mr. Gray," Isaac says.

"What do you mean by that?" Nadine asks.

"I mean, I've been going out and learning about artists of color." Nadine looks suspicious. "Where's your proof?"

"In my sketchbook," Isaac says. "You already know." Isaac gets up from the table and gets his sketchbook out of his backpack. He hands it to me first. I open it and scoot closer to Dad so he can see too.

After we all ooh and aah over Isaac's drawings, Chelsea says, "One of the bonus places I went to was the Bronx Documentary Center. I wrote a poem based on their exhibit *Spanish Harlem: El Barrio in the '80's* by Joseph Rodriguez. It's not finished yet. But I'm working on it."

"I'd love to hear it when you're finished," Dad says as he leaves the table, kissing me and Jason on our foreheads and Mom on her lips. "You all enjoy the rest of the night. I'm going to go rest." Dad goes back to his room, and I see worry spread all over Mom's face. Worry and sadness.

"We'll clean up, Mrs. Gray," Chelsea says. "Thanks for having us over."

Mom joins Dad in their bedroom.

Jason washes his hands and runs back to his video game in the living room. "Want to play with me, Isaac?"

"Of course," Isaac says.

The day sky has shifted now. It isn't dark or light, somewhere in between. Usually, this is the time of day Mom gets the house settled for the night—giving Dad his evening meds, putting away the dishes, closing the curtains. But I leave them open.

*　*　*

The weekend goes by too fast, like always. Monday is dragging. After lunch we're walking to our classes, and Chelsea keeps complaining about her club. "Jasmine, I'm serious. I don't want to go back to the All-We-Read-Are-Dead-White-Poets Poetry Club. But there's no other club I want to be in. What am I going to do? Ms. Hawkins says I have to decide soon."

"I don't know, Chelsea, what about Justice by the Numbers?"

"You know how much I hate math," she says as we climb to the second floor.

"But isn't it about learning statistics and understanding how those stats impact Washington Heights and other neighborhoods in New York?" I ask. "I think they talk about redlining, gentrification, and—"

"You lost me at statistics," Chelsea says. "Maybe we can start our own club?"

"We as in . . ."

"Me and you."

"I'm already in a club!" I say. "Besides, what would our club be about?"

Chelsea shrugs. "Aren't you tired of dealing with Meg? You could quit the ensemble, and we can do our own thing."

We get to my science class and stop at the door. James enters the classroom, and when Chelsea sees him all of a sudden she is no longer interested in a new club. She whispers to me, *"James Bradford* is in your class? You get to spend an hour with James Bradford every afternoon?"

It is so funny to me that Chelsea says James's whole name like he is a celebrity or a president, or someone important enough to be called by his full name.

"Why didn't you tell me James was in your class?"

"I didn't know you'd care," I say.

"Well, 'care' is a strong word. I'm just, I don't know. I didn't realize you had a class with him too," Chelsea says.

I give her a look.

"What?"

"Um, does Chelsea Spencer have a crush on someone and isn't telling me?"

"I, no. We're just friends—I don't, I don't even know if we're friends. It's just that I have a class with him, and I didn't know you two had a class together too. That's all."

"If you say so," I tease.

"Jasmine—"

"Payback for all the comments and jokes you've ever made about me and Isaac."

"Oh, please. You and Isaac are perfect for each other and just need to admit your feelings. James Bradford and I? We barely know each other."

"If you say so," I repeat. I go into the classroom and sit next to James. Our science class is officially called the Science of Social Justice. Mrs. Curtis is the youngest teacher in the school and is so honest with us that sometimes I wonder if she's supposed to be telling us everything she tells us. I had her last year, and I know there is no holding back in this class. We talk about the intersection of ethics, social justice, and science, and sometimes it gets kind of heated.

On the first day of class, Mrs. Curtis gave us our course

syllabus. The units of study this year will be "The Use of Human Subjects in Medical Research," "The Rising Rates of Childhood Obesity," and "The Environment, Climate Change, and Racism."

I'm excited to talk about all of these except the one about obesity. I hate talking about weight with skinny people. As a big girl it's like I'm invisible around skinny people; sometimes they make jokes or say things like "Oh my God I'm getting so fat," when really they wear a size small or medium, and no one who wears a small or medium—or large, for that matter—is truly fat. They don't know anything about being this big. And really, that's not what bothers me. What hurts is the disgust in their voice, the visceral fear in their tone, like gaining weight would be the absolute worst thing to happen to them. And so I just sit there, kind of in shock for most of those conversations.

It's completely opposite when I'm the only black girl in a conversation. If race comes up, people look to me to answer questions like I know everything there is to know about blackness. So pretty much my whole life is going back and forth from being super visible to invisible.

Mrs. Curtis starts class today saying, "Good afternoon, everyone. We've got a lot to cover today. Let's jump right in. I'd like you to write down four words that describe you. Don't think too hard about it. First four words that come to mind."

I write down my words, and when Mrs. Curtis tells us to share our lists with a partner, I am paired with James.

He goes first. "Um, I wrote down athletic, outgoing, generous, and then I couldn't really think of another one."

"You couldn't think of a fourth word?"

He laughs. "I don't really think about myself like that. I mean, who walks around thinking about words to describe themselves? What, you got like twenty words, huh?"

"Just four," I tell him. But I could have put down twenty. I really could have. I read my list. "Black, female, activist, actress."

"Damn." James leans back in his chair. "Why you and Chelsea always gotta be so deep?"

"What's deep about me saying I'm a black girl who likes theater and who cares about our world?"

James doesn't have time to answer—not that he'd have an answer—because Mrs. Curtis calls our attention back to her and says, "I want you to look at each other's lists and tell one another what you notice," she says. Then she adds, "And no judgments, just noticings."

We swap lists. I go first this time. "I notice that you didn't describe your ethnicity or gender," I say.

He jumps in with, "I notice that you did. You definitely did."

"No judging," I remind him.

"I'm not. I'm noticing that you almost always bring up race and gender no matter what the topic is."

"Well, the topic is to describe myself. So I did."

James says, "If our yearbook has a category for Most Likely to Start a Revolution, you and Chelsea will be tied."

I start laughing.

49

"What's so funny?" James asks.

"Oh, nothing. I'm just *noticing* how you keep mentioning Chelsea. Any chance you get, you bring her up."

Mrs. Curtis stands and calls our attention back to her. "Okay, so how many of you used adjectives that describe your personality?"

Hands go up.

Mrs. Curtis calls on a few students and writes their words on the board: *loyal, funny, generous*. Then she asks, "Anyone use words that spoke to a talent you have?"

More hands go up.

She writes *athletic, musician, poet, singer* on the board.

Then she asks if any of us wrote down words that describe our ethnicity. Not as many hands go up, and the ones that do are all people of color.

Mrs. Curtis puts the cap on the dry-erase marker, sets it down, and sits back in the circle. She gives us another handout. The top says "Science's Role in the Social Construction of Race." Mrs. Curtis says, "Even though race—especially in North America—is how humans get categorized, even though it's what divided our country and sometimes still does, race is a social construct. It's really true that on the inside we're not that different, and in this unit we're going to talk about that."

When the bell rings, James and I walk out together. He says to me, "I wasn't talking about Chelsea a lot."

"And there you go again," I say.

James laughs. "Okay, you've got a point."

"I get it. She's an awesome, smart, beautiful person. What's not to love?"

"Love? Whoa—who said anything about love? Anyway, I'm with Meg."

"What? Since when?"

"Last week."

I hope Chelsea meant it when she said she doesn't like James.

6
CHELSEA

"Ladies and gentlemen, let's go! I want to see you push yourselves to the limit here," Coach Williams yells in our general direction. I say that, because we are all scattered around the sweaty gym floor. It smells like a combination of BO and hairspray, and every time I breathe too deeply, I gag.

"Why would he want us to push ourselves to the limit? I don't even know what that means," I whisper to Nadine, who was forced to switch from band class to gym, since she'd already taken all her music credits. She was totally pissed, but it's currently making my life much easier, since I have someone to talk to when my obsession over James becomes too much for one woman to handle. I'm beginning to think that I am too much to handle, and besides the fact that he looks good and knows that we're in the same class, I have no real reason to even like him—I guess lately, it's giving me something to take my mind off missing poetry club, or clubs in general.

What I definitely don't miss is Jacob Rizer. Every time he sees me in the hallway, he asks me if I miss him, and the other day he called out: "You'll be back." No, I won't. After I quit, Ms. Hawkins told me that I had until the middle of October to choose a different club, and that it would have to be approved by her. She also let me know how disappointed she was, and how much she'd miss my "spunky personality." She actually said those words, which confirmed that Ms. Hawkins doesn't really know me at all, and made me feel way better about quitting. That is, until I realized I had nothing to do after school. So I've mostly been hanging out at Word Up and writing in my journal. It's like my thoughts and ideas have nowhere to go, and no one to listen to them.

"Just lean forward and pretend you're stretching your hamstrings," Nadine whispers back, actually stretching her impossibly long limbs toward me. She is wearing workout clothes, the kind that make you look both athletic and cute, and she definitely looks both.

"Gym is the worst," I say.

"Get ready for the best afternoon of your lives," Coach Williams shouts. He's always speaking in exclamation marks. "We are becoming road warriors this afternoon and turning our cross-country running into cross-city running. We're gonna be taking over Washington Heights today! So I need you all to get laced up and get ready to take to the streets."

"What? No!" I say, a little too loud. A few people look over in my direction.

"Spencer, you can do this! Here's the plan. You each have a partner and a route you'll need to take. This is part workout and part exploration. You will go on an easy two-mile run—each of you will have different paths, some with hills, some with parks, some around the block. It's your job to run fifteen-minute miles and take note of the things you see and hear. It's about creating a relationship with your city and using it as a place to make your body healthy and strong. Are you all with me?" Coach Williams asks.

A few people mumble yes, and a couple of kids on the track team high-five each other. I'm mostly panicked about the concept of running, and especially with some jock who believes that running on city concrete is the best idea on the planet.

"I've partnered you all up, and the list is right here." He unfolds a giant piece of chart paper. "Check to see who you'll be running with and where, and I expect to see you all back here at 3:05 p.m. so we can debrief and pack up for the day. All good?" He gives a thumbs-up and posts the chart paper. I find my name near the top and see "James B." next to mine.

"Who's James B.?" I ask Nadine, looking around the room. I'm sure I'm paired with a freshman who will likely run circles around me.

"James Bradford," Nadine says, looking at me wide-eyed. "Your lover." She smiles. We both look in his direction. He's stretching and hasn't looked up at the paper yet. Maybe I can still change it.

"Shut up. I don't even like him."

"Yeah, keep telling yourself that," Nadine says.

"I can't run with James Bradford. I'll puke before we even get out the door."

"Chelsea, you'll be fine. It's no big deal," Nadine says, trying to soothe my panic.

"That's easy for you to say. You're on the soccer team. You actually go running for pleasure. I only wanna run if I'm auditioning for a horror film," I say, trying to do a self-check of how I look. I'm wearing my old, beat-up tennis shoes and a T-shirt that says: Virginia is for Lovers. I thought it was really cool when I got it at the Goodwill, but now I'm not so sure.

"You'll be fine. Just keep a steady pace and don't say anything weird," Nadine says, patting my back like I'm a toddler.

"Are you serious? All I ever say is weird stuff. Crap, he's coming over."

"Good luck. Break a leg," Nadine says.

"What? You only say that in the theater . . . before a show . . . not before a run. If you say break a leg before a run, then someone could actually . . . oh hi," I say, looking up toward James.

"Let's do it," he says, holding up the route Coach Williams handed out.

Do you know how many times I have dreamed of James Bradford saying *let's do it* to me? Or even how many times I have imagined doing it with James Bradford? Not that I have any real context, since I've only ever been to third base with a boy, and it was on summer vacation with a dude I met at a teen dance party.

We made out on the beach. This is totally not the same thing, and in that case, I never saw the guy again.

"These will be your partners and your routes for the next month, so get used to them," Coach Williams says as if he's reading my mind. *Great*, I think.

"So look," James says, leaning down toward me. "We gotta head down Broadway to get to Columbia Presbyterian, and then cross over to Amsterdam and take that up past Highbridge and Quisqueya Park." He looks at the route closer. "There's a dude that sells coco helado right outside the park. That should prolly be our last stop."

"A coco helado after a two-mile run." I'm liking the fact we'll be running partners more and more.

"It's about balance, you know? Also, go easy on me, 'cause I sprained my ankle this summer, and I gotta take it slow before basketball starts. Hope that's cool."

Did he just ask me if I was okay with us running slow? Amazing. "Yeah, yeah, that's no problem. I mean, I'll have to slow way down, but I can do it." I smile.

We head out the front door and start to jog toward Broadway. We pass the Bon Bon bakery that smells like pastelitos and fresh juice and then the dollar store, loaded with baby clothes, kitchen utensils, and home furniture in the windows. The fruit stand on the corner is overflowing with avocados and papayas, most of them sliced straight through the middle to show their freshness. We pass the Mister Softee truck and little kids already out of school or daycare. They're holding cones piled high with chocolate sprinkles and SpongeBob ice cream bars with bubble gum eyes. I take it all in. We run past the Hot Looks store, where all the mannequins have hourglass figures and massive breasts, and I unknowingly let out a huge sigh.

"You okay?" James asks.

"Yeah, it's just so annoying every time I pass Hot Looks. Also, why is it called Hot Looks? It's so weird." He looks up, and we both pause to catch our breath, eye to eye with the super-curvy mannequins.

"They're hot," James says, and starts to laugh. I punch him in the arm. "What?"

"Okay, fine. They are stereotypically hot. They're like the male fantasy."

"Which is hot," he replies.

"Which is manufactured," I say. "It's absurd to think that all women should look or even want to look like that. It's fake. It's like some bottled, plastic version of women, and it's all on display. It's like this constant message telling us how we should look and dress and be in the world."

"But no one expects y'all to look like that. It's just . . . it's . . ."

"It's just wrong," I say, looking around for more examples. I see them right away when I glance at the magazine stand. "Look at this." He follows behind me, and I can smell him, a mix of cologne and sweat. Why does he have to smell so good? How does his sweat even smell good? "*Cosmopolitan* magazine. This is a magazine for women. *For women*," I stress, "and look at what the cover says: '10 Things Guys Crave in Bed,' and 'Inhaled the

Whole Pizza?—How to Not Gain Pounds After a Pig-Out.' I mean, what is that? And all these magazines are supposed to be created FOR WOMEN."

"Just looks like sound advice to me," James says, and starts to laugh.

I give him a look.

"No, I'm just messing with you. '40 Girlie Moves That Make Guys Melt,'" he reads out loud, "'The New Feminism: Would You Go Topless to Get a Pay Raise,' 'Mind Tricks That Melt Pounds.' Is that real? What does that even mean?"

"What does any of it mean? It's all about getting super skinny, or lean, working out, and then doing whatever it takes to please men. It's a setup! And *Cosmo* is not the only magazine trying to get into our heads." We scan the others. Most of them have super-skinny white women on the cover with some type of headline that suggests that women aren't enough. "I mean, how about some covers that read: 'Food Is Delicious—Ways to Love It'—or oh, oh, 'Ways to Have a Healthy Relationship with Cheeseburgers,' or 'Your Body = Perfection,' or 'Sex—The Way YOU Like It.'" I pause. I can't believe I said that last one out loud.

James smiles. "Those are good lines."

"Yeah, they are," I say, feeling confident. "Maybe I just need to start my own magazine, or club, or whatever, because this is the kind of stuff I really wanna be talking about—the kinds of issues that are the most important—to me, at least," I say, and I start to really think about it. Maybe other girls are feeling the same way as me and hate getting all the mixed messages from the media. Maybe I need to figure out a way to be talking about these issues more, and create a space where learning and talking about women is normal and doesn't get shut down right away.

"I'd read it," James says. "And maybe you can make one for guys too."

"What? It's totally not the same for guys. You all get all the positive messages—you're always celebrated and . . ."

"What? No, the same is totally true for men. You're just not looking out for it." He leans over his legs to catch his breath. "Come on, I'll show you." He runs ahead of me to 175th Street. We weave between people, dodging bicycles, babies in strollers, and old folks taking their sweet time. I smell coffee brewing at Floridita and pass the elderly man who sits in a wheelchair outside the restaurant wearing an old captain's outfit. He salutes me, same as he does every morning on my way to school. The city feels alive to me in a new way this afternoon, and I can't tell if it's because I'm running with my crush, or if it's because my heart feels like it's beating somewhere else outside my chest.

"Here," James says, pointing to the window of the Vitamin Shoppe. "Check this guy out," he says, looking up. "Six-pack abs, insane muscles—I mean, you gotta work for that."

"And maybe take steroids, right?" I ask.

"Yeah, or spend all your time in the gym. All I'm saying is that it's the same thing for guys. We got that pressure too." I give him another look. "Okay, maybe it's not exactly the same." We look in the window at the cover of a *Men's Health* magazine. It reads: "6 Moves for Six-Pack Abs" and "Make Good Sex Great." "I mean, that's a lot." He looks at me, glances at his watch. "Come on, we gotta go if we're gonna get back on time. So just, ya know, think about it—writing some stuff for us."

"Yeah, yeah, I'll think about it," I say, pushing past him to take the lead. We run down Broadway all the way to 170th Street, then take a detour to J. Hood Wright Park to look at the GW Bridge on the first landing. We decide that as long as we get back by 3:05, then it doesn't really matter where we go. The bridge looks massive from our landing, and the Hudson rough and wild below. We talk about our classes—the ones that we actually like, and the ones we're just suffering through. We both agree that calculus can suck it. And we talk about the neighborhood and how we both landed in it.

"I love the Heights. Can't imagine growing up anywhere else," James starts. We're on the way back to school on Amsterdam Avenue, having crossed over for the famous coco helado. "It's home. My grandfather came here from the Dominican Republic, and just stayed. He was a mechanic, and he made enough to send my dad to college and business school, so when my dad made enough money, he bought the shop, and now he runs it. It's home," he says again.

"What about your mom? What does she do?" I ask.

"She's an artist—sculpture mostly and some painting. And she lives upstate—Hudson Valley. My folks aren't together anymore—I'm their only one, so I live with my dad during the week and try to spend weekends with my mom."

"Oh, I'm sorry, I didn't . . ."

"Nothing to be sorry about. They're cool with me, they just couldn't work it out with each other. And my mom hates the city—can't stand the noise and all the people—anyway she likes all that space. She's always telling me I need to spend more time in nature. Always telling me what to do—kinda reminds me of you," he says.

"So you mean she's awesome," I say. James starts to laugh and nods his head. "I think our moms used to be on some Parent-Teacher Association together before your mom moved. My mom thinks your mom is really cool."

"Yeah, your mom's Italian, right? I feel like they were probably swapping recipes for sauce or something."

"You're probably right." I start to laugh. "But yeah, she's Italian, and I gotta say, she's a pretty amazing cook."

"Ah, that's cool. Maybe you'll invite me over to eat sometime?"

I smile to myself, imagining James sitting around the table with my family—how awkward it would be.

"Uh, yeah, maybe," is what I say.

"And what about your dad?"

"Irish. All the way. And my dad's actually a pretty good cook too. And they're both way too religious for me, but that's a whole other story," I finish.

"Ah, I didn't know all that," James says.

"There's a lot you don't know about me," I say. "Could I get a small mango?" I ask the man scooping ice into small paper cups.

James pulls a five-dollar bill out of his back pocket and orders a coconut. "I got this."

"No, no, you don't have to . . ."

"You can just get it next time," he says.

"Ah, there's gonna be a next time?" I ask, feeling confident.

"Yeah, I mean next week when we run again." He looks at me. "What did you mean?"

"What? Um, no, yeah, that's what I meant," I stumble through.

James looks right at me. We sit at the edge of the playground and eat our coco helado while watching people walk by. In my head, I can't believe I'm actually sitting next to a crush I've had for almost two years—and mostly can't believe we got the chance to talk—more than I've ever talked to him. I also can't really believe that our legs are touching, and that I haven't passed out from the electricity. I have no idea if he's even feeling anything at all. I have no idea what's in his head, and I want to so badly.

"Race you back?" he asks, and we both throw our cups out and run.

* * *

On my way home from school, I send Jasmine a slew of texts:

First of all, my legs are insanely sore,
because I ran (walked) two miles.

And do you know who I ran/walked with?

That's right. Maybe you're right. Maybe I am
in love with him. Who knows!?

Where are you? We gotta talk.

Come to my apartment on your way home
from after-school.

I have plans. Big, big plans.

She texts that she's on her way but says nothing about my
confession, and this is exactly why I didn't tell her. I didn't want
her to judge me for falling for some jock like James.

My dad is home early from teaching, and I can already smell
roast chicken in the oven when I walk in. "Smells so good," I call
out, unraveling myself from my jacket and book bag. "Jasmine's
coming over."

"And hello to you too," my dad says, coming over to watch all
my things pile up in the closet. "Is Jasmine staying for dinner?"

"No clue. We have work to do, though."

"Work? Ah, I see, I will stay out of your way," he says, starting to laugh.

"What's so funny?" I ask.

"Chelsea, nothing. You are so sensitive, you know that? I was
just thinking that it's nice that you are so focused . . . all the time."

"Yeah, we have to be, and sensitive is a good thing. It means I feel things."

"Yes, yes, you're right. You go. Work. I will stay out of it. Don't bother your sister, though. She had a rough practice."

"Where is she?"

"She's in the shower," my dad says.

"Are you kidding? Living with one bathroom is the worst situation of my life, ahhhh."

"Really? It's the worst situation of your life?" my dad asks.

"You know what I mean."

"Listen, kid, when you grow up and get your own apartment in New York City, you can get all the bathrooms you want."

"Ha-ha," I say, heading for the remote control and the couch. I watch two terrible episodes of the *Real Housewives of L.A.* Mia joins me for the second, and we laugh at the fights the women get into, and then hate ourselves for getting caught up in the ridiculous drama. Jasmine shows up just as we're about to start our third episode.

"Tell me you're not watching this trash," she says, always taking the high road.

"It's research," I say. "It's so I can make sure we rage against the system so that no one ever has to see a Botoxed face ever again."

Jasmine laughs, teasing me. "But you do see that you're watching it, so that's sort of like telling the network you love it, and you always say that you have to consume the world the way an activist does, and that we need to support the kind of projects that show women in powerful positions, and . . ."

Mia joins in, "And you also always say that this kind of misogynistic dialogue is exactly what puts women at odds with each other. This is the kind of garbage that paints women in a very unflattering and superficial way," she finishes, smiling at Jasmine and making room on the couch.

"Oh my God! Shut up, both of you," I say. "I don't need to hear myself repeated back to me. I sound like the worst."

"Not the worst. It's just . . . it's all complicated," Jasmine says.

"Yeah, this kind of women's rights stuff is real," Mia says. I look up. Mia hardly ever stays around when Jasmine comes over. It's not that she doesn't want to hang with us, but I never think she's interested in the kind of things we are. "Today at practice, Coach Murphy gave us all a talk about playing overseas and in the WNBA. I mean, she basically said that if we wanna go pro, we're gonna make a fraction of what the men make, and you can't make any money unless you put your whole life on hold and play in Poland or Germany or something. I mean, nobody even respects women—and if the WNBA can't respect us, then . . . I don't know."

"Yeah," I say, "that's exactly what I've been thinking!"

"Last year in our Battle of the Sexes unit, I learned that in most careers women make less money than men and aren't put into positions of power nearly as much. The percentage of CEOs who are women is like one percent or something ridiculous like that," Jasmine adds.

"This is what I've been saying."

They both look at me.

"I know I go overboard sometimes, and I know I talk too

much, but somehow I just feel like women's issues and women's rights are just getting buried at Amsterdam Heights. It's like the whole world is focused on women's rights now, and sexual discrimination and sexism, so why is it that our classes aren't talking about it? Our school is more focused on basketball—no offense, Mia—and freakin' music and dance, and a poetry club that is rooted in the eighteenth century," I say. I'm on a roll, so I decide to push ahead. "That's why I'm thinking we quit all our clubs, and . . ."

"You already quit yours," Jasmine interrupts.

"No, I know. But what if you quit yours too, and we start a women's rights club? And we talk about the things we want, and we write about the issues that matter to us. How has Amsterdam Heights gone this long without a club specifically for women?"

"We did have the Equal Rights for Everyone class," Mia says.

"Yeah, but that was for . . . everyone. You're right . . . there hasn't been anything," Jasmine says.

"Dinner's ready," my dad calls out, totally messing with my persuasive flow. "Jasmine, are you staying?"

"Oh, thanks, Mr. Spencer, but I can't tonight. I gotta get home. My dad's cooking," Jasmine says.

"You tell him I'm thinking of him," my dad replies.

"I will, thanks. Chelsea, we'll talk about it tomorrow, okay? Don't worry. We'll figure it out. We always do."

7
JASMINE

When I walk into science class I notice that Mrs. Curtis has rearranged the room. She's put the desks into a circle, and on the walls are big sheets of chart paper with words in the middle: *Ethics, Race, Poverty, Research, Cancer.* There are more words on the other side of the wall, all having to do with the unit we are studying, "The Use of Human Subjects in Medical Research." We've been listening to interviews and reading excerpts from *The Immortal Life of Henrietta Lacks* for the past few weeks to learn about the story of Henrietta Lacks, a black woman whose tissue was used for medical research without her consent.

Mrs. Curtis gives us each a marker and asks us to move around the room to respond to the words on the walls. "This is a silent activity," she says a few times. "As you write your responses, please take a moment to read what your classmates have to say." I look at the sheet that says *Race,* and I write: a social construct with real disadvantages and advantages.

67

I step back and make room for others to write. I stand for a moment and read the other comments.

HAS NOTHING TO DO WITH HENRIETTA LACKS. THIS WAS ABOUT CLASS.

I hate checking boxes that I don't quite fit in.

Racism exists everywhere, even in hospitals.

Under the word *Cancer*, I don't write anything. All I can think of is my dad. I read the words on the sheet. My grandma had cancer. The word "had" stings my eyes, and I walk away without reading the rest.

"Okay, finish the last word you're writing on and come take a seat," Mrs. Curtis says. "I wanted you all to connect to these words in personal ways, not just the scientific ways that we read about." Mrs. Curtis joins us in the circle. "I'd love to know what you are thinking and feeling about the story of Henrietta Lacks. Anyone want to share an excerpt from the book that stood out to you?"

Corrine says, "Black women save this country over and over and never get the credit. That's what I think."

"Word," Monty says. "So true."

"This isn't about race to me," James says. "It's about class, right? They didn't care about this poor woman, and so they didn't treat her body with respect—"

Nadine cuts James off. "Except it was the nineteen-fifties. So just about everything was about race back then, and I'm pretty sure if she was white this would not have happened."

Mrs. Curtis says, "Well, let's name what happened. We're kind of talking around it. Can someone give a recap just so that we're all caught up and on the same page?"

I definitely feel like this is Mrs. Curtis's way of making sure those of us who didn't read the book can at least have some clue of what's going on. I look at Remy, who I know never does the assignments, and raise my hand. "Henrietta Lacks was being treated for cervical cancer. While on the operating table, a sample of her cancerous tissue was taken for research without her consent. She died not knowing her cells were used for research," I say.

Mrs. Curtis asks, "And why is this a big deal? What did that research lead to?"

A girl named Rose says, "Well, because of her cells the medical field had major breakthroughs, like the polio vaccine, chemotherapy, and the creation of drugs that treat leukemia, influenza, and Parkinson's disease."

"Isn't that a good thing?" James asks. "I mean, one woman's body made it possible for so many others to have treatment. The greater good is—"

"The greater good?" I ask. "No, what they did was rob this woman of her humanity. And they were able to do that because in this country poor black women didn't matter," I say. "I mean, the woman who was assisting with the autopsy even admitted that at first she didn't think of Henrietta Lacks as human."

"No she does not. The book doesn't say that at all," James says.

People start reaching for their books, turning pages fast to find the section I am talking about. A girl named Lily raises her hand. "Right here. I found it. It's that part about her seeing Henrietta's red toenail polish."

"Read it, please," Mrs. Curtis says.

Lily clears her throat. "Okay, it says right here, 'When I saw those toenails. . . . I nearly fainted. I thought, *Oh jeez, she's a real person* . . . it hit me for the first time that those cells we'd been working with all this time and sending all over the world, they came from a live woman. I'd never thought of it that way.'"

"See," I say.

I've set off a whole debate now. Half the class thinks the assistant was just saying that working on bodies for the sake of science can desensitize you and that even if Henrietta was a white woman, the assistant would have said the same thing.

Mrs. Curtis says she'll take one more comment and calls on me. "I am not saying it was only about her being a black woman, but I believe that was a part of it. You can't erase her blackness from the story." When I say this, James looks at me like he is hearing me for the first time.

Mrs. Curtis says, "I'd like you all to do a personal response now. Think of the passages we've read and respond to it in any way you'd like. It can be creative—a poem, a visual response. It can be a traditional essay. However you want to respond, I'd like you to do that now."

I think about the conversation we just had. How it took red toenail polish for a black woman to be considered a real person, how she wasn't real just from the fact that she was once a human, a daughter, a mother. I open my notebook and start writing.

Red: A Pantoum for Henrietta Lacks
by Jasmine Gray

1 in case you need proof of black women's humanity
2 know that we bleed too, red.
3 our bodies are not for your experimentation,
   exploitation.
4 we cry and laugh and create
   and sometimes, we paint our nails. Red.

2 know that we bleed too, red.
5 know that we get sick and feel pain, like you.
4 we cry and laugh and create
   and sometimes, we paint our nails. Red.
6 black women are made of flesh and tissue and cells.

5 know that we get sick and feel pain, like you.
7 we breathe and die and leave loved ones behind who
   adorn our graves with red flowers.

6 black women are made of flesh and tissue and cells.
8 this is just a reminder

7 we breathe and die and leave behind loved ones who
   adorn our graves with red flowers.
3 our bodies are not for your experimentation,
   exploitation.
8 this is just a reminder
1 in case you need proof of black women's humanity.

* * *

After school, I go straight to the black box theater. My favorite space in this whole building. It is a place of possibility. I have created so many worlds here, in this room. I have shed myself, put on someone else's truth, and filled this space with my voice, acting as Rose from *Fences*, Camae, the angel in *The Mountaintop*, and Lady in Blue from *For Colored Girls*. I have worked up tears buried somewhere deep within me, tears I didn't even know I had. Somewhere in me there must be profound sorrow since it doesn't take much for me to play the roles that call for heart-wrenching wailing. Somewhere inside me there must be an inherited wisdom from my ancestors since I can muster up the ability to play roles that offer guidance and strength. Dad and Mom have seen me perform, and afterward they always say, "Where did that come from?" and "We didn't know you had it in you." I love releasing all that emotion on stage, but I am ready to release more than sadness and pain.

That's why I get so excited when Mr. Morrison says, "This year, I'd like you all to write your own theater pieces, which includes creating one-acts and solo performances."

When he says this, I think maybe I can turn the poem I wrote for Henrietta Lacks into a monologue or maybe write a solo show about black women—our bodies and the stories they hold. And not just poems of sorrow or angst. I want to write a solo show that has monologues where black girls stand up and speak out. Maybe I'll write something about what happened on the train. But instead of moving to another seat, my character will tell the man to stop licking his lips at women like we're pieces of meat. She'll turn to the other men on the train and ask them why aren't they saying anything, why are they letting a grown man disrespect a girl.

I'll have my characters say the things I couldn't say in the moment.

Mr. Morrison keeps talking. "Now, I know writing your own material can sound daunting, so I wanted to get some creative ideas going by doing a few improv exercises. Hopefully we'll find some inspiration in these spontaneous scenes and can use them to build from."

We are sitting on the floor in a circle, and Mr. Morrison asks us to open the circle so we can make a stage area at the front of the room. Mr. Morrison tells us, "We're going to do a few rounds of Freeze Tag." Most of us get excited about that. It's an improv exercise where two actors are acting in a scene and someone from the audience calls out, "Freeze!" The actors turn to statues, and the person who called out comes in and tags the actor of their choice. Then, a new scene is created, inspired by the body positions of the actors.

Several rounds go, and then Kyle and Kou, two freshmen who are twins, end up in a scene together. They aren't identical, so there's no problem telling them apart. They are working at a construction site, and Kyle is playing a character who is concerned about his immigration status. Both Isaac and I call out "Freeze" at the same time. I tell him to go. Gives me more time to think.

Kyle is frozen as a worker digging a hole with a shovel; Kou has his hands cupped at his mouth. He was yelling that it was lunchtime. Isaac comes in and takes out Kou. He cups his hands in the same way and then starts a new scene. "Yeah, yeah, yeah—here we go, here we go," he chants like he's a rapper and moves around the stage hyping the crowd. Kyle turns his shoveling arms into a wild dance.

The theater fills with laughter. This goes on and on, the two of them on stage dancing and rapping when it is clear they are not good at either. I call out, "Freeze," and take out Kyle, who is frozen with his arms stretched wide. I take on Kyle's pose—my arms are stretched open, as wide as they can go—and realize I have no idea what to do, so I just go with the first thing that comes to mind and reach out to hug Isaac. "I missed you. Welcome home!" I plan on building a scene where Isaac is my son coming home from college break, but the way he hugs me back, the way he pulls me into him and holds on, I think he is making up another scene in his mind.

He lets go and says, "Baby, I missed you too. I'm sorry this job takes me away so much."

I wasn't expecting that. I mean, I've never heard Isaac talk like this. I don't even remember hearing him talk about having a girlfriend. Ever. I have to go along, so I step back from him and say, "I don't like it when we're apart."

"Me neither. I think I know how to solve that," he says. He pretends to go in his pocket and pulls something out. He gets down on one knee. Isaac and I are frozen, looking into each other's eyes, my hand in his hand. I have never noticed how brown his eyes are, so big you barely see anything other than his pupils. So serious, like he has something important to tell me. Sad, like he is holding so much in. Isaac proposes to me—well, his character proposes to my character. And when I say yes, he stands, holding my left hand like he is adjusting the ring.

"Freeze!"

It's Meg.

I hear her voice before seeing her. She walks up to the front of the room and stares at us. "You can let her go now," Meg says.

Isaac lets go of my hand; Meg takes his position. "Here's a little piece for you, and the rest for me." She breaks away from me and pretends to eat something.

I don't get it. I just stand there.

Meg eyes me, egging me to play along. "Don't you just love a good cupcake? Splitting was the perfect idea, since we're both watching our figures."

I really want to walk offstage, go back to my seat, and replay the moment that just happened with Isaac and me, but I know I have to go along. "Oh, thank you. This is . . . this is so tasty. And since we had salads for lunch, this is the perfect reward."

Someone call freeze now, please.

We go on and on talking about vegan this, and salad that. This is the dullest scene I've ever been in. Just when I'm about to call freeze myself, Meg says, "I'm so proud of you for making this choice. Diets are hard, but we're in this together. And please know that you're beautiful, regardless of your size. Don't let anyone tell you that you're not."

Is she serious?

I can't play along anymore. "Who said I didn't think I was beautiful? Why do thin people feel the need to give me compliments like my self-esteem needs a boost? Why do you assume people are telling me I'm not beautiful? You're—"

"All right, thank you. That's good, that's good," Mr. Morrison says.

I keep going. "I don't need your fake compliments, your pity. I know I am beautiful. Inside and out."

A few students start clapping. My heart is pounding, my hands sweaty. We stand for a while like stone statues.

"All right, let's take a break," Mr. Morrison says.

Meg steps away, sits back down next to her fan club.

I sit next to Isaac.

Mr. Morrison jumps up, grabs a stool from the corner of the room, and says, "I am very impressed with what I've seen today. I'd like to develop some of these characters that showed up. Especially yours, Jasmine."

When he says my name, I am stunned.

Mr. Morrison continues, "You were giving us so much sass today. I think we should tap into that energy and keep going in that direction. I love your idea, Meg, of developing a scene around dieting and all the issues you young women face. And, Jasmine, your 'Girl with an Attitude' confidence is perfect," he says.

Perfect?

I raise my hand. "I, um, I actually have something I started in my science class that I'd like to work on." I tell the class about Henrietta Lacks. I tell them my idea of turning her story into a one-act or how I could do a solo piece. Only two people like my idea. And Isaac is one of them. I'm not sure if his is out of obligation.

Mr. Morrison says, "I think that's predictable for you. We haven't seen this side of you and, well," Mr. Morrison looks around the room and says, "I think you may be the only one who can pull it off in such an authentic way."

I can't believe that after the variety of roles I performed, he is most enthusiastic about me acting sassy and being an angry and emotional woman. Even after he's seen me perform Beneatha Younger's monologue—which was all about why she dreams of being a doctor, how she believes giving people medical attention is one of the most powerful things a person can do, how it is the closest thing to being God—all that resonated was sass and anger. And today, after seeing me in the arms of Isaac, after seeing my hand in his, the syncing of our eyes, all that stood out was sass and anger?

"I'm sorry, but I don't think this character would break any stereotype at all. It plays right into it. A big girl on a diet is the plot point for most movies, TV shows, and books. Why can't I just be big and be a character in love? Or be big and be a scientist? I am not playing a role where the big girl has to focus on losing weight."

Mr. Morrison doesn't respond, so I just keep talking.

"Mr. Morrison, if we're writing our own scripts, shouldn't I have some say about the character I develop?"

"I'm not saying no to your idea. I'm saying I'd like you to consider exploring this new voice you discovered today. I think there's some nuance we can build into that character. Plus we haven't seen you sassy and angry—"

"Please stop saying sassy—"

"Yeah, isn't that like, so offensive?" a freshman whose name I keep forgetting says.

"Thank you," I say to the girl.

Isaac adds, "It's definitely offensive."

Having them have my back makes me speak up even more. "Mr. Morrison, I just, I don't know. I'd rather play roles that are not stereotypical for black women. To be honest, I don't even want to play the sad, depressed role this year. The type of character I'm talking about is bold and strong in a way that is less about her struggle but more about her standing up for others and telling their stories. I want to write some pieces that just celebrate and—"

Meg sighs loudly and says, "Oh my goodness, can we just move on? This is not a big deal."

Another student says, "She makes everything about race."

"This is the August Wilson Acting Ensemble," I say. "Everything we do is about race. And it's not just about race for me—I am not going to be the fat black girl playing the angry, sassy woman—"

"Well, lose some weight then," Meg says.

The class erupts, some laughing, most sighing in disbelief that this is actually happening. Mr. Morrison stands. "Okay, all right. Listen, we are not going to be disrespectful here." He walks over to Meg and says, "I think you need to apologize."

I don't know if she does or doesn't. Before she opens her mouth, I'm out the door.

I am halfway to my locker when I hear Isaac calling after me. "Jasmine, wait up. Hold on." He is running down the hall. When he catches up to me, his chest is rising up and down, up and down. He doesn't say anything or ask any questions. He just walks with me to my locker. I open it, get my coat, close it. We walk, and I follow his lead to his locker. He gets his coat, puts his sketchbook in his backpack. We walk to the common area, where there are benches and murals and water fountains big enough for you to put your water bottle under the nozzle without bending it at all. We sit together, me swallowing tears I refuse to let fall. Isaac says, real low, almost a whisper, "I'm sorry that happened."

My phone buzzes. It's probably Chelsea. Clubs will be out soon, and she's most likely wandering the halls waiting for us to get out so we can hang out a bit before going home. I take my phone out.

It's Mom.

"Sorry, Isaac, I have to get this." I answer the phone and barely get hello out.

"Jasmine, your dad was rushed to the hospital. Not sure yet what's wrong." She is talking loud, raising her voice above the traffic and noise around her.

"Where are you?"

"I'm driving. On my way to the hospital. He went in an ambulance. Mount Sinai."

"Where's Jason?"

"With me."

"I'll meet you there."

"All right, okay." Mom hangs up before I can say goodbye.

I stand up, put my coat on. "I have to go," I tell Isaac.

"Your dad?"

"Yeah."

"I'm so sorry, Jasmine. Of all the days." He hugs me, holds me long enough to soften my stubborn tears. They fall quick, seep into his sweater.

I pull away—pull the sadness back in so that by the time I get to the hospital my eyes won't be red. Jason will cry if he sees me crying. I zip my coat. "Tell Chelsea for me, okay? I'll text you all tonight with an update." That's our routine. Every time Dad is in the hospital, I send a group text letting them know what's going on.

Once I'm on the train, I take my notebook out and start thinking up ideas for our new club. Something where all the parts of me are respected and honored. A place where Chelsea can

write the poems she's passionate about, a place where I can perform roles beyond what is already imagined for girls like me.
A club where students actually have a voice. A space where we
can make good on what this school promises to be.

8
CHELSEA

"Ms. Lucas, a club consists of three or more people, so as long as you are here, and at least two of us, then we are considered an official club," I say, repeating the line Ms. Hawkins used to keep the poetry club alive for so long. After Jasmine quit the August Wilson Acting Ensemble, we devised a new plan to start our own women's rights club, figuring that even if it was just the two of us, they'd have to agree based on the rules of *three's a club*. At least, we hoped that was true, and not just some nonsense that Ms. Hawkins made up.

"This is true," Ms. Lucas says. It's the end of the day, and she is cleaning up her classroom, straightening rows of desks, and sorting piles and piles of paper.

"And you are not currently an advisor to any other club," I say, having already done some research on who best would fit as the advisor for our new club.

"Not exactly, but I do look over all the clubs and work as the coordinator, so I'm definitely still involved," she says, then stops, leans on one of the desks, and looks at me and Jasmine, who have interrupted her at the end of the day. "What is it you're looking to do?"

"We want to start our own club—a women's rights club. A group that is dedicated to writing and creating work that supports women's ideas. Our club will write poems, monologues, scenes. We'll write essays and opinion pieces all about women, and get our thoughts and feelings out and into the world," I say, realizing I've been needing this for a long while.

"Oh," Ms. Lucas says, paying closer attention.

"Right now, the world is so focused on women—debating the issues of reproductive rights, paid maternity leave, women getting paid less than men, sexual discrimination issues, harassment, I could go on and on—and it feels like everyone outside of Amsterdam Heights is taking it very seriously, but here, it's like we think the work is done . . . but it's not," Jasmine finishes.

"Well, those are excellent reasons to start a club. I commend you for thinking of this and pushing through with it, but you two are already in clubs that you love, right? I've seen you both on stage for talent night reading poetry and performing. Why would you want to leave your clubs?"

Jasmine looks at me, as if to say *you go first*, so I do. "Well, we have both had some issues with our clubs."

"Oh, why is that?" Ms. Lucas asks.

"Just your average institutional racism and misogynistic attitudes about women and people of color, so—"

"Uh, well, what Chelsea is trying to say," Jasmine interrupts, giving me the look that says *stop talking*, "is that we have a different vision of what the clubs can be. We want something that's more in line with our ideas about women's roles and how we see ourselves in the media. We want to talk about issues that matter to us, and we need a space to do it."

I nod my head, understanding that complaining about our current advisors is probably not the best way to win over a future advisor. Also realizing that I should probably always let Jasmine do the talking. "And even though we both love poetry and theater, we weren't getting the support for the kind of creative and activist work we wanted to do."

"If you'd like to talk about this more, we could work with your advisors and come up with a plan. I would hate for you both to miss out on a solid, already-established club experience. You know, I've always thought that clubs are one of the best parts of Amsterdam Heights, and it's tough to get one up and running, even with all your passion," Ms. Lucas says. I can't tell if she's trying to get us back into our clubs because she really wants to fix things, or if she just wants us to leave her classroom.

"No thank you, Ms. Lucas. The club situations we were in will not work for us this year," Jasmine states. "We want to start a new club. We would love for you to support our vision and be our advisor."

We sit looking at Ms. Lucas, waiting for her next move.

"Well . . . okay then. I'm, um, I will, sure, I'll be your advisor. Let me tell you, I am pretty busy with the coordination of the other clubs, so you two will really have to lead this club and take ownership over it. Do you think you can do that?"

"Yes," I say, a little too loud, getting overexcited. "Yes, yes, we can do it. We're small but mighty. Besides, isn't this always the case—it's only a small group of people who've ever changed the world. The majority is always—"

"Yes, Chelsea, thank you for your enthusiasm. But there are some logistics you need to know about before starting a club. Do you two have a little time right now to go through everything?" We both nod. "Okay, well, the other important thing to discuss is what you want the focus of your club's blog to be about." Ms. Lucas goes to her desk to grab a manila folder labeled: Club Rules and Guidelines. "As you both know, each club has its own blog connected to the school's webpage. I know blogs can feel a little dated to some of you young people, but there have been clubs that really take it to another level, with videos, interviews, personal art, and things like that. There are ways to make them very cool spaces, and I'm sure you two have some ideas! Students or advisors are responsible for uploading essays, photos, upcoming events, and any exciting information about their club to share with the student body. You'll have to post at least once a week. This is a student-led page," she tells us. "I think for poetry and theater, the advisors mostly did the posting, but that's not the case with every club. Some of them have more student authority, and this one definitely will since I can't be at every single meeting. You two will need to set up your own posting schedule and manage the content." She hands us each a sheet of paper and says, "Oh, and you need to sign this."

CLUB RULES AND GUIDELINES:

Be kind to your readers and yourself: don't post anything that you wouldn't want the world to know. What you share on the internet will live in public space forever. Be respectful and try your best not to offend anyone in your posts. Please remember to do the following:

- **Use appropriate language.**
- **Check your sources and do not plagiarize.**
- **Spell-Check and edit your work.**

I acknowledge that breaking any of these guidelines could lead to any of the following consequences:

- **a warning from my club advisor**
- **deletion of a portion or all of the post**
- **temporary or permanent loss of blogging privileges at the discretion of my club advisor**

_____

Jasmine and I sign the paper, and then Jasmine says, "So what should we call our blog?"

Ms. Lucas says, "How about the Amsterdam Heights Collaborative Community School Women's Rights Blog."

Jasmine and I look at each other. My face can never lie. *Um . . . no,* I think.

"Um, well, I think we want something a little more . . . catchy," Jasmine says, saving me.

"Oh, I see. The old lady will just excuse herself from this conversation." Ms. Lucas laughs.

I stand and get a marker to write down our ideas on the dry-erase board. Neither of us can come up with anything much better than the one Ms. Lucas had.

We cross out all the ones we absolutely hate and narrow it down that way. It gets down to Our Words, Our Voices and Write Like a Girl. We decide on Write Like a Girl. "Because people are always trying to silence girls, tell us how to talk, how to act. You know how people say someone throws like a girl or fights like a girl? Well, we write like girls—we write about issues that matter to us," I say.

"Yeah," Jasmine adds. "And it's not about stereotypical girl topics written in sappy, cliché ways."

"Write Like a Girl. I like it," Ms. Lucas says. "Yes, I like it a lot."

I type in the school's log-in page and start setting up our blog.

"So, just to do a quick brainstorm here, every club should have some themes, and I know you two have already been

87

thinking about this. So tell me more about your ideas." She grabs her notebook and pen.

"Well, we want to talk about how crazy movies and TV are, and how they show us in totally crappy ways. It's all a bunch of stereotypes that magazines and shows are serving to us. I want to do a bunch of posts on commercials that just show women as housewives, cleaners, caretakers, and nannies. I want to talk about colorism and body shaming too. Also, I'm thinking about violence against women and social inequality—not necessarily in that order," I say, taking a breath.

"Whoa, okay, good, good. That's definitely a start!" Ms. Lucas says. I lean back in my seat, realizing that I am getting way too hyped and talking way too much.

"Besides the blog, what else do you want the club to do? Any thoughts from you, Jasmine?" Ms. Lucas asks.

"Besides the blog," Jasmine says, "I was thinking we can put on events and performances. I learned a little bit about guerilla art at my theater camp, and I think we could do some of the actions like street performances and placing art and quotes in unpredictable places. I mean, we wouldn't go on the street, but we could do an impromptu performance or chant or something during lunch in the cafeteria," Jasmine says. "I haven't really thought it all out."

Then I say, "Maybe we can also highlight women activists and artists that people may not know."

Jasmine gets excited about this idea. "Yeah. I didn't see any black or Latino playwrights on our syllabus at that summer camp. And only one woman," she tells us. "I can work on that."

Ms. Lucas smiles. "I have to say, it usually takes a while to get a new club up and running, but you two are off to a great start."

"What should our first post be about?" I ask.

"I have the perfect idea," Jasmine says, and I know she's thinking about writing something about the ensemble.

"I am excited to see what you both come up with." Ms. Lucas looks at her watch. "Sorry to be the bearer of bad news, but I have to get home and to start dinner."

"See, Ms. Lucas, there you go, falling into gender stereotypes. Why is it that you have to be the one to cook dinner for your husband? You have to rage against that kind of stuff," I say, joking, but also kind of serious.

"Chelsea, I love to cook, so that's why I make dinner. And as for a husband, I'm married to a woman, so that's not an issue for me." She smiles at both of us. "I think you still have some things to learn about women's rights, huh?"

"Oh, uh, sorry about that. And yes, you're definitely right. We will explore all of that in our club. For sure. And we can meet here in your class for clubs, right? And we're official?" I ask.

"Yes. Chelsea and Jasmine, Write Like a Girl is official."

9
JASMINE

WRITE LIKE A GIRL BLOG

Posted by Jasmine Gray

Acting Like a (Black) Girl

I am a girl, plus.

Which is to say I have to deal with all the sexist
expectations, stereotypes, and assumptions that all girls
face *plus* all the racist expectations, stereotypes, and
assumptions about my blackness.

There is an invisible but ever-present checklist to measure
if I am acting like a girl or not. Boxes built to keep me in my
place. These boxes show up in every area of my life, even in
a theater class where the whole point is to play a role, to
become something imagined. But the more I attend theater

camps and auditions, I am reminded that society has a hard time imagining women outside of roles that keep us in the box of being some kind of caregiver, sex object, or victim (who can only be saved by a man, of course). And then there's the unrealistic beauty standards that we have to measure up to.

And so there is a way to act like a girl: be needy, be emotional, be loving (unconditionally), be superficial, be soft spoken, be beautiful and sexy—which also means be skinny—and also means be white (if you are not white, be a lighter shade of brown).

And there is a way to act like a black girl: be loud, be bossy, be emotionally strong (so strong you never cry or complain because whatever comes your way, you can handle it), be aggressive, be oversexualized, be wise, always having advice and answers (usually for white characters who are playing more important roles than you).

I wish I was making this up. I wish that when I googled "stereotypical roles for black women" nothing came up. But instead, there are several articles and documentaries on the history of representation for black women.

I would hope that at a school like Amsterdam Heights, these roles would be studied and exposed, that we'd create scripts that dismantle these caricatures. I would hope that

91

at a school like Amsterdam Heights, a teacher would never, ever say to a black girl, *"It will be great to develop something where you can really go full-out 'Girl with an Attitude.' We don't really have anyone in the ensemble who can do that as well as you just displayed."*

But sometimes (dare I say most times), hope is not enough. So along with my hope for a better school, let me make this real clear. If I am going to be cast in any plays, one-acts, improv scenes, or staged readings, if I have to play any of the following, I will not "act like a black girl."

1. The Jezebel: The Jezebel is a promiscuous female with an uncontrollable sexual appetite. The Jezebel image also declares that young black women are unlovable and cannot be taken seriously. During times of slavery the bodies of African American women were sexualized in order to demean them. When illustrated, their features were exaggerated to comical lengths in order to make them seem worthless. We have the Jezebel stereotype to thank for every scene that portrays black women only as objectified sexual beings for the pleasure of men. I will never be cast as a Jezebel type. I am too dark and too wide (see "Mammy" to get a better understanding of how this all works).

2. The Sapphire: Evil, angry, and stubborn (especially toward African American men). This is the loud-mouthed, finger-snapping, black female character who often brings

92

the comedic relief. The caricature of the Sapphire has been said to act as a warning or punishment for going against society's norm that women should be passive, nonthreatening, and unseen. (Can I also say that given the hurtful stereotypes that exist, there are actual reasons that might make a black woman angry? I am not saying we should never show the emotion of anger in a scene but to paint us as angry beings—just because? Do better.)

3. The Mammy: This is the overweight, deeply religious, maternal woman (most of the time dressed in unattractive/ plain clothes and usually a good cook). People generally love the Mammy character. She actually has some authority, but she still knows her place. You can find her being a maid for a white family or the sidekick best friend who has all kinds of advice to give (she even has advice on love, even though she has never had a successful relationship).

Let me repeat: I will not "act like a black girl." Not unless she is nuanced. Not unless she is imagined to be more than tired tropes and predictable clichés.

----

terryann liked this

bluesky liked this

bluesky reblogged this from **tonyavwells**

93

bluesky commented: I can totally relate.

hannahbee commented: This also applies to books & movies. I am Puerto Rican and so tired of seeing us portrayed as maids or oversexed vixens.

artandstuff commented: Awesome post!

artandstuff reblogged this

girlsandghosts commented: That theater teacher sucks! Hope he/she reads this.

girlsandghosts liked this

rodneyharvey commented: Wow. Had no idea there were actual names for this. Thanks for sharing.

rodneyharvey liked this

tonyavwells reblogged this

tonyavwells commented: yaaaassss!

harlemchick commented: OMG. This needs to be reblogged a million times!

harlemchick reblogged this

brownpoet commented: something similar happened at my school. Except it came from a "friend" not a teacher. I thought maybe I was being too sensitive, but this proves that I was not. Thank you.

rollerderbygirl reblogged this from **girlsonly**

websteravenue reblogged this from **herheights**

websteravenue liked this

herheights reblogged this

herheights commented: YES!

mixedbag reblogged this

blackdreamer212 liked this

girlsonly reblogged this

girlsonly commented: I am sorry this happened to you. I wish this was the first time I heard something like this but unfortunately I've experienced it and so have other black actors I know. We have to do something.

gweber liked this

gweber commented: This IS doing something.

sunshineandrain commented: So tired of stereotypes in books, film, and theater about ALL people from marginalized groups!! Thank you for speaking up.

gweber commented: I hate the term "marginalized" but I feel you sunshineandrain!

firegirl reblogged this

writelikeagirl commented: Thanks for your feedback. Keep checking back! More posts coming soon.

10
CHELSEA

"Whoa," I say, opening my computer and pulling up our blog site. "Do you understand what a big deal this is, Jasmine? I mean, you posted this last night, and we each posted about it on social media—but . . . we've had more than a hundred visits to our blog site." We are at school early, waiting for Ms. Lucas to arrive and open her classroom so we can work on the blog and create a schedule of posts.

"Chels, can we focus? What are you saying?" Jasmine says, sitting down next to me and eyeing our metrics page.

"What I'm saying is that you posted this at 9:07 p.m. and this morning when I checked the stats, just because I was curious to see if anyone even noticed we had a new club and blog, our site had been visited more than a hundred times, and look—every time I refresh, the number goes up." I refresh again, and the number bumps up to 153. "People are reading it as we speak, which means people are talking about it and visiting, and reposting, and the day has just started! Write Like a Girl is a hit!"

I pause and look at Jasmine. "I'm so glad you wrote it all down. I'm sorry it happened, but I love that you put it all out there. I wish we had named names. I'd love to call out Mr. Morrison and Meg—who does she think she is, anyway?"

"I know," Jasmine says. "She's the worst. I can't believe James is going out with her."

"What!? No! No, no, no. That's not even possible." Of course I know it's totally possible. Meg sings like a freaking angel and is one of the strongest actors in the school. Not to mention she's definitely one of the most beautiful girls at school (I guess I should have started with that one). But she acts like the whole school rotates around her, and according to a handful of her close friends, it does. I can't believe James is into that. So pathetic. But I guess I really have no idea what kind of person he'd be into. I just wish he'd be into me.

"I'm sorry," Jasmine says. She gives me a hug.

"I don't even know why I'm upset. It's not like we're even a thing. I just, I kind of wish we were," I add, feeling like an idiot for liking someone who clearly has no feelings for me.

"I know. I get it." But then Jasmine's eyes fill with tears, and Jasmine never cries.

"What's wrong?"

"My dad's still in the hospital. I feel like nothing even matters because all I want is my dad to be better," Jasmine says. "I just want to feel like myself again."

I put my arm around her, and we sit together, watching the whole school start to file in and wake up.

"Hello, girls," Ms. Lucas starts. "You two are here early. Did we have a plan to meet this morning?" she asks, looking confused.

"No, but we figured if you were here early, we could work in your classroom and plan some things for our club. Is that okay?"

"Of course, yes. Come in." She looks at us again and can see Jasmine wiping away tears on her shirtsleeve. Ms. Lucas walks to her desk to grab a box of tissues. "You still have about fifteen or so minutes until the first bell rings. Stay as long as you want. But can I ask you two what's wrong?"

"My dad's in the hospital," Jasmine says. "He has cancer. Stage four."

"I'm so sorry, Jasmine. I had no idea you were dealing with that. What can we do? How can we help?"

Jasmine shrugs. "There's nothing anyone can do right now." We are quiet, and I really want to think of something to say. Jasmine beats me to it. "On a positive note, the blog is blowing up," she says, and we all start to laugh.

"It is?" Ms. Lucas asks. "After just one post? What did you write? I didn't even read it before you posted it," she says, sounding concerned.

"Oh, it's just your average takedown of Hollywood's extremely superficial and stereotypical roles black women are assigned in the movie industrial complex that is basically ruining our lives," I explain. "She also called out the August Wilson Acting Ensemble, which was named after a prominent social justice playwright, who is black, I might add."

"We know that, Chelsea," Jasmine says.

"Yeah, I know *we* know that. I'm just saying it out loud, okay, because it seems like most of the people in the acting ensemble . . . I'm sorry, the *August Wilson* Acting Ensemble, don't seem to understand that."

"Yeah," Jasmine cuts in. She tells Ms. Lucas everything that happened. "That's the story we didn't get into yesterday when we told you we wanted to start our own club. He basically wants me to act the stereotype, which is just . . . it's just wrong," she says.

Ms. Lucas and I both look up.

"I'm done. I'm totally and completely done," Jasmine says. "I'm tired of being invisible to people who only want to make me visible for specific roles. I'm not playing anyone's parts or ideas of me anymore. And I'm going to say what I need, and I'm gonna start saying what I want too. I gotta get ready for class. Let's talk more later?" Jasmine asks.

"Sure," I say. "So you're gonna see James this morning?" I ask, a little too casually, mad at myself for even bringing his name up again.

"Of course I'm going to see James, Chelsea. I'm gonna see him every morning in the same class that we're gonna have together all year—every day."

"I know, I know, I was just confirming that you'll be seeing him," I respond. "Maybe you should remind him that Meg sucks, and that your awesome friend Chelsea is unique and kind of quirky . . . and hot . . . say I'm hot too. And remind him that Meg sucks," I add again, stumbling over my words.

"Yeah, maybe I will. I'm going to tell him he needs to get his act together and drop Meg and her punk ways," Jasmine says. "I'm going to tell him exactly how I feel. I think I might even tell him how you feel," she says, standing up and packing her bags.

This is a new Jasmine.

"I'm going to start telling people the way it is." She gives me a quick kiss on the cheek, waves to Ms. Lucas who has been staring at us wide-mouthed for the last few minutes, and walks out.

I don't even have time to say, "Hey, maybe don't tell James I'm into him because I'm trying to play it cool," and then I think, *I've never played it cool, so whatever.*

* * *

By lunchtime, the school is humming. I rush through the cheeseburger line, which is the fastest line because it's also referred to as the barf line (though I've never actually barfed from the burger). I go to our normal table and pull out my phone. I've been dying to refresh all morning long, and I see that the number is 452. Four hundred and fifty-two people have read the blog, or at least they've clicked on long enough to see Jasmine's perfect title, and if they saw that, I know they had to read on.

"Hey, I saw the new Write Like a Girl blog. That piece Jasmine wrote was soooo good," Isaac says, crashing into me with his tray. He has opted for the taco boat, piled so high the cheese is tumbling into his applesauce, which, I have to say, looks a lot more appetizing than my meal.

"Uh, yeah, your girl raised the bar about a trillion degrees," I say, stealing a sliver of cheddar from his tray.

"That doesn't even make sense, degrees, trillion . . . anyway, she's not my girl," Isaac says.

"Well, I don't know about that. I heard about the scene, you know . . . the love scene." I bust out laughing.

"What do you mean? What did you hear?"

"Ah, you're curious, huh? I mean, I heard you went full-on relationship in the scene. You, too, raised the bar about a gazillion levels."

He starts to laugh with me this time. "I did, I totally did." He high-fives me, which tells me he's as proud of himself as I am of him. I've always seen Isaac as my brother. How amazing would it be if Isaac and Jasmine actually started dating?

"A lot of good it did, since Jasmine quit the ensemble. I feel like I have you to thank for that," Isaac says.

"Uh, I think you have Mr. Morrison to thank for that. He's the one that lost his mind in class, which in retrospect was perfect, because now we have our own club. Ha!" I say.

"Well, if that first post is any indication of what's to come, I think y'all have some good ideas, and a whole bunch of people are talking about it."

I hear a voice say, "Congrats on your new club." I swivel around in my seat. It's James. He's standing behind me with his tray in one hand and a basketball tucked inside his other arm. It's such a cliché, and I'm falling right into it. "Hey, man," James says to Isaac. They both nod.

"Yeah, it's pretty cool," I say, smiling a little too wide. "How did you . . . how did you hear about it?"

"Jasmine told me all about it this morning," James says, looking right at me. I have no idea what Jasmine said to James, and now I am wondering if she went full out. "She showed me the post, and in my second class, pretty much everybody was talking about it, and when half the basketball team's talking about a blog post from some new club, then you know it's making its rounds," he says.

"Half the basketball team? Really?" I ask, and look around the lunchroom. It's not as if everyone is looking at their phones, but there's something about the intimate conversations and the huddles in small groups that makes me think this post has some staying power, or at least has pushed the conversation in some intriguing ways.

"You wanna sit?" Isaac asks James. I stare in his direction and can't believe he asked James to sit with us.

James looks around the cafeteria for a minute, then back at us. "Sure." He puts his tray down and slides his basketball to balance between his feet. He lets his book bag fall to the side between Isaac and him, and he's sitting right next to me. Our arms would be touching if I'd stop being such a weirdo and start eating, but instead, I take a couple gulps of my iced tea and just sit. His tray has two burgers and a taco resting on top of each one. He starts to devour them.

"You wanna take a breath?" I ask, watching him in wonder.

"What? I'm hungry," he says, laughing. "I gotta get my energy up for our run this afternoon. I was thinking we could just run down to the Chipped Cup and get a doughnut today. We could get there and back easy."

"You two are going out this afternoon?" Isaac asks, looking at me like I've left something out of the story. "I didn't know you two were . . ."

"Gym class. We're running partners until the end of the month," I say, realizing that I'm already kind of sad that the month will end.

"For Halloween, we should run up and down 181st and get candy at all the stores. That'd be so cool," James says, polishing off his first burger.

"So for gym class everybody just gets to run around the city and do whatever they want?" Isaac asks. "Uh, why did I take gym in the tenth grade? All we did was play volleyball and do burpees. This sounds way better."

"Yeah, well, we're really supposed to stick to a specific route, but we have it down to a science, so as long as we go twenty minutes in one direction, we can get back in time. The other day we caught the M4 down to Jackie Robinson Park to get on the swings and check out the empty pool and then raced the bus back." I start laughing, thinking about James fake crying behind me, complaining about his ankle and limping along. "We've been pushing the limit each week."

It's true. Every time we get outside, we come up with a new plan and some new way of seeing the city. And we talk. We talk about when we were little, we tell stories, talk about the things we wanna do when we graduate. Somehow we never run out of things to say. I think that's the reason I like him the most.

"And I also get schooled on about a hundred issues that are important to women today," James says, smiling at me. "What do you always say? Down with the . . . down with the . . ."

"Patriarchy," I finish, punching him in his ridiculously muscular arm. Oh, his arms, another reason I like him.

"Down with the patriarchy. That's what you say, right?" James looks at Isaac. "The patriarchy is a system where men have all the power. And we're a big part of the problem," he adds, showing off.

"Oh, I know all about the patriarchy," Isaac says. "And yeah, man, we're definitely part of the problem."

"Yes, I am so glad you two are seeing the ways of the world. Now if I could just convince everyone else, we'd be all good."

"Well, get to it," James says. "What's the plan for your next post? You were all fired up about all those magazines we saw a couple of weeks ago."

"Oh yeah, it's coming. Watch out for it. And I'm also writing a piece about the princess industrial complex," I say, starting to feel comfortable and finally eating my food like a normal person.

"The what?"

"The princess industrial complex. The way the media convinces us that we should dress and act like royalty so we can get popular, get the guy, have a true love story, and on and on. It's a setup."

"Yeah, well, my mom is obsessed with the princess industrial complex. I think it worked on her, because she loves all that kinda stuff, so I guess I never thought it was that big of a deal," James says.

"Oh, it's totally a big deal," Isaac says, shaking his head.

"I guess for me, it was just a way of telling me how to dress, how long to wear my hair, the kind of things I should say and do. It's this whole idea that if you are a certain type of girl, you will always win, you know what I mean? And it starts when girls are as little as two and three years old," I say.

"No way," James says, finishing his last bite of burger, wiping his mouth, and looking around the cafeteria. I'm not sure what, or who, he's looking for, but I keep on, trying to make my point.

"Yes! My little cousin is five years old, and she thinks that girls should wear dresses, her favorite color is pink, and she told her mom she wants to grow her hair long like Rapunzel so she can swing from it," I say, looking straight at James now.

"Well, that's just good thinking . . . she's using her hair to get places." He laughs. "No, no, I see what you're saying. I do. I just don't know if it's that big of a deal. It seems a little over the top."

"Uh, no, it's real. All the princesses I grew up with were thin and white and had long straight hair—all of them. I didn't see myself in them. That's the main problem—when you don't have any diversity. You just have these generic models of women, marketed and manufactured to little girls all over the world, who are meant to value and want to look and act like those women.

And what if you don't look like them? Then where can you even see yourself?"

"I just didn't think any of it was that serious, but I get your point."

"Yeah, it affects men too . . . because it makes you think that's what a woman is supposed to look like and act like. And all these princess stories include being saved by men—sometimes by a kiss, or sometimes by true love. That sends a message that women literally can't save themselves. Look at freakin' Rapunzel! She has to get a man to CLIMB up her hair to save her. There is nothing more sexist than having a man use a woman's body part as an accessory to save her. It's ridiculous," I say, looking up and realizing that James is standing and gathering his bag and tray.

"I am right there with you," Isaac says. "Because for guys . . ."

"Hey, sorry to interrupt, and I'm totally with this—we can talk about it on our run today, but I gotta get out of here. I'm meeting a . . ." Meg walks up behind James and puts her hands over his eyes.

"Guess who?" she says. He swings around and puts his arm around her waist. It's not really in a boyfriend/girlfriend kind of way, but it's definitely more intimate than anything we've done together.

"You all know Meg, right?" James asks.

"Of course I know them," Meg says. "Isaac is in the ensemble with me. How's Jasmine doing, by the way?" she asks, eyeing me. She knows we're best friends, and also that the blog post was written with Meg and Mr. Morrison in mind.

"She's great," I say. "Totally great."

"Tell her I read her post, and that I had no idea she would take everything so seriously," Meg says, lacing her arm behind James. He looks uncomfortable and starts to walk away, but she pulls him back. "You can also tell her that all stereotypes come from some form of truth. So they had to be based on something. Maybe Jasmine just looks the part."

"Nope, nope," I say. "Stereotypes are all fake. They aren't real. They're a way to lump people together and create bias about a whole group. That was Jasmine's whole point. And it's not a joke. None of it's a joke. Her feelings, my feelings, are real. And if you think it's no big deal, or that stereotypes can't hurt people, then you're part of the problem." I stand up a little too fast and stumble as I try to collect my tray. James puts his hand on my elbow, but I brush it off.

"Me, part of the problem?" Meg calls after me, and I can hear her laugher echoing through the lunchroom as I walk away.

WRITE LIKE A GIRL BLOG

Posted by Chelsea Spencer

Princess Industrial Complex: What I learned from Rapunzel

Women with hair that is a long blond rope
have magical, mystical powers,
& can do most all things,
but they will always need to be saved
by a swashbuckling, bumbling man.
Rapunzel is thin as nothing,
paper fine, petite & small design.
She will learn when you cut your blond locks,
your powers will vanish & your tresses
will turn a drab & lifeless lackluster brown
(and short), but she will learn that princes
sometimes prefer brunettes & all will be well.

But here is what I say.
Hair can be an animal sometimes, up and off
your precious, precocious head in a flash.
Reckless & jumbled.
Women aren't fairy tales, fluff, filtered
into fugitives trapped with their own powers.
My own hair is repugnant & revolting,
it's ruthless & ravenous—relentless

slithering, sly & slick, bodacious & funky.
Yeah, repugnant as in take your breath,
lungs, heart. My hair won't be your swing,
your sexy, can't be teased or trotted out, your
perfection is not attached to my skull. Back up.
You can't dye me to fit your pleasure.
I'm not sunflower, pure diamond, hot toffee,
sparkling amber, auburn dream, platinum crystal,
vanilla icing, caramel kiss, copper shimmer.
I'm not sprayed or straightened. I'm a bully.
My hair's got you in the corner. Don't dainty me,
don't gel me up for the perfect curls.
Don't you dare try to climb up me—to save me.
I'm keeping myself alive just fine.

----

magicalme liked this

loulou commented: The PRINCESS INDUSTRIAL COMPLEX!
WHOA! I have never heard it compared to other industrial
complexes—like this whole system that is set up to teach women
how to act, how to think, what to wear . . . whoa! I am shook by
this! I just looked through my old Halloween costumes and I was
some type of princess from ages 3-9. What is that?! Wish I had
been almost anything else. This is deep!

sophiamays commented: Same for me. I would ONLY wear
dresses in pre-school because I thought girls were supposed to

look pretty all the time, and in middle school, I stopped answering so many questions because I was nervous about being too loud or a know it all. Was princess culture—being quiet, calm, pretty—a part of that?

ginawilson72 liked this

wondergirl commented: Agree princesses are super problematic, and I'm so glad your school has a space for you all to write and critique what is happening in your worlds. Bravo!

writelikeagirl commented: Thanks so much!

firenexttime reposted from sophiamays

brandilux commented: Can I use this in my media class at school? We are studying how racist and sexist the media can be—it's soooooo corrupt! I mean, look at the kind of girls they celebrate and put on magazines and in commercials. Always the same color, always the same size. I know people are trying to change that, and sometimes it happens, but not nearly enough. We need to be out there even more! I've even started to write some of my own poems. Thanks for the inspiration!

writelikeagirl commented: Yes, yes! Please spread the word!

marymarymary liked this

WRITE LIKE A GIRL BLOG

Posted by Chelsea Spencer

Beauty Magazine Redux

Beauty Magazine—Found Poem
You won't be able to stop checking out your butt, but
be brave this year. This year look Hot! Hot! Hot!
in your jeans. Girls Gone Wild (for less). Less
is more. More is more. But how far must a girl go
to get his attention? Hot Abs. Hot Arms. Hot Thighs.
How far must a girl go? His attention? How hot hot
hot is his attention—*girl*? Get Instagram Instaglam. Oh!
Fashion, beauty & body tricks. Tricks of the beauty trade—
Bikini Body Confidence. Blitz. Glitz. Gutz. Butz & Bendz.
Slutz & Steady Glamor. Sexy cuts. Sexy tone. Sexy sexy
sexy sexy sexy sexy. Sexy. Amazing shine. Shine & get
the guy. Get flat abs. Fast. Get major confidence. Get:
Gutted. Get: Guilty. Get: Major stressors. Get smooth
skin fast. Get 625 pretty looks for YOU. Party hair. Party
skin. Party boobs. Party bod. 763 fashion tips & beauty
tricks. Boost your bra size in one month. Boost your hot
flat abs. Boost your confidence. Boost your mood w/
659 new luscious lip colors. Learn to kiss. Sexy like.
This issue is for YOU.
This issue is for YOU—
Is this issue

for YOU? Who

is this issue for?

How about—

Arithmetic paradoxes & aerial coordinates & butterflies.

You won't be able to stop mastering quadratic equations.

This year be Brilliant! Brilliant! Brilliant!

How 'bout his attention is secondary

to your valedictorian speech,

class president, National Honor Society, so let him choke

on your algebraic dust. His attention? Over it. *Girl.*

Get Instagram Instasharp. All knowing & resourceful. Oh!

Coding, programming & tech tricks.

Tricks of the job trade—

Yoga Body Confidence. Smartz. Slickz. Prowess.

Prodigy & Precocity. Brainy moves. Brainy body confidence.

Brainy flair. Brainy knack. Brainy. Brainy.

Brainy. Brainy—Brainy. Get the grades.

Get a 4.0. Get the gold medal in the 400-meter dash.

Get jacked biceps. Get the glory.

Get 625 genius moves for YOU.

763 ways to find & pleasure you. Learn to love

your boobs. Bod. Homage the muscles in your mind.

Boost your IQ in one month. Boost your peptides,

peripheral nervous system. Learn how to be a CEO, CFO,

executive direct like a boss. Do it all Brainy like.

No, this is the issue for YOU—

----

bepretty commented: I am ALWAYS THINKING THIS HERE!!!!!!!!

wahibabeee commented: truth telling—that is all. and you all are on a roll. i am loving all these posts and poems. thanks for starting these conversations. and it's gonna make me look at magazines in a whole different way—it also makes me want to get in the system to try and change it!

marymarymary reblogged this

mattcooper commented: Interesting read—I never thought about this

mslucas commented: This is one of my favorite poems so far—very cool.

writelikeagirl commented: Thanks so much for reading our posts! Be sure to check back often. We'll be posting 1-2 times every week!

tamirb commented: guys have it just as bad—write one for us!

brooklynforever liked this

brandilux commented: YES! I saw a quote in my Media Studies class that said: A Woman's Place Is in the Resistance. And you both are doing it! I looked through some of my mom's home and garden magazines and used your poems as inspiration. Here's mine:

A woman's place is not:

> in the kitchen
>
> or in the garden
>
> or in the bedroom

or cleaning the bathroom

or cleaning the counter.

She's not an Easy-Bake Oven

or a dollhouse

or a doll.

A woman's place:

is in the resistance

is in the existence.

I exist.

writelikeagirl commented: Oh, we LOVE this poem! Thanks for sharing. Maybe when we bring Write Like a Girl to the world, you will come and write with us! Yes! Keep sharing.

jrock liked this

wahibabeee commented: You know I'll be coming back to this blog. This is the only relevant blog at Amsterdam Heights anyway. Who cares about photos of the basketball club or the Environmental Club? This is where it's at!

writelikeagirl commented: Thanks! We're not trying to put any other clubs down, but we appreciate your comments. Come back soon!

WRITE LIKE A GIRL BLOG

Posted by Jasmine Gray

What It Be Like: on being a girl

It be like men telling you to smile when you're all out of sunshine. Like your mouth being more familiar with saying yes than no. It be like hiding sometimes, wrapped in puffy coat, too-loose dress, nothing clinging or low cut. It be like wanting to be seen and not wanting to be seen all at once. Like knowing you have the right answer but letting him speak anyway. It be like second-guessing your know-how, like fact-checking your own truth. It be like older women telling you how to get a man even if they don't have a man, even if you don't want a man. It be like learning how to play hard-to-get, how to entice, how to be sweet honey always. It be like being told you are too sweet, too loose, too woman and not enough girl, too girl and not enough woman.

It be like knowing all the world is expecting you to be nurturer, when maybe you want to hunt. It be like a wild flame trying to burn, burn while everyone else wants to extinguish it. It be like being told it's okay to cry, but it never be like rage unfiltered, anger expressed.

It be like trying so hard to hold everything in: emotion, brilliance, waist. Breathe in always, never let out.

It be like stomach cramps and bloated belly, like cravings and moods that change like spring days. It be like trusting the mirror when it shows you your beauty. It be like trusting your heart when it tells you who to love, who to walk away from. It be like knowing you can always start again, that you can always create and make something because you are made for birthing.

It be like meeting other women—older and younger, living and no more breath. It be like their spirits are inside you, remaking you into something better and bolder every time you say their names, read their poems, learn their legacy. It be like knowing you are what praying women had in mind when they travailed for tomorrow.

It be like knowing you are a promise, a seed.
It be like knowing that without you
planted and watered and nurtured
the world can't go on.

----

alexjsimms liked this
danawashington liked this
bronxbeauty commented: It really be like this! Word.
harlemgirl commented: This poem is giving me life. And I mean that literally. It gives me something to look forward to. It's making me think about how being a girl affects me.

jeremiahbbox commented: My new favorite blog.

lizfreeman commented: The world can't go on without us women! Yes.

jokelly reposted this

sydjohnson reposted this

sydjohnson liked this

wonderworld19 liked this

wonderworld19 commented: This part right here "fact-checking your truth." Girl, yes.

sugarhillforever commented: Why can't I like this a million times? So good.

mslucas liked this

bepretty reblogged this

beme reposted this

jrock commented: I hope you all do something with these poems and posts and not just let them store up online. These words need to be spoken out loud.

WRITE LIKE A GIRL BLOG

Posted by Jasmine Gray

Playtime for Fat Black Girls

I

Mom wouldn't buy me Barbies because there weren't many black Barbies to choose from, and the ones that were painted brown had white girl features and hair, fake girl bodies. Mom made dolls instead, gave me brown cloth dolls with big brown eyes. Dolls that looked like my aunties and the women who sat at the window of Harlem brownstones. Dolls with twists and dreads, pressed hair and hair wrapped in fabric with African print. Dollies made just for me, black. But none of them were fat.

II

The only fat doll I had was a white baby doll that I got from a sidewalk sale. It was something to play with when pretending to be a mommy, something to feed and rock and lay down gently in a crib. The fatness was cute in a chubby, rosy cheeks kind of way. I knew it was okay to be a chubby baby but not a big-boned girl, a fat teen.

I knew my body was not normal.

Not even in make-believe did girls look like me.

III

I was never called on for stick ball. Maybe because I am a girl, maybe because the other kids at the park didn't think a big kid like me could run fast. Maybe that's how I got so good playing by myself in my journal, in my bedroom, in front of a mirror putting on shows for my teddy bears. My imagination was my playground.

IV

I pretended to be Storm and all the women who saved the day in the reruns my grandma watched—Bionic Woman, Wonder Woman. I did not pretend to be princess, in my make-believe I was queen.

V

I played make believe.
I made myself believe.
I believed what I made.
I made me.

----

firenexttime reposted
mslucas commented: Just so good to see this perspective, Jasmine. Thank you!
magicalme commented: So for real. This is my story. Thank you for putting words to my experience.

loulou reposted this

brandilux liked this

wondergirl liked this

sophiamays liked this

sophiamays reblogged this

sydjohnson commented: "I made me." I am thinking about this statement. How do we make ourselves and stay true to who we want to be?

jokelly reposted this

jokelly commented: You two make me cry every time!

11
CHELSEA

"Come in, come in," Ms. Johnson tells us. I am walking, reluctantly, into my STEAM lab, which is my least favorite class. Science, Technology, Engineering, Arts, and Mathematics—um, only one of the words in that sequence is interesting to me. I am an artist—that's who I am, and that's my role in the world. I am definitely not going to be an engineer or create a start-up tech firm and not because I'm a girl, but because I don't like science, technology, engineering, or math. Period. Besides, in the next week, we have an open mic to plan for, and the big Halloween dance, which I cannot wait for. Also, our blog gets hundreds of visits every day. Ms. Lucas said it's easily the most visited and commented on blog in Amsterdam Heights history, and she's serious. She asked us to start thinking about a chapbook or zine component and said she'd help us raise some funding for it. My mind is on Write Like a Girl all the time, so I don't have much energy for STEAM.

Ms. Johnson motions us to take a seat in the big circle of chairs set up around the room. This is not your average room design. I take a seat next to a couple of other juniors.

"Please take a seat anywhere in the circle. There will be one less chair than we have people. I will actually be playing our first game with you all, so just go ahead and sit, and I'll be the first one in the circle." *Great*, I think, *a game*. Ms. Johnson is forever trying to make her classes fun, which usually backfires big-time. We all take our seats—there are about twenty-five of us, all looking around the room wondering what's next.

"First, let's keep talking about why STEAM actually matters. I want you to continue to open your minds about this class. This is about dialogue, critical thinking, and using our information to take thoughtful and exciting risks in our work, to engage in experiential learning and begin to really collaborate and push each other to become twenty-first-century learners."

"Boo," Ramel calls out, laughing. Ramel is one of James's best friends, so I feel like I'm at least one degree from James.

"Ha-ha," Ms. Johnson says, giving Ramel a look. "All I ask is that you keep pushing yourselves in this class. Now, today we are going to break down misconceptions and stereotypes about the tech industry and really take a look at gender and race within these fields. We are gonna take it all apart and figure out how we can fight against these issues."

Now *this* is interesting. I didn't really think about any issues of gender or race in the tech industry, so I sit back and let Ms. Johnson explain the game—besides, I'm all about women getting more jobs and elevated roles—actually becoming CEOs and bosses. And since my semi-fight with Meg, I've been thinking more and more about what I could have said differently, how I could have changed her mind about stereotypes and where they come from, and who they benefit and who they hurt.

"So, this is how the game works. It's called—Do You Love Your Neighbor."

"Yes, but only if she's hot," Ramel calls out.

"Enough, Ramel. And also, that's a sexist statement, so cut it." She gives him a serious look this time.

"Ah, sorry about that," he says, and sits up a little taller.

"Everyone will have a chance to stand in the middle of the circle, and once you're there, you will share something that is true for you, and if that's true for anyone else in the circle, then you will jump up and switch chairs. The person without a chair is the next one up. Make sense?" We all nod. "I'll go first so you can see. And you start it like this. Get ready . . . I love all my neighbors who love science," she says. About five kids actually admit to loving science. They stand awkwardly, and then when Ms. Johnson steps out of the circle and removes a chair, they realize it's a game of death and start rushing to other chairs so they don't have to stand alone in the middle. Alex Perkins, our resident science fanatic, ends up standing.

"What do I do now?" he asks, looking around.

"Think of something that is true for you, Alex, and something that's related to STEAM—let's keep thinking of bringing it back to that, yes?" Ms. Johnson says. "And I have an added challenge. This can't be anything that people can see on the out-side. It has to be something on the inside—something that we don't know by looking at you. I want you all to use this game to reveal yourselves. That's what this whole class is about. It's finding out things we didn't know existed, and unearthing things we didn't know were there." She smiles. It's clear that this is the class of Ms. Johnson's dreams, and the more she talks, the more excited I am about it.

"Okay, so, I love all my neighbors who like to play video games," he says. All the boys get up to move, and a couple of the girls. I stay seated.

"Interesting. Keep an eye on who moves. Did you all notice that more boys than girls moved on that question? Let's keep thinking about gender roles when we think of technology, and also how it starts," she adds.

Everyone gets a chance in the middle. Ms. Johnson pauses after each one to ask us who moved, what that means, and how we can shift our perceptions. She tells us that this game is about breaking down assumptions, and that we should get to know each other rather than making snap judgments. After class I stay to ask Ms. Johnson about sexism in the tech industry, since I think it might be something we could write about.

"Chelsea, please just google 'sexism in Silicon Valley,' and see all the madness that comes up. You will be shocked," Ms. Johnson explains, setting the chairs back up for her next class. "I am so glad you and Jasmine have started the women's rights club—I mean, it's about time! You know, what happens is that people think that there's equality—women can vote, feminism is a hot trend, equal rights for all—and then they gloss over it or think there's no need for a club or for pushback. That's when things start to go off the rails, you know? That's when people stop thinking about harassment and sexism in different sectors. Well, let me tell you, we will be talking all about it this year. There's a big push in tech for women to be telling their stories and raging against the status quo."

"The status quo?"

"The existing state of affairs—the way things are run, basically. And in the tech world, things have been mostly run by men. And it's very problematic. Read the Google memo that went out to all the employees that suggested that women aren't suited for tech jobs for 'biological' reasons, and that they're prone to 'neuroticism'—higher anxiety, lower stress tolerance."

"What?" I say. "You're kidding me. Is that for real?"

"Yes, and no I'm not kidding. Try reading *Gizmodo* for a week. I bet Alex Perkins is reading it. Get in there, Chelsea. The only way to change things is from the inside out."

At the end of the day I find the Google memo. I can't even believe it's a real thing. I choose the most bizarre section, print it out in the computer lab, and start an erasure poem, a poem where you cross off lines to make a completely different point. I love the results, so I decide to post it on our blog.

WRITE LIKE A GIRL BLOG

Posted by Chelsea Spencer

James Damore's Google Memo—An Erasure Poem

Personality ~~differences~~
Women, on average, have more:

- Openness ~~directed toward~~ feelings ~~and~~ aesthetics ~~rather than~~ ideas. Women generally ~~also have a~~ stronger ~~interest in people rather than things, relative to men~~ (also interpreted as empathizing). ~~vs. systemizing).~~
    - ~~These two differences in part explain why~~ women ~~relatively prefer jobs in~~ social ~~or~~ artistic ~~areas. More men may like~~ coding ~~because it requires~~ systemizing ~~and even within SWEs, comparatively~~ more women work ~~on front end, which deals~~ with both people and aesthetics.
- Extraversion ~~expressed as~~ gregariousness ~~rather than~~ assertiveness. Also, higher agreeableness.
    - This leads to women ~~generally having a harder time~~ negotiating salary, asking for raises, speaking up, and leading. ~~Note that these are just average differences, and there's overlap between men and women, but this is seen solely as a women's issue. This leads to~~

126

~~exclusory programs like Stretch and swaths of~~
~~men without support.~~
- ~~Neuroticism (higher anxiety, lower stress tolerance).~~
   - ~~This may contribute to the higher levels of~~
   ~~anxiety women report on Googlegeist and to~~
   ~~the lower number of~~ women ~~in high stress~~
   ~~jobs.~~

----

loulou reposted

magicalme commented: Can't believe someone would even write something like this. Makes me so angry! Thanks for sharing.

mslucas commented: I was just reading about this, and am appalled! So shocking and disheartening. Would love to see more of these erasure poems. Very interesting form!

brandilux commented: Never even knew what an erasure was, and now I'm trying it out all the time. I have even started sharing some of my poems at school, and my teacher asked if I wanted to share at our next assembly. I can't wait. Keep sharing and posting please!

writelikeagirl commented: So glad you're writing. Can't wait to see some of your new poems!

cindyb liked this

elreyes commented: I had the same situation in my STEAM class last year. The teacher only called on the boys in the class, and when a coding program came to our school, he only recruited the guys—he did this openly. He told me he didn't think the girls would be interested, and that there was already a fashion and songwriting program after-school, and we might like those better.

brooklynforever liked this

writelikeagirl commented: So sorry to hear this. Let's keep spreading these stories!

m.barns reposted this

The only way to change things is from the inside out, I say to myself. It's the end of the day, and I love the way Write Like a Girl is shaping up. I'm already thinking about doing a whole series of erasure poems around the tech industry. I'm sure I'll find a ton of material.

"Spencer, should I be worried about you? First, you blow up in the cafeteria, and now you're walking around talking to yourself? I feel like you're starting to go a little crazy," James says.

"Don't call me crazy. That's a way men have been silencing women for decades. Please don't fall into the group of men who put all women who don't fit into their nice and neat little box into the category of crazy. You're too smart for that."

"Thanks," James says, suddenly serious. "Nobody ever calls me smart. Fast, good at sports, hot obviously." He smiles. "But not smart. I like that."

"You're definitely smart. Way too smart to be hanging out with Meg," I say, surprising myself. James doesn't reply. "No, I get it. And just to be clear. I didn't blow up at Meg—she pushed me, and I responded. Calmly."

"Chelsea Spencer is always calm," Isaac says, walking over to our lockers. I smile at him. I know he's messing with me, and he knows how amped up I can get, but I could care less. I appreciate him being here again.

"Hey, those poems you posted are FIRE," Isaac says.

"Oh yeah, I read those. You pretty much take down that whole princess industrial complex you were talking about. I showed it to my mom. She said she knew that loving princesses was not great, but that seeing someone so young talk about it kinda shook her," James finishes. "What I'm saying is, you've finally created some buzz."

"Oh, I already had buzz," I say.

"No, no, you're right. I'm gonna stay thinking about Yoga Body Confidence. Smartz. Slickz. Prowess," he adds. Did James Bradford memorize a line of one of my poems, and is he repeating it out loud, back to me? *Whoa.*

"Hey, man, you going to the open mic on Thursday at Word Up?" Isaac cuts in, and I turn around to give him the death stare. I can't believe he asked James about the open mic, which I am definitely going to, especially since I've been planning to read my "Beauty Magazine" poem.

"What open mic? I didn't even know about it," James starts. "You didn't tell me about that." He looks directly at me. I blush. I know it, and I can't help it. "Are you reading?" he asks.

"Yeah, she is," Isaac says.

"Did you write a poem for me?" he asks, smiling as wide as his outstretched hand palming the basketball.

"Um, no," I say, completely lying since I've written about fifteen poems for him. "Did you write one for me?" I ask.

"Maybe," he says.

Isaac looks at me and shrugs his shoulders. "You should come then. It's a cool scene," he adds, and only Isaac, with his comic book T-shirt that says He Comes from the Future with the Power to Destroy the Present, could convince James to come to an open mic at an anarchist, volunteer-run used bookstore.

"I'd love to hear it . . . if you wrote one," I add.

"Maybe I'll stop by. I'd like to hear you read that poem," he says, and walks away.

Isaac looks at me, takes a bow, and says, "You're welcome."

12
JASMINE

After school Chelsea says, "I need to buy something to wear to the next open mic. Want to come shopping with me?"

Nadine teases, "You *need* to get something or you just want to wear something new for James?"

I laugh. "Where are you going?"

"I was thinking we could walk 125th," Chelsea says.

We get on the train and head downtown to Harlem. Walking up the stairs with Nadine and Chelsea gets me winded because Nadine's legs move like she's in a speed-walking race. When we get to the top of the stairs, we squeeze our way through the people coming and going. A trail of incense fills the air, and from the distance a man shouts out, "Got your oils right here. Got that tea tree oil, got that coconut oil, right here, right here."

We haven't even walked a block before Nadine is stopping at a street vendor's table to try on earrings. "Can I try these on?" she asks the woman at the table, holding up big wooden earrings that look like single teardrops. I would have never picked those up, but they look good on her. Nadine has an eye for fashion, and after all these years of being her friend, you'd think it would have rubbed off on me, but it hasn't.

Nadine tries on five pairs of earrings, looking at herself in the handheld mirror from every angle possible, then decides to get two pairs, the wooden earrings and a pair of oversize copper hoops.

We continue down the street until Chelsea says, "Let's go in here."

We walk into Rubies and Jeans, a store that just opened about six months ago. It's got a high-end feel to it, but the prices are reasonable. There's a mix of casual and dressy clothes, and the atmosphere makes you feel like you are shopping in a classy, trendy boutique even though it's a chain store. Chelsea goes straight to the escalator. "The clearance racks are downstairs," she says. Nadine and I follow her, and when we get off the escalator, Chelsea walks over to the rack under the Forty Percent Off sign. She pulls a bunch of tops and jeans off the rack and tosses them over her arm. Nadine is looking through the bins of jewelry, picking out rings and bracelets. "I'm going to try these on. Be right back," Chelsea says.

"Okay." I roam around the store looking through the sea of clothes and see a section far back on the right side of the room with a sign that says Plus Sizes. I didn't even know this store had clothes that would fit me. I walk over to the plus size section, wondering why my sizes have to be in a special section of the store and not mixed in with the other sizes. There is a definite divide, as if a shirt with a 3X tag will contaminate the other clothes. I look through the clothes—there's not much to choose from. Just two racks compared to a whole store full of options for thinner girls. Just as I pick up a sweater to try on, I see the advertisement on the wall. A model with full cheeks and curvy hips is standing with that half-smile, half-serious look that models give. In a room full of fat people, she'd be considered thin. The caption under her half-smiling, half-serious face says: *Rubies and Jeans Plus: Because every girl deserves to look beautiful.*

A store clerk sees me and says, "Not finding what you're looking for? We've got a bigger selection of plus size options online. Free return if it doesn't fit." She gives me a sympathetic smile and walks away.

Online? Why can't I try on the clothes here in the store? Why are these two racks hidden in the way back of the store?

I read the ad again: *Rubies and Jeans Plus: Because every girl deserves to look beautiful.* I think about the word "deserves" and wonder what they mean by it. How about: I am beautiful. The way I am. For a moment—just a moment—I think about taking out my black Sharpie marker and rewriting the statement:

Because every girl is beautiful.

Because every body is beautiful.

And then I think about crossing out the word "beautiful," because what does that even mean? This is a clothing store. It's just clothes. Wouldn't that be a good ad?

Rubies and Jeans: It's just clothes. Come try something on.

I look back at the poster one more time before walking away.

I study the girl's body. She isn't thin, but she is definitely not a big girl like me. I wonder why girls with bodies like mine can't even model the clothes that are made for us. Most times when I see body types like mine on advertisements, they are on posters like the ones in the subway—big body, sad face. Sometimes they are the *before* picture in a weight-loss success story, but bodies like mine aren't often seen with happy faces, stylish clothes. I put the sweater back on the rack. I don't really need anything anyway. I always waste money when I'm shopping with Chelsea. While she's trying and buying clothes, I usually stick to the accessories section looking for earrings, things to put in my hair, or cute wallets. That's usually the option for a big girl in most stores. And I think maybe I buy something every time because I want to feel normal, don't want Chelsea asking, "Why aren't you getting something?" It's been this way since the sixth grade. The first time we went shopping together, I remember trailing behind Chelsea, going rack to rack, Chelsea's arms full of options, mine empty. Chelsea noticed I wasn't picking out anything to try on and she said, "What's the matter, not finding anything you like?" I knew in that moment that she didn't even realize that I actually *can't* get anything from the stores she shops at. She kept on asking me, "You're not going to get anything?" And so at the counter when she was paying for her clothes, I picked up a pomegranate-mint lip gloss. I think I only used it once.

I walk over to the dressing room. Chelsea is still trying on clothes, and now Nadine is in the room next to her. I sit on a chair in the waiting area, scrolling through my phone, not really looking at anything important. When Chelsea and Nadine come out of the dressing rooms, they both have a handful of clothes in their arms. They stand in line, buy them, and we leave. On the way out of the store, Chelsea says, "I think this is my new favorite store."

* * *

At home, it's just Dad and me. Mom and Jason are at his karate practice. I start making dinner so when Mom gets home that's one less thing she'll have to do. Dad comes into the kitchen just as I am filling a pot with water.

"What are you making?" he asks.

"Spaghetti."

He reaches up on the top shelf and takes down the glass jar that has dry noodles in it. The jar is half-empty, so I can hear the noodles shift and rub up against each other, sounding like the music shakers Mr. Morrison has in the prop box at school.

"Thank you," I say. I could have got it down myself. Well, I would have had to use a stool, but I could have. Dad walks all over the kitchen gathering ingredients and setting out the dishes I will need. "You don't have to help, Dad. Just sit here and keep me company." The more he exerts energy, the more tired and miserable he'll feel tonight.

"I'm okay, Jasmine. I'm having a good day today." He chops garlic on the cutting board, then opens a can of fire-roasted tomatoes. None of us are the best cooks, but we can doctor anything up and make it taste good. We buy spaghetti sauce from the market and add our own stuff to it. Dad works on the sauce while I break the noodles in two so I can dump them in the boiling water. "You don't have to be scared of me, Jasmine. I'm not going to break."

"But you're going to die." I didn't even mean to say that. It just came out as quick and easy as the tears streaming down my face. The steam from the hot water hits my face, and I don't move. "Sorry—I—"

"Don't apologize," Dad says. "It's true. Eventually, I'm going to die." He sprinkles salt in the boiling pot of noodles, then stirs the simmering pan of sauce. "But not today. I am not going to die today. Today we are cooking together, and we'll eat dinner. And I'll probably eat too much but still want some ice cream, and your mom will fuss at me, but we'll share a bowl anyway. And since it's Friday, maybe we'll watch a movie tonight, the four of us. Something Jason can handle, of course. That's what's happening tonight."

I step back from the stove, trying so hard to hold in my sadness, but it spills out of me. Dad puts the spoon down, turns the burner all the way to simmer, and takes me in his arms. He lets me get it all out, and over and over he tells me, "It'll happen. And there's nothing we can do about it. But not tonight. Not tonight, sweetheart."

13
CHELSEA

Isaac and I show up for the open mic just in time. Word Up hosts a Teens Only open mic once a month, and it starts promptly at seven p.m. They are pretty strict that it's twenty performers only, and I say performers loosely because you're pretty much allowed to do anything on stage. I've seen people juggle, read monologues, perform with their dogs, sing a cappella, swallow fire (that one was actually banned from the bookstore—understandably), but you get the idea.

Nadine always brings her phone and connects to the speaker system. Currently she is on an old-school eighties and nineties kick, so Prince and TLC are in heavy rotation. Tonight she's wearing her super-short hair slicked straight back. She has five earrings in her left ear and one in her right that holds a long feather that rests on her shoulder like a bird. She has a bright purple scarf wrapped around her waist like a skirt and a neon-green bra that shows through a black sweater riddled with holes. I could never pull that off. "Yes, yes, yes," she says as soon as she sees me. "So glad you made it. I already signed your name on the open mic. You're set."

"Thank you," I say, kissing her cheek.

"Where's Jasmine, though? She should be here—you two are like the stars of the internet right now."

"It's her dad again," Isaac says, and moves to grab a doughnut and pour cups of coffee for us. The bookstore is already filling up, and I can tell they're about to start. Nadine shakes her head and shuffles through her phone at the same time. None of us can stop thinking about Jasmine and how she's handling everything. I see Isaac move to text her, and I peek at his phone—*We miss you. I miss you*—it reads.

I love it.

"I'm so sorry about her dad. I hope she's okay. I hope she's writing and getting her emotions out there, because people are studying you two big-time. Everyone is loving the posts," she says, looking behind me. "I love everything you've been posting. I wanna make a Write Like a Girl playlist. Will you post that if I do?"

"What? Yes! We will definitely post that. I love it. Make it tonight, and I'll post it in the morning. People like to check in the mornings, or at least that's what I've noticed, since I check our stats all the time. It's like googling yourself."

"I definitely don't google myself," Nadine says, starting to laugh at me.

"Anyway, it's like that—and people visit it all the time!"

"Yeah, because it's good. And not cheesy. That's the problem with Music that Matters. Our advisor only posts out-of-focus photos and video clips of us playing. It's so boring."

"We kinda lucked out with Ms. Lucas. She's so busy with coordinating all the clubs, and she totally trusts us, so we have a lot of freedom with what we post." I shrug my shoulders, already thinking about when I'm gonna share Nadine's playlist and who will be watching for what we post.

"Welcome to Word Up Teen Night, folks," Leidy Blake says from the stage. "Come in, make room. We have a packed house tonight, and the list is almost officially full, so make your way to the front." Leidy hosts every month, and she is amazing. She's basically the godmother of the bookstore and has been in the neighborhood since she was born. Her long silver hair is wrapped up in a bun on top of her head, and she has a crystal necklace on and a few chunky rings on her fingers. She's exactly what I want to look like when I get older. She is a local's local, and nobody cares that she's in her sixties.

"Hey." I look around and see James standing behind me. "Did you go up already?"

"Not yet," I reply.

"Uh, James Bradford is here . . . to see you," Isaac whispers over at me. I start to laugh. Nadine is eyeing me from her corner spot and holding both hands up to air high-five me, which I try to do secretly, since it's getting even more crowded in here and I don't really want anyone to see me air high-five my friend.

"How's about we get our first performer up on the stage,"

Leidy starts. "Please welcome one of my personal favorite poets: Chelsea Spencer."

When I say I killed it, I'm not trying to brag, seriously. I am just saying that I am good at only a few things: gathering good people, creating womanist/feminist blogs that rock people to their very core, and writing and performing poetry. That's really it, so yes, I nailed it. I performed it just the way I'd been practicing, and the crowd loved it, at least I think they loved it. Leidy Blake calls up the next performer to the stage, and I walk back to take my seat.

James leans toward me. "Thanks," he whispers in my ear, and I can feel my whole body shiver. Nadine instantly starts playing "I Wanna Be Your Lover" by Prince, and I start to laugh. She knows me so well.

"You gonna get up there? Read that poem you wrote for me?" I ask.

"Well, after that performance, I think mine needs some work. Maybe next time. Glad I caught you, though. I like that poem." He squeezes my shoulder, then walks out.

"Let's keep it going. Next up, please welcome Rachel from the Incarnation School," Leidy calls out, shaking me from my James Bradford haze. *Did he come here just to see me?*

"Thanks. So, I'm here tonight to talk about this new blog: Write Like a Girl, because it's what all of us have been talking about all day," she starts, and the crowd starts to clap and yell again.

I was still reeling from James showing up to hear me read,

but now I'm even more in shock. People at other schools have been reading the blog?

"Most of us are fed up with the sexism happening in our schools. We're also dealing with racist teachers, racist principals—it doesn't stop. And what Jasmine Gray wrote told the truth, so I'm here to read it now for those of you who didn't read it, and for those of you who still don't get it. My name is Rachel Lewis. I'm a black girl who will not be put into anyone's box. I am no Jezebel, Mammy, or Sapphire. I am my own woman, and I'll act any way I want to. I am not . . ." She starts to read every description Jasmine wrote.

I look at the crowd; about fifteen people have their phones up and are recording the reading.

Isaac comes up behind me and says, "I think you and Jasmine have officially created buzz."

An Almost Love Poem
for James

by Chelsea Spencer

You
my shine
galaxy
of breath & lungs
all of me a wave
crestfallen over you
the planets shift when you're near
I count their revolve, a tremble
to know your heart bumps up against mine
hope it will stay steady this whole long time.

WRITE LIKE A GIRL BLOG

Created by Nadine Abdul

Write Like a Girl Top 10 Playlist

1. "Respect"—Aretha Franklin
2. "Run the World (Girls)"—Beyoncé
3. "Doo Wop (That Thing)"—Lauryn Hill
4. "Cranes in the Sky"—Solange
5. "The Greatest"—Sia
6. "Queen"—Janelle Monáe
7. "U.N.I.T.Y."—Queen Latifah
8. "Girl on Fire"—Alicia Keys
9. "Bad Reputation"—Joan Jett
10. "You Don't Own Me"—Lesley Gore

14
JASMINE

This Halloween is the worst ever. I'm spending the night at the hospital with Dad so Mom can take Jason trick-or-treating. He was not at all impressed with the treats the nurses are giving out—small bags of apple slices, tiny boxes of raisins, black licorice.

The plan for Halloween was going to be me and Chelsea dressing up as Gloria Steinem and Dorothy Pitman Hughes. One day, when Chelsea was over and we were making buttons for our eighth grade end-of-the-year project, Dad overheard us talking and said, "You two are little versions of Dorothy Pitman Hughes and Gloria Steinem." When neither Chelsea or I knew who Dad was talking about, he made us look them up, and that's when we saw the iconic photo of the both of them holding up their fists, with a confident defiance on their faces. Chelsea and I promised each other we'd replicate the photograph for this Halloween. Although I wasn't sure anyone would actually know who we were. Unless we walked around side by side all day with our hands in the air in fisted protest, I doubted we'd be easily guessed. I think this made Chelsea want to do it even more. She likes for people *not* to know who she is dressed up as. We decided to emphasize our hair and clothes—Chelsea would wear a long wig, parted in the middle, and I would wear my hair out in an Afro. We even went to the Goodwill on 135th in Harlem to find seventies clothes.

Now that I am not going, Chelsea said she's not dressing up at all, which will be the first time ever in life that Chelsea has not been in a costume for Halloween. I've seen pictures of her as a baby dressed as a ladybug, a sunflower. Always something.

"You don't have to stay, Jasmine," Dad says. His voice is scratchy and weak.

"I know."

"You're going to miss your school's dance," he says. "And you already missed the open mic thing. And weren't you and Isaac going to go to the Schomburg Center? You can't keep missing everything because of me. You really don't have to stay," Dad tells me.

"I know," I say. I turn the TV on, flip through channels trying to find something that isn't depressing, like the news or one of those animal shows. I know I'm missing out on a lot of fun, but if I go, I'll just wish I was here anyway. Plus, I'm really scared of something bad—really bad—happening while I'm away. I don't know what I'd do if I was at some silly dance and my father died. And I know that sounds extreme, like what can I do anyway if

I'm here? I'm not a doctor. But I am his daughter. His first and only girl. I need to be here.

When I turn to the station that shows reruns of classics, Dad says, "Leave it here." *A Different World* is on. Dad and Mom swear this is one of the best shows ever to be made. They watch it for nostalgia's sake, reminiscing about their college days at Clark Atlanta. Mom is always pointing out an outfit, saying, "I used to wear that back in the day," or "That style used to be fly."

Used to. Key words.

Dad reaches for the remote and moves the bed up a little so he can see the TV better. It's weird to me that the controller for the television and the bed are all in one. "I was cool like Dwayne Wayne," Dad says. He musters a laugh out; it is faint, but it is there.

"Dad, Dwayne Wayne wasn't the cool one. Wasn't his character considered a nerd?"

"Nerd or not, he got the girl in the end," Dad says. "Just like me."

I laugh.

When the commercial break comes on, Dad lets out a deep sigh. "She didn't sign up for this," he says. It almost sounds like he doesn't remember I am here, that I can hear him. But then he turns to me and says, "I know our vows said for sickness and in health, but we assumed sickness would come much later. Much, much later. I just wish—" Dad's voice cracks. It isn't until I look at him that I realize he's crying. Actual tears. I have never in my whole life seen my father cry. Just the sight of it makes me crumble to pieces. I don't know what to say to him—the man who always, always knows what to say to make me feel better. I can't just let him sit in the bed crying, alone and full of frustration. I get out of my chair and sit on the edge of his bed. I take his hand, hold it in mine. Just as I squeeze his hand, my phone buzzes. It's sitting on the windowsill, so the vibrating is loud and obnoxious.

"You can answer it," Dad says. He sniffs his sorrow, clears his throat, and sits up stiffer.

"I know," I say, but I don't move.

We watch the show together.

My phone buzzes again.

And again.

My phone is shaking and spasming on the windowsill.

"Whoever it is, is just going to keep calling until you answer," Dad says.

"I know," I tell him. I turn the volume up. By the time the show ends and the commercial comes on, Dad has fallen asleep. I let go of his hand, but I stay in the bed with him.

A nurse comes in, my favorite one, Ann. She smiles at me like nothing is wrong, which is actually more comforting than sad smiles that are full of pity and worry. "You're on overnight duty tonight, huh?"

"Yeah. My mom needed a break, and my brother needed to go trick-or-treating."

"I'll bring a cot and some blankets."

"Thanks."

147

When Ann comes back, she's also brought a few boxes of apple juice and packets of saltine crackers. "A little midnight snack for later," she says.

I'm two more episodes into the marathon of *A Different World* when Dad wakes up. He coughs the sleep out of his throat. The first thing he says is, "Is that your phone again?"

I didn't even notice it buzzing. I forgot all about it. I go to the window, pick up my phone, and look through the notifications.

Dad asks, "So who's that calling? Got a new boyfriend you haven't told me about?"

Isaac comes to mind, and I look down hoping maybe it's him that's been calling. "You'll be the first to know," I tell Dad. Well, Chelsea will. And then Mom, but Mom and Dad are basically the same people so he's high on the list. I look at my phone: sixteen text messages; five missed calls.

Something is up.

15
CHELSEA

"How do I look?" I ask, studying myself in the full-length mirror in the hallway.

"Well, you look good, but I'm still slightly confused," my mom says, looking me up and down. "What's with the cat ears? I thought you weren't planning to dress up this year."

"Mom, it's catcalling. See? I have a telephone. And I just couldn't let a Halloween go by without being in costume. It's one of my things."

"Okay, I see that now, but that's why I thought you were a phone booth. Geez, Chelsea, it's a little confusing."

"Ah, Mom. I'm not a phone booth. Those don't even exist anymore."

"Well, I thought that was why it was funny. Is it supposed to be funny?"

"No, it's supposed to be thought provoking."

"Oh, it's definitely thought provoking," she says, pulling me in for a hug.

"It is! See, I'm actually a cat calling, and the joke is that this is the only kind of catcalling that should be allowed in the world. An actual cat calling someone, and not, ya know, catcalling."

"Right, yes, I do see it. I'm just sorry you and Jasmine couldn't go as Gloria Steinem and Dorothy Pitman Hughes. But I am glad she's with her dad tonight."

"Me too. And there's no way I could go as Gloria without my partner. It would've been totally confusing."

"You're right. This costume is much clearer," Mom says. "Enjoy your night. Are you meeting Isaac and Nadine?" The door buzzes just as she asks, and they walk in, both dressed as their favorite superheroes. Isaac is Black Panther with black pants, a black T-shirt, and his hair slicked back, and Nadine is Katana from the *Suicide Squad*. She has on black jeans, a leather jacket, and Katana's mask that has the Japanese flag across it and is holding a fake samurai sword that looks pretty real to me. They both look amazing.

"You two look so good," I say, standing back to take it all in.

"You too," Nadine says, "I love it. You're a cat in trouble, right? Like a cat in a tree?"

"What? No, I'm catcalling. See? I'm a cat. And I have a phone. So I'm catcalling."

"Yeah, well, it's not totally clear, Chels, but don't worry. We'll be with you tonight. We'll help get that message across," Isaac says.

"Great," I say, "always misunderstood. I should've gone as a big question mark."

"Now that woulda been funny," Isaac says. I roll my eyes and push them both out the door. I don't want to miss any of the dance, and I definitely don't want to miss seeing James. Ever since the open mic, I've been feeling even more like something could happen between us. I know he's sort of dating Meg, but for some reason, I feel like that's gonna be short lived, especially since we've been talking more and more, and even though our month of runs is over, we've already made plans to get coco helado next week. Things could still happen.

* * *

We walk in, and the gym is totally transformed. The lights are low, and there are strobes in the corners and a makeshift disco ball above us. There are fake skeletons, pumpkins, and black and orange streamers all over the bleachers. The back table is loaded with cookies, popcorn, and soda, and the music is already playing, with most of the seniors out on the dance floor, since they've been here setting everything up.

"This looks soooo good," Nadine says. "I love it. We could stage a whole creepy photo shoot in here. Chelsea, look at me. Be a cat, and now pretend you're calling someone." I make my best cat impersonation and hold my phone up.

"Make sure you hashtag it with #catcalling. The internet will understand."

Nadine keeps her phone open and goes to Instagram to post it. "Whoa," she says as soon as she opens her app.

"What?"

"This." She holds her phone up so Isaac and I can see it. It's Meg and two of her best friends. They're all dressed up like princesses. Meg is Rapunzel, with a long wrap of blond braid trailing down her back. Her friends are Snow White and Cinderella. They're clearly the sexy versions of these princesses, dressed in short skirts, with tiaras and sheer tops on. Underneath the photo it says: #princesslife #princessesrock #goodlife #princesslikeagirl #squadgoals #whysoserious #jokesonthem

"What the . . ." and before I can finish, Nadine holds up her phone again.

"Is that?" I ask, and look closer. It's another photo that Meg posted of some kids from the acting ensemble. One is dressed like Mammy, with a long dress and scarf and holding a box of Aunt Jemima pancake mix in front of her, and one is holding a movie poster of Pam Grier from *Coffy*. She has an Afro wig on and is wearing a red tube top. Both of the girls are white. Underneath them it says: #mammyrocks #mammyspancakesarebest #sweetsapphire #jokelikeagirl #jokes #soserious.

I take my phone out and start texting Jasmine.

Just checking on you. Hope your dad is
doing better.

I'm here with Isaac and Nadine. They both
look awesome. Black Panther and Katana.

I'm dressed as catcalling. I'm sure you're

laughing your head off right now, since I
KNOW you get those kinds of jokes.

Guess who else is on their way?

I send the screen shot of Meg and her punk princess power.
James isn't here yet. Where is he?

Just when I'm in the middle of sending texts, I look up and
see them all walk in. Angie Marshall is dressed like a princess
too, with a fluffy dress on and a tiara. I can't believe she's with
them. She's actually one of the cooler members of the group, and
one of the only ones who reached out to Jasmine when she quit
to tell her how messed up Meg's comments were—she's also one
of the only other black girls in the group. Her boyfriend, Corey
Finn, another guy from the ensemble, walks in with her.

OMG. Angie Marshall is dressed like a
princess too!

Not cool!!!!

Okay, something weird is happening. This
dance is taking a turn.

"What are they wearing?" Isaac asks.
"Oh, they're just wearing your basic sexist and racist costumes," I say.

153

"And it looks like they're targeting you all," Nadine adds.

I pull out my phone to go on Instagram too. I look up the photo they must have posted when they were getting ready. It says #jokesonyou #partylikeagirl #PrincessAllDay #PrincessPower.

"Oh no, no," I say when I see them walking toward us. I can see Isaac clenching his fists.

"You okay?" I ask.

"No," he answers, and I can see he's pissed, not just because of their insanely racist costume choices, but because they've also taken Jasmine's and my work and made a big joke out of it.

"Yo, Angie, what's with your costume?" Isaac asks as they make their way over to us.

"Back off, man. It's really not that serious. It's a joke," Corey says, starting to smile.

"Yeah, it is serious. You all need to take those costumes off. They're offensive for a whole bunch of reasons," Isaac says, moving closer.

"Come on. We're just messing around. It's just a costume, and we wanted to play around with stereotypes by becoming some of the unique characters written about on the very serious Write Like a Girl blog," Angie says, laughing.

"The work there IS serious, and it's changing a lot of people's attitudes, and thoughts, and—"

"Dude, take it easy. What's the big deal? What's up?"

"Don't worry about him. He's just got a crush on Jasmine," Meg says.

"What?" Corey asks, really laughing now. "I didn't know you were into fat girls."

And that's all it takes—all it takes for me to see that Isaac really is in love with Jasmine, and all it takes to confirm that he's not about any of this trash. He pulls his arm back and punches Corey right in the face.

"Isaac," I shout. A group has gathered around both of them. Corey stands up and pushes Isaac back into a pile of balloons with skeleton faces all over them. Isaac lunges for Corey again and grabs him by the shoulders. They wrestle, knocking over the entire bowl of fruit punch. Fizzy pink liquid sloshes to the ground, and two of the princesses slide while trying to stop the fight. Meg's wig gets caught on the leg of the overturned table, and it pulls her long blond hair to the ground. I can see a few of the other guys move in to stop the fight, when suddenly the lights turn on, and Principal Hayes is standing between them with one of the chaperones.

"Get these two out of here," Principal Hayes says. "We'll be dealing with both of you on Monday."

"Wait, no, it's not his fault," I say, pushing through the crowd and stepping all over Rapunzel's now sticky wig.

"Excuse me?" he says, looking right at me.

"They're the ones who instigated it. I mean, just look." I gesture at Angie, who is nursing Corey's bloody lip.

"They what?" Principal Hayes asks.

"They came dressed as the stereotypes. There's Mammy and Sapphire," I say.

"It's called a joke," Meg says, taking a step forward. "Can't you get that? Get over it," Meg says back, so calm, but at the same time, she kicks her wig in my direction. As if I'm an afterthought, as if I don't matter at all. All of a sudden, I move toward Meg. I don't know if I'm gonna try to hit her or launch into a speech, but I'm mad in a way I've never been before.

"Enough," Principal Hayes shouts. "This dance is officially over. Please see yourselves out. Done. This. Is. Over." Everyone groans, and a few people kick the balloons around the space. Some of the seniors start to clean things up.

Just then, James walks into the cafeteria and looks in my direction. He sees the lights on and the punch spilled all over the floor. "What happened?" he mouths in my direction. I point my finger at Meg and her group, who are gathering their wigs and sashes, and shrug my shoulders. He holds his hand up to his ear and mouths, "Call me." I don't know if I will, or even want to, after this.

Principal Hayes tells me he'd like to see me in his office. Nadine and Isaac wait for me outside, and as soon as I finish getting a ridiculous talking-to, I meet up with them and call Jasmine.

It only rings once. "Jazz? We might be in trouble," I say. "Um, so, yeah. I mean, well, *I* might be in trouble."

"What did you do?" Jasmine asks.

"Well, Principal Hayes ended the dance—which I didn't think was fair because, I mean, it wasn't like everyone showed up like that, and it was only halfway over anyway. It wasn't fair, and he also didn't understand what a big deal those costumes were."

"So what got us in trouble?" she asks.

"Well, I was pissed. I told Principal Hayes how I didn't think it was fair."

"That's it?"

"I may have said a little too much."

"What else did you say?" Jasmine asks.

"After Principal Hayes told me I needed to act in a more mature way to get my point across, he said something about how he couldn't believe something like this would happen at *this* school. And so I told him that there's a lot of messed-up stuff that happens at our school. He actually looked surprised, and said, 'Like what?' so I told him."

"You told him what?"

"That he needed to fire any racist teachers—like Mr. Morrison, who clearly should not be teaching at a school like this. And I may or may not have said that you were going to send your blog post to the *New York Times* and every other major newspaper in the city if he didn't do something."

"Chelsea!"

"I know, I know. I said too much," I admit. I can see Isaac and Nadine giggling beside me. I know Isaac is relieved that Principal Hayes dropped any punishment due to the sensitivity of the situation. "He wants to talk to us about our blog. He thinks we've been writing things just to be instigating these kinds of situations."

"Where is all this coming from? We haven't instigated anything. Has anyone posted anything negative in our comments section?" Jasmine asks.

"I don't know, I haven't checked in a couple of days. I was too busy getting my costume right, which totally didn't work, by the way."

"Well, can you check?" Jasmine asks. "Do you think there might be something under my first post?"

"I'll check as soon as I get home," I say. "I'll call you back." I hang up without even mentioning James or asking about her dad.

daisymae commented: one question?? who cares!!??

purplelipstick commented: lies. lies. lies! these people are always trying to start something . . .

vagabond commented: maybe if they all didn't act like jezebels, sapphires and whatever else, then Hollywood wouldn't cast them all in those same ole parts.

chrometilt commented: ths pst actlly fls RACST to me!

lenabee commented: how about you learn how to spell racist? also, this blog is NOT RACIST. it is simply commenting on how RACIST the movie industry actually is. how about get educated first before you start commenting on intellectual blog posts. thank you.

chrometilt commented: BITCH. Did I spell that right???

vagabond liked this

lenabee commented: What does the academy value in a black performance? The NY Times actually posted a video about THIS SUBJECT! Of the 10 black women up for best actress Oscars, all played characters in poverty. 9 were homeless or nearly so.

harlemchick commented: #TRUTH

chrometilt commented: #CRAP

wahibaby commented: Learn how to ACT!?? Then maybe you'll get other parts?

harlemchick commented: shocked at how ignorant people can be

websteravenue liked this

blackdreamer212 liked this

hudsondreamer commented: this post is as ignorant as this blog.

daisymae commented: and again—who cares!? no one's gnna watch this girl on stage anywy! who's gnna cast hr?

harlemchick commented: seems like YOU care since you keep commenting. I G N O R A N T!

chrometilt commented: some girls just need to shut the hell up! like this dumb-ass blog.

vagabond liked this

purplelipstick liked this

honeydew liked this

hudsondreamer liked this

wahibaby liked this

girlonfire liked this

NOVEMBER

16
JASMINE

I've rehearsed with Chelsea ten times how to apologize to Principal Hayes. We have it all planned out and go over it an eleventh time on our way to his office.

"Got it," Chelsea says. "I'm sorry if I was disrespectful, but I do believe our school has some issues that need to be addressed," she repeats.

"Perfect," I tell her.

When Chelsea and I get to Principal Hayes's office, he is sitting at his messy desk, which is cluttered with file folders, books, pens, and Post-it Notes. His tie is loosened, and he's leaning so far back in his office chair that it looks like he could fall out of it. He's swiveling from side to side until he sees me and Chelsea walking in. "Ladies," he says. "Come on in. Have a seat." Principal Hayes stands and walks around his desk, joining us in the section of his office that has four chairs around a small coffee table. "I'm glad we could talk," he tells us.

Like we had a choice to come here. We should be eating lunch right now, but during first period we both got a notice from the office saying we needed to come see him at lunchtime.

Chelsea and I sit down beside each other. Principal Hayes sits across from us. "So, I wanted to follow up with your, uh, concerns, Chelsea. I am sorry you feel that this school—"

"I don't feel it, I know that this school has some racist teachers and that it was unfair—"

I pinch Chelsea, clear my throat.

She talks quieter but finishes her sentence. "I think our school doesn't actually live up to its mission, and we should do something about it."

"I appreciate your zeal, I do. But you have to understand that you can't just make accusations about staff here and think I'm immediately going to fire someone. It doesn't work like that, Chelsea. And that's not actually what I want to talk with you about."

"Of course it's not," Chelsea says.

"Consider this your official warning. Your club will be shut down if you continue to incite discord throughout the student body."

I lean forward. "What do you mean 'incite discord'? It's not our fault people showed up to the dance dressed up in offensive costumes."

"Well, now, perhaps you are not fully responsible for it, but your blog is stepping outside the lines of the parameters set for school blogs," Principal Hayes says. "I mean, take a look at the other Amsterdam Heights blogs—they mention upcoming events, they share club photos from field trips. You two are being instigators—"

Chelsea interrupts. "You mean we're encouraging discussion and dialogue."

"No, I mean you're curating a space that encourages people to be disrespectful. Why didn't you report the inappropriate comments on the blog to your advisor?"

Chelsea answers, "We just—I wasn't checking the comments. I had no idea people were responding that way. But still—we couldn't have known all of this would happen."

I add, "Principal Hayes, we can change the settings. We can make it so no one can leave comments."

Principal Hayes considers this. He leans back in his chair, turns from side to side.

Then he stops and says, "Girls, the comments are not the only issue. It's some of the actual posts I have a problem with." He looks at me.

My chest rises, and my palms get sweaty. "What was wrong with my post?"

"You said derogatory things about a teacher. Students showed up to the dance in direct response to *your* post. We can't have you two inciting these kinds of incidents. This school cannot be seen as a place—"

"Are you telling me that because I gave information—truthful information—about a personal experience I had and because I shared the history behind why that experience was so painful,

I am in trouble?" Now my voice is rising, and Chelsea is the one nudging me in my side.

"I am telling you that my expectation is for you to be respectful of this school and its staff and monitor student comments. Can you do that?"

"Yes," we say in unison again.

"Consider this your warning. If there's another incident because of your blog, I'll shut it all down. You're dismissed," he says.

Chelsea opens her mouth to argue, but I stop her. On our way down the hall to the cafeteria, she says, "I just want him to admit that we didn't instigate anything."

"It's fine, Chels. It's only a warning. I wanted to leave it at that before he changed his mind."

"Humph," Chelsea says. "If he thinks our blog is starting something at this school, wait till he sees what we post next."

"Um, Chelsea, let's—let's not push it. We have to be smart. Strategic. Let's post something less controversial but still in line with our club's mission."

Chelsea doesn't respond, so I know this means she is not liking my idea.

"We need to switch it up a bit anyway. We can't do the same thing every time."

"We don't always post the same thing," Chelsea says.

"I know. I meant, I'm just saying maybe we can take the focus off us for a few posts. Share something about other feminists."

Chelsea gives a hesitant "okay."

"Trust me," I tell her. "I've got some ideas."

WRITE LIKE A GIRL BLOG

Posted by Jasmine Gray

Feminist Spotlight: Sarah Jones

Because there are contemporary artists creating work
about what's going on in today's society.

Because there is power in inventing
and reinventing yourself.
Because the experiences of immigrants
need to be documented, honored.
Because women need a space to share their truths,
a space to be seen.

Because Sarah Jones is a Tony Award–winning playwright
that everyone should know.

Today's post features Sarah Jones, a biracial performer best
known for creating multicharacter one-person shows that
tell stories about sex trafficking, immigration, and human
rights. Sarah Jones was born in 1973 and was educated
at the United Nations International School and Bryn Mawr
College. Here's a quote from her TED Talk. Get to know
her work and be inspired.

> "To what extent do we self-construct, do we self-invent?
> How do we self-identify, and how mutable is that

identity? Like, what if one could be anyone at any time? Well, my characters, like the ones in my shows, allow me to play with the spaces between those questions."

—Sarah Jones

----

sophiamays liked this

magicalme liked this

wondergirl reposted this

firenexttime commented: OMG. How many voices did she do in that TED Talk? Amazing.

writelikeagirl commented: Right? If you close your eyes, you really think there are different people talking.

brandilux commented: Heard your principal almost shut your blog down. Glad you two are still at it.

hearmeroar commented: I love that you're highlighting contemporary artists. Not all poets and writers are dead white men. Yes!

harlemgirl14 commented: My mom took me to see her show at the Nuyorican Poets Café. SO GOOD.

robincanton commented: Art that matters, that makes a difference. Love this.

peaceandlove commented: Just when I thought your blog couldn't get better.

principalhayes liked this

WRITE LIKE A GIRL BLOG

Posted by Jasmine Gray

Feminist Spotlight: Natalie Diaz

Because language is power.

Because language desires to survive.

Because nothing is singular.
Because Natalie Diaz is an award-winning poet
that everyone should know.

Today's post features Natalie Diaz. Natalie Diaz was born
in the Fort Mojave Indian Village in Needles, California.
She is Mojave and an enrolled member of the Gila River
Indian community. She has a BA from Old Dominion
University, where she was awarded a full athletic
scholarship. She played professional basketball in Europe
and Asia before returning to Old Dominion, where she
earned an MFA. She is the author of the poetry collection
When My Brother Was an Aztec. Diaz has worked with the
last speakers of Mojave and directed a language
revitalization program.

Here's a quote by Natalie Diaz. Get to know her work and
be inspired.

"I don't believe anything in me is singular. I need to be more than singular. I need to find myself in others, not as a mirror image, but as a wild thing, a thing that is in a forest beyond my self and your self. Maybe because I grew up on a reservation, or in a large family, or always on a team, or as less than 1% of the American population. Or maybe because I believe that the energy in me is the same energy in every other living thing. If I could remember this more, I might hurt people less. I might love people better."

—Natalie Diaz

----

hearmeroar liked this

brandilux reposted this

magicalme liked this

sophiamays commented: This blog is the best! Learning so much about people I never heard of.

wondergirl reposted this

firenexttime commented: I want to get her poetry book ASAP. Love this!

robincanton liked this

harlemgirl14 commented: Read some of her poems online. She might be my new favorite poet.

peaceandlove reposted this

principalhayes liked this

WRITE LIKE A GIRL BLOG

Posted by Jasmine Gray

Feminist Spotlight: Reena Saini Kallat

Because no one should be forgotten.

Because ocean is body, body is ocean.

Because art is memorial, art is witness.

Because Reena Saini Kallat is an innovative visual artist that everyone should know.

Today's post features Reena Saini Kallat. Reena Saini Kallat was born in Delhi, India, and graduated from Sir J.J. School of Art, Mumbai, with a BFA in painting. Her art explores the role that memory plays, in not only what we choose to remember but also how we think of the past. Her series using salt as a medium explores the tenuous yet intrinsic relationship between the body and the oceans, highlighting the fragility and unpredictability of existence. Kallat has worked with officially recorded and registered names of people and objects that are lost or have disappeared without a trace, only to get listed as anonymous and forgotten statistics.

Here's a quote by Reena Saini Kallat. Get to know her work and be inspired.

"Our ideas and understanding of the world are definitely shaped by who we are, and where we may be located on the planet, so I am certainly aware of how my experience of being a woman contributes and informs the work I make—even though through the work I try and explore ideas that look beyond nationality and other stereotypes."

—Reena Saini Kallat, *Culture Trip*, 2015

----

peaceandlove commented: I love the line "Because art is memorial, art is witness." Agree!

kingslegacy liked this

calebalexander reposted this

wondergirl liked this

harlemgirl14 reposted

firenexttime reposted this

brandilux commented: thanks for including women of color on your blog. #inclusive #diversity

hearmeroar reposted this

robincanton commented: Agree with brandilux! #representationmatters

principalhayes commented: Great post, girls!

17
CHELSEA

Chelsea, dinner's ready," Mia shouts down the hall. "Mom made your favorite—spaghetti and meatballs. You're so spoiled," she continues as I walk into the kitchen, which is only about five steps from my bedroom, so I have no idea why she's even shouting.

"Well, at least that's one thing that's going in my favor," I reply, and slide into my seat at the front of the table, which is right next to the oven and an arm's-length away from the fridge, so I could basically fry an egg and pour myself a glass of milk all at the same time. Our apartment is on the small side, and when something happens to one of us, everyone seems to know.

"Don't be so dramatic," my mom says, shoving me to the side to pull a loaf of garlic bread out of the oven.

"Why does everyone keep saying that? It's like women aren't allowed to have any emotions," I say. My mother closes her eyes and looks like she's trying to meditate, something she does a lot lately.

"Chelsea, not everyone is out to get you," she says, opening her eyes and starting to serve everyone.

"Principal Hayes is trying to shut us down, Mom. Completely and totally shut us down. Do you understand that?" I ask.

"Shut who down?" my father asks, closing the door behind him and slipping his shoes to the side. He's clearly sweating as he takes his jacket off. He throws his satchel, full of student papers, into the closet. He's a professor of education at City College, and this time of year is rough with grading lesson plans and helping students get better at teaching. "Jesus, it still feels like Indian summer out there. How's that even possible at the beginning of November?"

Mia and I give each other a look. "Dad, you can't say Indian summer."

He moves past us to wash his hands, while giving my mom a kiss. It would be pretty idyllic if only the principal of our school wasn't trying to silence the voices of women, and my dad didn't just walk in the house spewing some old-fashioned, racist term.

"According to our People's History class, there're a bunch of terms and sayings that have super-racist origins. Like, the etymology of Indian summer was based on the idea that Indians were deceitful—as in—as crazy as summer in November. So even though you think it might be harmless, you just made a statement based on a historically stereotypical and racist statement," Mia says, leaning back in her chair and smiling at me.

"Well said," I say, already looking forward to taking that class my senior year. "You could just say, 'Jesus, it feels like global

174

warming out there,' and then you'd really seem like you were socially conscious."

"And it would also make you seem like you know a thing or two about science," Mia adds. I love when she gets all social justice-y. "You two are the ones who sent us to the revolutionary high school."

"I stand corrected and will officially never use that term again. Can I blame my stupidity on being old?" he asks. We shake our heads.

"Excuse me, could we refrain from saying Jesus in that way? Please," my mom adds, glaring for a moment at my dad.

Jesus, I say in my mind, but I stop myself from rolling my eyes. "By the way, I wouldn't say our school is so revolutionary," I add, "especially since the school, or should I say the principal, decided that our women's rights blog was too derogatory and was inciting incidents of unrest."

"Incidents of unrest?" my father asks. "What do you mean?"

"She means that they've been writing some awesome poems and posts about women's rights, racist teachers, and the basic takedown of systems of oppression. And truthfully, some people, no matter how woke—and I hate that term—"

"Right? I mean, I feel like if you say, 'I'm so woke,' it's sort of like saying the opposite. Like I'm so with it and in the know, and whatever," I add.

"They think they are, but they're really just same old, same old. They can't get with the system, and they definitely can't get with it when a woman is behind it," Mia finishes.

"Can we please pray before we eat," my mother asks, clearly

annoyed. "While I appreciate you all sharing your days with us, I'd like to eat, myself. It has been a long day for me." My mom is a social worker, and it seems like all her days are full of other people's problems, so when it gets to us, she's already had enough. "Our Father, who art in heaven," she begins, and she ends by asking God to watch over us and guide us in the right directions in the weeks to come.

I try not to say anything, I really do. I know my mom was raised super Catholic, and that she truly believes a healthy dose of Jesus (coupled heavily with guilt) in our lives is beneficial and makes perfect sense, I just don't know if I can get behind it. It's not that I don't believe there's some type of higher being, but I just don't know who or what that higher being is, and besides, I'm so fed up with everything and everyone that I can't take it anymore.

"Mom, what if God's a woman?" I ask, piling my plate high with meatballs.

My father eyes me from across the table. "Don't start, Chelsea," he says. Mia nudges me. She's heard this conversation before, and it never ends well.

"It's completely fine if your God is a woman, Chels. Pass the spaghetti, please."

She's not gonna fight with me, so I try again. "But I mean, why does your God have to always be a man? If God is a spirit, then why can't that spirit be embodied by a woman? And since a woman is the one that gives life, and not the father, which is what the Bible always tries to make us believe, then I just don't understand why you wouldn't say, 'Our Mother, who art in heaven,' especially since you're a woman, and . . ."

"Enough," my mother shouts, slamming her water glass on the table. "I understand you're upset about your little club, but you do not have the right to pick a fight with all of us tonight."

"My *little* club? It's not a little club. It's the Hotbed of Cultural Women's Issues—the Nerve Center of the World, the Command Post of Politics Pertaining to the Pussy," I shout. I can see my father trying not to smile, and it makes me even angrier. "I know you all think it's some little joke that Jasmine and I are running, but it's not. It's a big deal, and it means something to us."

"Chelsea, I hear you, but you can't just go around starting fires, you can't act like a child every time . . ."

"A child? I'm not acting like a child, Mom. Have you read any of our posts? Do you even know what we're fighting for? It's the same issues you couldn't get over, because you were so obsessed with beauty and looking a certain way, and you ended up putting that on me, so that even when I was trying to not care about being pretty—because that's what you told me to do—it's all I could ever think about."

"Don't start this again, Chelsea," my father chimes in, adding nothing else to the conversation.

"And you," I motion to my dad, standing up now. "You're both so concerned with us speaking our voices and standing up against injustices, but now, now that I'm really doing it, you're telling me I'm acting like a child. Well, I'm just getting started.

And we're not going away," I finish. I stab another meatball with my fork and shove it into my mouth before I head to my room. I figure the kitchen will be closed after the way I've acted tonight, and I don't wanna have to run into my mom or dad again. I slam my door and start on a new poem.

Grown Up

No frilly dresses
or shoes that pinch. No candy,
lemonade, cartoons.

See me grown—my own
attitudes, opinions, thoughts
all mine, don't disturb.

Who you think I am?
The woman I'm becoming
I'm already her.

Yes, adult enough
running up against 18
won't you see the whole

me, a history
I'm crafting in front of you.
Writing down my dreams.

A map to lead you,
directions for who I am
free out in the world.

18
JASMINE

Fall is my favorite season. The crisp air is refreshing after four months of unbearable heat. I love watching the changing leaves and wearing sweaters that are warm enough to wear as a coat because it's not really cold yet—not winter kind of cold. I throw on an oversize green sweater and head out to meet Isaac at the Schomburg Center. We're going to view the Emory Douglas collection that's on display. Dad has officially resigned, so there are no more special private viewings. The closer I get to the center, the slower I walk. I didn't think going would be emotional, but with each step I take it hits me that Dad will not be in his office when I get there. My heart starts pounding once I get to the corner of 135th and Malcolm X Boulevard. Will Dad's colleagues give me those sad "I know your dad is dying" eyes? I keep getting them at school from teachers, and it just makes me want to look down at the floor—anywhere other than in someone's eyes.

I step inside, and instead of the sad eyes, my favorite security guard gives me a hug, like he always does. The pounding settles, and I go inside to find Isaac, who is sitting on a bench inside the lobby.

"Hey." I tap him on his shoulder. "Have you been waiting long?"

"I got here way earlier than planned. No train issues, imagine that," Isaac says. "You never know coming from the Bronx." He stands and hugs me. "Glad you could join me for my last Brown Art Challenge outing. I know your dad said it won't count, but I mean—it's the Black Panther Party. I gotta get some points for this. Plus, he's not the one who told me about it. I found out about this one myself, especially after seeing the exhibit on Puerto Rican Freedom Fighters at El Museo. It just blows my mind that all these communities of color were building off each other and making art to form this big resistance . . . together." He laughs. "So you can see I'm into it. You ready?"

"Ready."

We go inside and enter the exhibit room on the main floor. I feel small walking past these massive posters, so big you have to stand back to see it all. The first poster I see has a young boy holding up a newspaper that says All Power to the People in one hand, and *The Black Panther* in the other. The boy's mouth is open, like he is shouting something out. There's a white square next to the print that explains more about the image. It talks about the Black Panther Party and how art was used as a means to get their message across. I am sure to take notes in my head because I know Dad will ask me what I learned when I get home.

Isaac is standing in front of a print that is a collage of different patterns all making up a hat that sits over a black child's face. The rims of his glasses have other children in them; in the left lens, a woman holding a little girl's hand; in the right, a group of children eating at a table. There are so many little details hiding in this one big poster. The longer I stand there, the more new things I see that I didn't catch right away, like the words at the very top that say We Shall Survive. Without a Doubt. I am struck by the confidence in that statement. I take a photo of the poster, making sure I get the top. I want to keep that saying at the forefront of my mind this school year, and always. I will survive. Without a doubt.

Isaac shakes his head and says, "Did you read this?" He points to the summary next to the poster. "Did you know the FBI tapped Emory Douglas's phone? That's how powerful his art was. They thought of it as combative and too critical of the U.S. government. That's like, a whole new level of what it means to be an art-ivist," Isaac says.

We keep moving through the gallery, but as slow as we're going, I doubt we will see the exhibits upstairs. We can only stay for an hour. I stand at the next poster forever just looking at the bold blue background and the brown faces emerging from the left side of the page. People are holding signs that say Freedom Now and U.S. Gov't Stop Killing Black People Now!!! "This could have been made last week," I say.

"Yeah. That's so messed up. These posters were made in the seventies. We're still holding up the same signs."

I keep walking; Isaac stays behind. He sits on the floor, takes his sketchbook out, and starts drawing. Just like he does sometimes at school, in the hallway, leaning up against his locker during lunch. His pencil moving fast across the page. His eyes glancing up at the poster, then back down. Isaac notices me staring at him. "Come join me," he says.

"I can't draw," I remind him.

"Write something," he says. "Pick one of these images and just . . . write."

I hesitate and then join Isaac on the floor. I lean against the wall that has no art and take my notebook out of my bag. I focus on one of the smaller framed images. It looks like a comic, except there is no color and the squares aren't connected. There's a story linking all the drawings together. A story about the conditions of living in the projects. It's called Public Housing USA. Each tenant speaks, and Emory Douglas's art amplifies the words. The story starts off as a letter and goes into all the things that need to be tended to in the projects—rats, stopped-up toilets, leaking sinks, nowhere for children to play. The first line says *Hello, Public Housing Authority. This is a tenant of your slum housing calling you again.* The word "again" stands out to me. I start writing.

We sit together, drawing and writing, as people walk by. Isaac says, "I don't even care about the Brown Art Challenge anymore. It was just nice to come and do this."

"Yeah," I say.

"I'll have to tell my dad. He'll want to come see too. The

Young Lords were inspired by the Black Panther Party. He'll love this exhibit."

"Can I read what you wrote so far?" he asks.

I hand him my notebook and take his sketchbook. We take each other in. I think how if I had to plan out a perfect first date, this would be it. Maybe lunch or dessert afterward, but when this is over, we're meeting up with Nadine and Chelsea. Maybe friendship is enough. Maybe I want more.

If I take Chelsea's advice, I should just say something to Isaac. Stop waiting for him to make the first move. I don't know why women are taught to be pursued, chased. What's the worst that could happen if I tell Isaac that I have feelings for him? I think about telling him right here, right now.

"What are you thinking about?" Isaac asks.

"Oh, nothing. Just, just taking all this art in," I say. He doesn't know I am referring to him when I say this.

* * *

Isaac walks home with me so we can meet up with Chelsea and Nadine. My house used to be the hangout spot, but it's kind of hard to enjoy movies or game night with the soundtrack of Dad vomiting or moaning in the background. The whole house feels sick. No matter how much Mom and I clean, or light candles, or water the plants, or display bright-colored throw pillows on the sofa, there's a sadness and staleness that hovers here.

I hate that Jason is growing up in a home so unlike the one I had in elementary school: a home with Dad standing over the grill in the backyard, drizzling his special secret sauce over chicken or steak. A home with bedtime stories read radio-theater style, with Mom and Dad acting out all the voices. Jason won't have memories of dyeing Easter eggs and being so jealous of Dad who knows how to mix colors and create one-of-a-kind designs. He won't remember Saturday mornings eating Mom's french toast—the rare time we eat as a family at the dining room table. None of those things happen anymore. But today, I asked Mom and Dad if Chelsea, Nadine, and Isaac could come over, and they said yes.

When Isaac and I get to my block, we walk up the steep steps of the brownstone. I need to rake; leaves are covering the sidewalk, the steps. I open the door and go inside. Mom says hello to both of us and calls out from upstairs, "I put out some snacks in the kitchen." And by snacks she means she prepared a whole spread of food for us, like she used to do: two types of wings, barbecue and spicy, mozzarella sticks, chips, fruit.

"You can start eating," I tell Isaac.

Just as I say this, the doorbell rings. Chelsea and Nadine are here, and as soon as Mom hears their voices, she comes downstairs. Mom gives Chelsea the biggest hug, and Jason runs over to Isaac and wraps his arms around his legs.

"I love your haircut, Mrs. Gray," Chelsea says.

"Thank you. I'm still getting used to it," Mom says. Mom cut her hair last week. I've never seen her with short hair, not even in the photos from her childhood. Her hair has always been long and flat-ironed bone straight, but she said it was too much to manage with all that's going on, so she cut it. I have been thinking about that ever since, how even just washing and straightening hair has become too much since Dad's been sick.

"How's your mom, Nadine?" Mom asks.

"She's fine."

"Tell her I said hello. I owe her a phone call." Mom takes out plates from the cabinet. "Help yourselves," she says. "Come on, Jason. We've got to finish this math."

Jason and Mom go into Jason's room.

I sit in the kitchen with Chelsea, Nadine, and Isaac and feast on the food Mom put out. Then we make our way to the living room. Isaac takes out his sketchbook and starts doodling as we talk. He always does this—draws while talking. It used to annoy me, made me feel like he wasn't listening, but I think it actually helps him focus.

Nadine sits on the floor and leans her back against the sofa. "So, how are things with the women's rights club?"

"We still have the club," Chelsea says. "But I feel like Principal Hayes is watching everything we do. He basically gave us a warning that if our blog causes any more trouble, he'll shut the club down."

"But Write Like a Girl didn't start all that drama," Isaac says.

Chelsea looks at me. "See?"

"I agree. I know it's not our fault, and I definitely think we should keep speaking out. I just want to be smart about it. And, well, I want to do more than just the blog. We should think outside of just what the school requires us to do. If we really want to make a point that women's voices deserve to be heard, that our school has to do better—let's take action."

"What could we do?" Chelsea asks.

"Okay, so Isaac and I just came back from the Schomburg Center," I tell them. When I say this, Chelsea smiles, but I don't even acknowledge it. I just keep on talking like I don't see her over there gushing and looking at Isaac.

Isaac's eyes light up like he knows what I'm about to say. His wrist slides back and forth as he shades in something on the page.

"They have an exhibit up right now on Emory Douglas and the Black Panther Party." I tell them about the newspaper the Black Panthers had, how art was a big part of getting messages across and how they had a list of demands of things they wanted.

Isaac erases something, blows the dust off the page, and holds up his sketchbook. "They looked something like this," he says.

Chelsea takes his notebook and looks his drawing over. "This is . . . wow, Isaac, you are so talented. I mean, look at this—" She hands the book to Nadine.

"So, I was thinking Isaac could draw something for our club, and we can make buttons or something—something with a quote about our voices being important and how we cannot be silenced," I say.

"Yes, because him *warning* us is threatening to silence us," Chelsea says. Then she says, "Isaac, what do you think? Can you draw something for us?"

He takes his sketchbook back, closes it. "A button might be too small, but I like the idea of us wearing something. Maybe I can design a T-shirt. We can get a small order made and have people wear them at school."

"Yes!" Chelsea says. "We could all show up to school wearing our shirts and we won't even have to say a word. Whatever quote we choose will speak for itself." Chelsea takes her phone out, and I know that she's looking up quotes already.

Nadine says, "That's perfect. It's like responding to the idiots who wore disrespectful costumes. We'll wear something that speaks against that."

I ask Isaac, "Are you sure you have time for this?"

"Of course. I'd do anything for you."

Nadine can't help herself. She blurts out, "Oh, you're doing this for *Jasmine*. Not for us, for women's rights, for the cause? Oh, we see how it is."

Isaac throws a pillow at her. Chelsea is spilling over with

laughter, and all I can do is shake my head and act like I didn't also catch that Isaac just said he'd do *anything* for me. Just as I am about to ask if anyone wants something more to eat or drink, I hear the bedroom door open. Dad walks slowly out of his room. He looks thinner today, even thinner than yesterday, and he is walking like every part of his body is in pain. He says hello, and I can see the fear and sadness and anxiousness in everyone's eyes.

I look away from Dad, stare at the yellow pillow lying on the floor that Isaac threw. Focus on the brightness, try my best to hold on to its light.

* * *

Once everyone is gone, Dad comes back into the living room and sits on the sofa. "So I see you and Gloria Steinem have gathered your troops." He smiles, but it looks painful on his face, not like his normal, joyous smile.

"So much is going on at school, Dad. Every day it's some new drama with our club."

"Sounds like you all are figuring it out. I read what you wrote for the blog."

"You did? Do you think I was disrespectful?"

"Now you know I would have said something to you if I did," Dad says. He shifts his body, getting more comfortable against the throw pillows. "I think you stood up for yourself, and that was brave."

I walk across the living room and sit next to Dad on the sofa.

"You've definitely got the Gray gene," he says. "Speaking up,

189

standing up for what you believe in. That kind of courage runs in your veins." I know Dad is thinking of his father, who was a preacher, and his grandfather, who was a community organizer who worked on voting rights. Dad turns the television on. We watch *Family Feud* and yell out answers at the TV. We get more right than either team. Something else that runs in our genes, I guess.

Dad falls asleep before the final round. I lay my head on his chest, like I used to do when I was little. I can hear Dad's heart beating. I listen to his drum beat on and on. He is my favorite song.

19
CHELSEA

It's Saturday. The one day of the week when I can sleep in, so I take full advantage and roll over again. I've been trying to get the image of Mr. Gray out of my mind ever since I saw him a couple of weeks ago. Try to forget how thin he is and how he moves so slow. I try to see him the way he was before the cancer, making loud jokes and dancing in the living room with Jason and Jasmine. I used to love going to their house after school. They used to listen to music during dinner, which I thought was so cool. When I tried to attempt it at my house, my mom shut it down right away, saying there was too much noise in her life, and she needed some quiet at the end of the day. I remember Mr. Gray's laugh the most, and while he still tries, I can feel the tension. I miss the way it used to be.

When I finally pull myself from the covers, I see that Mia has flung hers onto the floor, and she's already up. When I get to the kitchen, she's eating the most massive bowl of Fruity Pebbles I've ever seen.

"That's disgusting," I say, grabbing the box and reading how many grams of sugar are in one serving.

"Shut up," she mumbles, "I don't have time for your food justice this morning. Besides, you know you want some."

I pour myself a bowl. "Where is everybody?"

"Mom went to yoga. She's gotta manage some of that anxiety with some meditation. I forced her to go. And Dad's grading papers at the library."

We eat in silence. The to-do list in my head is growing. Shower, get dressed, finish my poem for afternoon workshop—Leidy Blake teaches a class called Radical Acts for Beginners at Word Up every week, and I'm her best, and sometimes only, student—pick up the shirts from T-Shirt Express on the Upper West Side, and then head to workshop. I can't wait to see how they look. Isaac pulled a couple of all-nighters last week to finish our original designs—he's a total champion for the cause. We chose five powerhouse women who've changed the game. It took hours to decide, so we had to use a massive chart to make sure we were inclusive of art forms, ethnicities, and work for and about women. They had to truly represent womanist/feminist interests and ideals. We got into a pretty heated argument about Janet Jackson and Beyoncé, but we had to pull it back because we wanted to have more history and less pop magic, although I'm still gonna try to get Isaac to make me a shirt that says, "No, my first name ain't baby, it's Chelsea," and on the back, "Ms. Spencer if you're nasty." That would be sooo awesome.

"You have basketball practice today, right?" I ask Mia, who's slathering a bagel with extra cream cheese.

"Yup, two p.m. at the gym. I gotta go for a run first."

"Okay, cool, you think I could drop off some of those shirts I was telling you about? Maybe the team would wear them next week to school?"

"Sure, I can definitely let them know it's for my little sister and her crew. I think they'd do that for you, and all your little weirdo friends."

I show her a couple of designs. Isaac has used a composite of the women and highlighted their faces on the front along with their names below. On the back it says *Woman Warrior* and an awesome quote from each of them—this is who they are and what they say:

AUDRE LORDE

Your silence will not protect you.

SANDRA CISNEROS

I've put up with too much, too long. And now I'm just too intelligent, too powerful, too beautiful, too sure of who I am finally to deserve anything less.

FRIDA KAHLO

Feet, what do I need you for when I have wings to fly?

MAXINE HONG KINGSTON

In a time of destruction, create something: a poem, a parade, a community, a school, a vow, a moral principle; one peaceful moment.

RUBY DEE

The kind of beauty I want most is the hard-to-get kind that comes from within—strength, courage, dignity.

And at the bottom, just a little smaller it says Write Like a Girl—Join the Conversation. It's just radical enough, I think. I take a gulp of Mia's orange juice and get in the shower.

I run to the train downstairs and jump on the A, studying the ads right away. There's one that's particularly gross—an ad for plastic surgery where one woman holds oranges in front of her breasts with a super-sad face, and another woman right next to her holds melons in front of her breasts, and of course on her face, there's a massive smile. Every time I see that ad I get so depressed about the state of the world, but when I get up closer, I see that someone has written across the top, "Or love yourself, and donate to breast cancer instead." *Yes,* I think. I take my phone out and snap a shot to send to Jasmine. I compose the text:

> This is what I'm talking about—live actions!
> I mean, that's what we need to do, we need
> to be taking down crappy ads and media
> and men who are setting out to totally
> destroy our self-worth.

I switch trains at 125th Street, and along with the Poetry in Motion posters, which I so want to have one of my poems on someday, I see the ads for Thinx, the period underwear, which I love.

It says: Why Are There Period Ads Everywhere? And below, it says, *The better question is, why shouldn't there be? There's a 1 in*

12 chance that you're on your period now, yet we rarely discuss men-
struation outside of whispers from woman to woman. Today we can
change this. I take my journal out and jot down some notes for
later.

> To the ads in the subway that try to tell me how to
> change my body—
>
> My body is a tornado. Nor'easter.
> The eye of every storm. Yes, my body
> a cacophony. Song. Hydrant of butterflies
> Collective. Not meant to be revised or edited.
> Just exactly right the way it is. My body
> is a rallying, an assembling. It cannot be
> shut down or silenced. Won't be. We
> live holy & raucous in our skin, we
> are not made of fruit—there's nothing sweet
> about me. My body is a hurricane. Natural
> earth moving & shaking—we who don't shut up
> or down other girls & the kinds of noise our bodies
> make. We are a protest of bones & will not be shushed
> or quieted. We've got our hands & mouths & teeth
> & breasts & blood all the way up & shining
> & blistering on up & into the great big blazing sky.

By the time I get off on 96th, I'm practically skipping. No
one is gonna take us down. We have all the power. The shirts

are ready as soon as I get to the shop. I take a few out and spread them on the counter.

"Very cool shirts," Dave, the guy who's working on the front desk, says. "My girlfriend would love the Frida Kahlo one. She's into that kinda stuff."

"I love them," I say, unfolding a few to see which size would work for me.

"So, you have extra-small, small, medium, and large, and then a few of the men's large as well. Does that work?"

"Yes," I say. "Thank you." I walk out of the store and hail a cab, since the shirts are way heavier than I expected. We ordered enough to sell next week. I haul the load into the taxi and text Jasmine that I'm on my way to Word Up, and that she should meet me there so she can help me unload the shirts.

Jasmine is sitting on the front stoop of the bookstore when I arrive. She has her journal out, so I know something's already on her mind. I give her a quick kiss on the cheek, and we haul the boxes inside. The bookstore is still empty, since bilingual story time doesn't start until one p.m. It's just Derrick, one of the grad school volunteers who works the checkout desk, and Leidy, who is setting up in the back. She's setting out notebooks and pens, and is clearly way more ambitious this week, since she has nearly a dozen laid out on the tables. We say hello, and I instantly read my poem to Jasmine, who loves it, and thinks we should make a video this week. I pour all the shirts out.

"So cool," I say.

"A reminder that class is about to start, so please respect the space," Leidy says, eyeing the shirts, "but I am loving these shirts. Nice job!"

"Thanks, and you know nobody ever comes to class, Leidy. It's like every week it's our special one-on-one," I joke.

"Well, I am hopeful. So please think about someone other than yourself, dear," she replies, and walks to the back of the store.

I roll my eyes, then notice Jasmine, who is studying the tags on each shirt. By the look on her face, I can tell something isn't right. "Did they get a quote wrong? I knew I should have checked them all before I left. What'd they mess up?"

Jasmine looks at me. "You didn't check them?"

"Oh, I mean, yeah, I looked. They looked great to me, but . . ."

"And you checked the sizes? I mean, you *ordered* these sizes?"

"Yeah, they're all there. Jeez, I thought you meant the quotes were wrong, but yeah, the sizes are all here. I got 'em all." I smile. "We are really doing this."

Jasmine is silent. She pushes the chair back and folds her arms.

"What?" I ask.

"You really don't know."

"Catch me up, Jasmine, because I have no idea what the problem is. I mean, I spent all last week helping Isaac with the design, and then the whole freakin' morning going downtown to pick these up, and now you're annoyed—so what's the big deal?"

"The *big* deal is that I can't wear any of them, Chelsea."

I look down at the shirts and see that Jasmine has laid out all the tags on the women's sizes. "You didn't even think about me, which means you didn't consider anyone who doesn't fit into the standard sizes, which is *messed up*." She whispers that last part so Leidy doesn't hear us arguing.

"Oh, crap," I say, gathering them up to look at all the labels. "I'm so sorry, I didn't even, I just . . . I didn't even think about getting the bigger sizes, or the plus sizes, I mean—"

"Well, you should have, and if you looked at anything other than your favorite magazines, then you'd know there's a whole market for curve models, and women and girls who occupy space with their bodies in different ways."

"I know, I know, I just—"

"You don't know, and it makes me feel like you don't even see me, Chelsea."

"Intersectionality," Leidy sings from the back of the store, clearly listening in on our conversation. "You must learn to look at and see each other—you have to come together over race and class and color and nationality and sexuality and size and ability, and so on," she begins to hum.

I roll my eyes again. "I got men's large, okay? You can wear that, right? It's fine."

"No. It's not fine. And by the way, for someone who's so into fashion, I think you'd know that a men's shirt is cut differently, and so no, it's not gonna fit me. And Leidy's right. We have to start thinking about everyone, and not just ourselves all the time. You have to do better," Jasmine says, grabbing one of the women's large. "I'm gonna get Nadine to make this work for me. And you, you need to do some edits on that poem."

20
JASMINE

When I get home, I sit at the kitchen table and try to start my homework, but all I can think about is my conversation with Chelsea. I can't stop thinking how girls like me hide in plain sight. Chelsea has known me since middle school, and in middle school I was fat. I wasn't thick or plump or big-boned. I was fat. The biggest kid in our grade. Always. How could she not see that? All these years of taking the subway together, hasn't she noticed that when she points out that there's a seat and I say, "That's okay, I'm fine, you sit," that I am not just being polite but that I actually can't fit, can't squeeze in between two people on a crowded train?

I have always felt so close to Chelsea. In the fifth grade, a white girl told me that my brown skin was just dirt and that if I took a bath, it would come off. Chelsea slapped her. Of course, we later learned about the whole nonviolent movement, but for me it meant Chelsea was my real friend. That she wasn't going to make excuses for anyone's racist comments. She has always had my back. Always.

I'm so distracted by my thoughts that I don't even notice Mom has come into the kitchen. She has bags of groceries in her hands. "Can you help me with these?"

I take the bags and start unpacking them.

"We're having sandwiches for dinner," Mom says. She sets out pastrami, salami, turkey, and cheddar and provolone cheese.

I unpack the pickles and all the condiments she bought.

Mom slices sourdough bread, then takes out serving dishes and prepares the meat and cheese on the plates like she's getting ready for guests to come over, even though it's just us.

"What's wrong?" Mom asks.

"Nothing. Why?"

"What's wrong?"

"Mom, I'm fine." I bring the trays of meat and cheese into the dining room.

"Humph." Mom dumps potato chips in a bowl and brings it to the table.

I call Jason and Dad to come eat.

I wish I could just make my sandwich and go to my room to eat. Every time we have dinner together, we share our peaks and pits of the day. Today, there are no peaks to share. Just pits for me. And I don't want to talk about it, especially not with Mom. She has nagged me about my weight since I was a chubby seven-year-old. *You need to get that weight off of you*, she says. She's eased up on it now that Dad is so sick. But still, I know she wishes she had a normal-size daughter.

I can feel myself about to cry, and I am so tired of crying. So tired of stressing about if I am going to fit in a booth at a restaurant or if the reason why Isaac hasn't actually asked me out is because he'd be embarrassed to claim the fat girl as *his* girl.

But I am more tired that all these things are superficial and have nothing to do with my actual health. The last time Mom insisted I go to the doctor because she was so worried about my weight, the doctor told her I was healthy. That, yes, incorporating healthy eating and regular exercise would be important but that all my vitals were where they needed to be. Still, though, she nagged the whole way home. "You need to get that weight off of you." Like it is so easy.

I don't care what Mom says, losing weight isn't about my health. I know this because whenever she gains half a pound, she looks at herself in the mirror with disgust and says, "Oh God, I am getting fat." And when she was pregnant with Jason all she kept talking about was the fear of not losing the weight afterward, as if staying big would be the worst thing that could happen to her.

"Jasmine, would you like to start us off?" Dad asks.

No. I really, really don't.

I think for a long while.

"Come on, Jazz," Jason whines. He eats a chip, and Mom gives him a look, then looks at me.

"Um, I'd rather not talk about today." I haven't even told

Mom about anything that's happened at school with the blog or quitting the acting ensemble, so explaining why we made shirts wouldn't even make sense to her. She'd probably just say what she always says whenever I complain about the roles big girls get cast in, "Well, Jasmine, you know how the entertainment industry is. If you want a different kind of role, you have to look a certain way. That's the business." No outrage in her voice.

"There's no pass," Jason says. "Hurry up."

Dad says, "It's okay. Tonight, Jasmine gets a pass." He smiles at me.

Jason says, "My pit was not getting chocolate milk at lunch today because they ran out."

"And your peak?" Mom asks.

"Chips for dinner!"

"You have to eat your sandwich first," Dad says.

Mom shares about her day. "My pit was the looong line I had to stand in at Whole Foods, but my peak is sitting here, eating dinner with you all."

Dad drinks from his glass of water and says, "Your mom and I have the same peak tonight, I guess." Then he looks at me, "My pit is that something's upset my daughter." When Dad says this, I smile—which is kind of strange. I have never felt joy after someone shared their bad thing. Dad prays over the food, and we eat. Mom compromises with Jason, telling him as long as he eats two squares of his sandwich he can have some chips.

After dinner, I go to my room. I am finally in a better mood and am able to get my homework done. Just before I go to bed, there's a knock at my door. "It's me," Mom says.

"Come in."

She doesn't step into my room. Instead, she talks through the half-opened door. "You don't have to tell me, but I just want to make sure you're talking to someone."

"I'm fine, Mom. Just a misunderstanding with Chelsea. We'll be fine."

Mom's shoulders relax. "Okay. Just, just checking. I love you."

"I know you do. I love you too."

Mom closes the door.

I lie in bed, trying to fall asleep, and I think for today's peak I could have said Mom and Dad.

21
CHELSEA

Our shirts are a hit. There are nearly thirty of us who show up in all the different designs. I wear Maxine Hong Kingston, and Jasmine wears Ruby Dee. Isaac and Nadine got some of the people from their clubs to wear them, and then Mia got the entire girls varsity basketball team to come in rocking our Woman Warrior T-shirts. I watch them all walk in together—a whole mix of the women on their shirts—and see the surprised look on the security guard's face.

"These look nice," Ms. Sanchez says, eyeing all the designs as we walk in. She stops me to admire the quote on the back. "Wow, I love these! Where did they come from?" she asks.

"We designed them," I say. "Well, I mean, a bunch of us did. Isaac, Jasmine, and Nadine—we all figured it was about time people celebrated revolutionary women," I finish.

"You kids did this, huh? I love it. Let me get three of the Sandra Cisneros shirts, please. For my granddaughters. They know how radical I am. They will love these. You have to teach 'em when they're young," she says. "We came here from the Dominican Republic, and once you arrive, they try to take all your history away from you. Whitewash it all. Maybe put Julia Alvarez on the next batch."

"We're on it," I say, unloading three shirts for her right then and there.

Who knew Ms. Sanchez was so political. And by second period, I am getting text message requests for shirt sizes and styles. We beg Ms. Lucas to use her classroom, and then we post on her bulletin board that we'll be selling some of our shirts, and if we run out, or need different sizes, then we're taking any future orders during lunch. We get to the room to set up—unfolding the shirts that Jasmine and I packed up in our backpacks in neat piles. We each brought twenty-five shirts in all different sizes to make sure we had a variety for everyone. We didn't know if people would want them or not, but we wanted to be prepared. As soon as the bell rings, kids come filing in and we don't stop the whole time. We sell all fifty shirts. Lots of folks love the women we have chosen, but others come in with special requests: Shakira, Tina Charles (from one of Mia's teammates), Gloria Steinem, bell hooks, Gloria E. Anzaldúa. And then there are requests for everyday women warriors. They tell us stories about women who make life better—moms who wake up early to make sausage and eggs for their kids, and aunts who show up to school plays and make clothes, sisters who help with algebra homework. When Meg and her best friend, Michelle, walk in to buy a shirt, I know the mood in school has lifted.

"Can I get two shirts? Uh, the bright yellow one and the hot pink one . . . the one you're wearing."

"All sold out," Jasmine says, not looking up.

"But we could take an order," I add, nudging Jasmine while in my mind trying to figure out why Michelle would even want to be a part of our movement. "This is Audre Lorde, and I'm wearing Maxine Hong Kingston. If you don't know them, you should totally look them up," I say.

"These are . . . I really like the shirts," Meg says, pulling her wallet out of her bag. "And for what it's worth, I'm sorry. We really were just joking."

"Thanks for that," I say.

Jasmine doesn't say anything at first, then as Meg walks away she calls out, "If you're going to wear these shirts, you really should look up these women. You could learn something."

* * *

By the end of lunch, Ms. Lucas is as excited as we are. "I'm just overwhelmed . . . ," she says. "Did you hear how many people shared stories about the strong women who make them who they are?"

I take out a sheet of paper before we leave and write: *To join the revolution, visit Write Like a Girl*, and jot down the website for our blog before pinning it to the bulletin board.

"You can't use the word 'revolution,'" Ms. Lucas says, eyeing the paper over my shoulder.

"But that's what it is. You saw how many people showed up here today, right?"

"Listen, I am here for you all, since I am your advisor, but 'join the revolution' is very different from 'join the conversation.' Let's get back to the dialogue, and everything will be fine." She finishes packing up her room and walks out with us. "Let's keep it all on the up-and-up."

"Okay," I say, frustrated that I can't change her mind. "I gotta run to my locker before my next class. Maybe we can talk about this later?" I add. Ms. Lucas nods as I rush out.

I run upstairs to the third floor to grab my textbook before STEAM. I've been reading a ton of tech blogs, and I can't wait to bring some of my newfound poems to class. I only have a few minutes before the lunch bell rings, so when I see Jacob Rizer near his locker, I almost turn around and leave my poems, but he stops me.

"Chelsea Spencer—poet, activist, T-shirt designer—she does it all," he finishes, starting to laugh.

"Did you wanna buy a shirt? Because we actually SOLD OUT. Too bad you missed your chance," I say.

"Oh, I probably still have a chance," Jacob says, and I take a step back. If he's flirting with me, and I think he is, then he's doing it in a creepy way. I give him a look and open up my locker.

"Whatever," I say.

"So you miss us in poetry club?" he asks, pushing his shoulder up against mine for a quick second. It's not too hard, but it's definitely uncomfortable, and way closer than he's ever gotten to me. Jacob was always such a jerk in class, and now I'm wondering if he was acting like a kid—like how my dad once told me when a boy really likes you they're mean to you.

"Nope, I'm pretty good where I am, thanks," I say, and move to grab the book inside my locker and get out of the hallway, which is still empty since lunch hasn't let out yet.

"Come on, admit it, you miss me just a little, right?"

"Oh yeah, I really miss all the times you talked over me in class, and when you'd make fun of what I said . . . yup, I really miss that."

"Ah, I knew you missed me. But I guess now you're too busy writing your sweet little poems about how hard the world is for girls. Poor little girl," he says, and pats me on the head like I'm a puppy or some small animal.

I don't know what it is, but something snaps in me, and I shove him off me, hard.

"Jeez, Spencer, you can't even take a little joke?"

"It's not funny," I say, "and don't touch me." Tears come to my eyes.

"Yeah, everyone is right about you and Jasmine. Always taking everything so seriously. And always making it about you."

"Shut up," I say, struggling to find a better comeback, but mostly just trying to walk away. I shut the locker door.

"Don't worry, I won't bother you anymore."

"Thanks," I say, trying to push past him. He's standing so close to me that it's hard for me to move away.

"You can go ahead and keep working on the next Feminist Manifesta," Jacob says, starting to laugh again, and as soon as I turn around, he slaps me . . . on my butt . . . right there in the empty hallway, with no one around to witness. I don't even turn around. My whole body feels like it's burning, like I'm on fire, and I can't catch my breath, and the tears are coming down for real now. I keep walking faster and faster.

"It was a joke, Spencer. A JOKE. Come on, lighten up," he calls after me.

I make it as far as the bathroom at the end of the hall before I'm behind one of the stalls trying to control my sobbing. I lean against the door and start to take deep breaths. I know what I have to do, and I take a few more minutes before pulling myself together. When the end-of-lunch bell rings, I walk down the stairs and straight for Principal Hayes's office.

"May I help you?" his secretary, Ms. Potts, asks.

"I'd like to speak to Principal Hayes, please. It's important."

"And remind me of your name, dear."

"Chelsea Spencer."

"Oh, yes, I have been hearing your name quite a bit," she says, smiling, "and reading that very smart blog of yours and Jasmine Gray's. Very smart indeed." She nods in my direction like she's in on a secret with me and lets Principal Hayes know that a student is here to see him.

"Well, to what do I owe the honor?" Principal Hayes says, standing in his doorway.

"I, um, I just wanted to talk to you about an incident," I say.

"Okay, I'm all ears," he says, "and Ms. Potts, could you go ahead and set up that conference call for me—it's in about ten minutes."

"Oh, um, well, it's uh, I would like some time to talk, because it was a pretty big deal," I say.

"I'll decide on that," he answers. "Because, Chelsea, you understand that there have been several issues that you've been involved in lately, correct?"

"Yes," I answer, refusing to say *correct*, and feeling like I'm being talked down to for the second time today. He waits, looking from me to Ms. Potts, who is watching, trying to pretend she isn't paying attention, even though it's obvious that she is.

"Okay, well, I need to report that Jacob Rizer smacked me."

"He smacked you? Jacob Rizer? Our senior class president, National Honor Society member, Jacob Rizer *smacked* you today?"

"On my butt," I add, trying to keep it clean but hoping to get Principal Hayes to understand what actually happened.

"Excuse me?"

"Yes, it happened, just now in the hallway upstairs. I was at my locker, and he came over and was asking all these questions and getting really close to me, and he just, oh, and he also patted my head too."

"I see," he says. "Well, I cannot imagine Jacob would ever do such a thing, but . . ."

"But he did. I am telling you right now that he did."

"And I appreciate that. Who else was in the hallway with you?" he asks.

I don't even want to think about why he's asking.

"No one," I say.

"And why were you both in the hallway during lunch?" he asks.

"Because Jasmine and I were selling shirts, and . . ."

"That's one of the problems right there," he starts. "Neither of you asked me if you could do that. You and Jasmine think you are above the rules, but you cannot sell your shirts on our property during school time to make a profit."

"But the National Honor Society and the cheerleading team and the basketball team sell stuff all the time to support their clubs, so what's the difference?" I ask.

"The difference is that it was approved by me, and it was clear what they were raising money for. There are protocols that you and Jasmine don't seem to understand," he says, obviously frustrated with me.

"Okay, well, that's really not the point. The point is that he physically put his hands on my body, and I feel like we need to do something about it," I say.

Ms. Potts interrupts. "It's true. I have seen that young man be a bit handsy with young women in the hallways."

"Uh, thank you, Ms. Potts. I will handle this, and could you please call up my conference? Chelsea, I hear your complaint loud and clear, and appreciate you coming to me with this."

"Right, because you said you didn't want any more drama online, and so I figured I needed to come right to you with this. So here I am."

"Yes, agreed. And thank you. And I will certainly be talking to Jacob to get his side of the story as well," Principal Hayes finishes as he starts walking back into his office.

"His side of the story? What? His side of the story is that

212

he smacked my butt and patted my head, as if he had ANY right to touch my body however he wanted," I say, not moving anywhere.

"Allegedly," Principal Hayes says, and it's that word that tells me the fight is bigger than this moment, bigger than me, or Principal Hayes or Jacob Rizer. It's bigger because not enough men listen to women, or believe women, or honor what we have to say. Ms. Potts is looking down at her desk. I don't want to cry in front of them, so I gather my book bag and turn to walk out.

"Not even a thank-you?" Principal Hayes calls after me.

* * *

"Allegedly: used to convey that something is claimed to be the case or have taken place, although there is no proof," I read from my phone, while taking a massive bite of a bacon cheeseburger, and coating the fries with our favorite ketchup and hot sauce mix.

"I cannot believe he did that," Jasmine says, shock in her face. "And I can't believe Principal Hayes just brushed it off. It's as if we're moving backward, you know?"

"Yup, exactly, and I feel like he did it on purpose, just to prove a point. And I would've gone to Ms. Lucas, but I feel like maybe she's not all about it either, and I didn't go to anybody else because I just don't even have the energy. I don't wanna go through a whole he said, she said. Why should I have to do that?"

"You shouldn't. And it makes me feel bad for our teachers, who have to deal with him every day. He's so cocky too, like he always knows everything. Ms. Lucas has to deal with Principal

213

Hayes, and you know when you went to see him, he was already mad at us for wearing those shirts today."

"And for selling them. He told me all about that. Do we need more food? Wings? Cheese fries?" I ask. "I'm starving." We are sitting in The Uptown. It's our favorite diner, and right on the corner of Wadsworth and Broadway, so it's one of the best meeting spots.

"Listen, we had to skip lunch for the cause, and I'm thinking we have a lot more to do now," Jasmine says, taking a bite of her BLT. "And yes, more food is a must, but I'm thinking we save some room for dessert. Chocolate cake would go so well with this meal."

Jasmine takes her sweater off, revealing the slightly off-the-shoulder look that Nadine designed. Nadine cut the sides and added an extra panel from one of the other shirts, so it's fitted and includes colors from the others. She also opened the collar, so it falls off the left side just a little.

"That shirt looks so good," I say, looking down at my plain shirt, which looks pretty dumpy in comparison. "Maybe I'll see if Nadine can fix mine up."

Jasmine gives me a look.

"What? I can't have a cute shirt too?"

"Chelsea, you can have all the cute shirts in all the cute stores, okay? Forever 21 should be called Forever Extra-Small, and Urban Outfitters? And Uniqlo? And Rubies and Jeans? Please. You can have all the cute shirts in the world. Leave Nadine to help me!" She laughs.

"You're right. I didn't think about that. Look, I'm really sorry. I messed up something that was supposed to be a big group action."

"Don't worry. It was still a big group action, and it worked. I mean, you definitely messed it up, yes, but thanks for saying that. And besides, I do look really good in this shirt," Jasmine says.

We both bust out laughing.

Then Jasmine says, "But next time?"

"I know, I know. I'll get all the right sizes next time," I say. We order a chocolate cake with a side of vanilla ice cream.

"I still can't believe what happened with Jacob," Jasmine says, shaking her head, "or with Principal Hayes."

"Me neither, and after it, I just kept thinking: Am I making too big a deal of this, or was it me that provoked it, and then I was pissed at myself for even thinking that. How could I think that?" I ask.

"Because this is complicated," Jasmine says. "And it just shows us that we need to do more."

Nadine and Isaac walk in. "It's sooooo cold out there," Nadine says, squeezing next to me in the booth, leaving Isaac to awkwardly sit next to Jasmine without getting all up on her. It's awesome to watch. They both order coffee and load it up with cream and sugar. "Today rocked," Nadine says, hugging my shoulders.

"Yeah, y'all made everybody start talking," Isaac says. "And I'm really feeling this new design on the shirt," he says, eyeing Jasmine.

"It looks so cool, right?" I ask.

Isaac blushes then changes the focus off Jasmine. "My dad asked me to make a bunch for our family reunion, with all the women's faces from the Rodriguez family."

"Oh, I love that," Jasmine says.

"So then what's next?" he asks, eyeing both of us.

"We're figuring it out. Something really big has to happen," Jasmine says. We tell Nadine and Isaac about Jacob.

"Are you gonna fight it?" Nadine asks.

"Yeah, I'm gonna fight it with you all, with something we decide to do. I don't want to have to bring a teacher into it, and I definitely don't want to talk about it with Jacob Rizer—he's just gonna totally deny it anyway," I say.

"Yeah, something's gotta change here. But if I were you, I totally wouldn't let Jacob off the hook," Isaac adds.

"You're right," I say, sitting back. "I know you're right. We gotta come up with something. What. Is. Next?"

"We can wear the shirts to the next open mic at Word Up. Maybe poets from the other schools will want to get some," Jasmine says. "Chelsea, before you perform your poem, you can talk about why we made these shirts."

I tell her, "*You* can talk about the shirts, too, after *you* perform one of your poems."

"Yeah," Isaac says. "You've been writing a lot lately. I want to hear some of your words."

Jasmine doesn't say yes to our idea, but she doesn't say no either.

Nadine says, "I can film the performance so you two can post it online. This can be our next action."

"And we need a statement or a list of demands. What was that you said earlier, Chelsea?" Jasmine asks. "Something about listening to women, and . . ." Jasmine grabs a pen and motions me to start talking. We spend the whole afternoon coming up with a plan.

22
JASMINE

It's the week before Thanksgiving, and we're all together at Word Up. I usually sit back to enjoy the open mic. I love seeing Chelsea up there mesmerizing everyone with her words, how she is so bold and confident. Sometimes I get nervous with her. I know her poems by heart as much as she practices them with me. So when she is reciting them, I move my lips along with her, sending her all the good vibes I can muster. It's one thing to be in a play and have a whole cast of people supporting you, but standing alone on stage in front of a mic? That's a whole nother talent. One I am not sure I have, but still, I am going to do this anyway because I promised Chelsea I'd read one of my poems.

I am good at pretending to be someone else, of getting in their skin and finding their voice, mannerisms. But tonight, I am standing here in my own brown skin, no costume, no stage makeup. Just me. Just me and my words, no playwright's thoughts or director's notes.

I am standing in front of the crowd, and this is the worst stage fright I've ever had. The audience here in this tiny bookstore is closer than they'd be if I were on a stage and they were sitting in the audience. They can probably see every roll in my belly, my thick legs shaking, my chubby hands holding the mic.

I don't want to do this.

I look out into the crowd and see Chelsea on the edge of her seat looking at me like, *You got this, you got this.* And Isaac is doing the same. I clear my throat and begin.

* * *

This Body

SKIN: NOUN
1. Sensitive. Dry.
See Dove soap, Oil of Olay, shea butter.
See middle school pimples plumping up
the night before picture day.
Always on the chin or nose.

2. Dark. See slave. See Negro.
See age 7. See yourself
playing on the playground
when a white girl says,
you must eat a lot of chocolate
since your skin is so brown.

HAIR: NOUN

1. See assimilation.
See smoke from the hot comb crocheting the air,
burning a sacred incense.
Your momma parting your hair, bringing iron to nap,
"Hold your ear, baby," she tells you.
So she can press Africa out.
When black girls ask, "Is it real?" Say yes.
When white girls ask, "Can I touch it?" Say no.

2. See natural. Reference Angela Davis,
Dorothy Pitman Hughes.
Comb yours out. Twist yours like black licorice,
like the lynching rope
used on your ancestors' necks.
Let it hang
free.

HIPS: NOUN

1. Reference Lucille Clifton and every other big girl
who knows how to work a Hula-Hoop.
See Beyoncé. Dance like her in the mirror.
Do not be afraid of all your powers.

2. You will not fit in
most places. Do not
bend, squeeze, contort yourself.

Be big, brown girl.
Big wide smile.
Big wild hair.
Big wondrous hips.
Brown girl, be.

* * *

For the past week I have been replaying my performance over and over. How nervous I felt before I did it, how when the audience clapped for me it sounded like a rainstorm moving through the room. How Isaac looked at me like he wanted my body, wanted me. The way Chelsea hugged me so tight afterward. We haven't seen each other for the past few days. It's Thanksgiving, and both of our families are serious about holidays. Mrs. Spencer doesn't even like for Chelsea to use the phone to call friends when it's family time. Mom agrees. "You see Chelsea just about every day. You can give your family one weekend," she said to me this morning when I asked what time dinner would be done. Mom assumed I wanted to go over to Chelsea's, but I was asking because Isaac wants to go to the movies. We don't have school tomorrow—maybe she'll let me out of the house then.

The whole brownstone smells like bread. Mom's buttermilk biscuits are baking in the oven, the last thing she's making before she calls us to the table. Every year she cooks a feast, and every year she says, "This is the last time I'm doing all this cooking. One of you needs to come in here and learn the recipes so I can retire." But every time I ask her to teach me how to make stuffing or how to bake her perfect peach cobbler, she never has the time. I don't think Mom will ever stop cooking. The kitchen is her favorite place in the house. When she cooks, she kicks us out, telling us, "I'll call you when it's ready."

But today, she's at least letting me sit in the kitchen with her. Which feels like a privilege since she kicked Jason and Dad out because they kept asking to taste food as she was cooking. They are playing video games in the spare room upstairs that's basically Jason's game room. Mom doesn't let me help though. I mean, she tries to let me help, but she can't stop looking over me as I chop the onion. She took the knife out of my hand and said, "No, sweetheart, like this," and pretty much cut the onion in the same exact way I was cutting, so I just finished and didn't ask for anything else to do because I know cooking is Mom's way of taking care of us.

She is standing at the oven, peeking in at her biscuits to see if they are browning when I say, "Mom, do you ever feel like Dad makes you cook, like he expects you to be the one to prepare all the meals?"

"Of course not," she says. She opens the oven, letting the heat escape. Now that the biscuits are out and sitting on the cooling pad, the kitchen smells even more like fresh bread. "Your dad and I don't *make* each other do anything. I like to cook, so I cook. If I didn't, I wouldn't." Mom spreads butter on top of the biscuits.

The doorbell rings, and she motions for me to get it. It's Grandma Gray and Aunt Yolanda. They are always the first to arrive because Grandma does not like to be late, so she shows up about thirty minutes early to everything.

By the end of the day, our home has been visited by too many people to count. Mostly family, but a few members of our church stop by to check on Dad. One of his colleagues from the Schomburg Center comes by with a sweet potato pie from Make My Cake. "Couldn't come empty handed," he says. He's the fifth person that's come by today, bringing food with him but not staying to eat it. "I just wanted to say hello and see how you were doing," the man says.

Mom takes the pie and goes into the kitchen, mumbling, "What am I going to do with all this food?" Then, even quieter and with more venom in her tongue, she says, "All these people visiting like this is a wake. He's not dead yet."

DECEMBER

23
CHELSEA

"Chels, wake up," Mia calls. I've been taking my sleeping- and downtime seriously, and since all the drama happening at school, I feel like I've just needed a break—from everything. "What are you doing in here?" Mia asks, pulling the covers away from me. "It's Christmas Eve—we have stuff to do. And dinner tonight. Grandma's already on her way. Get up!"

I slowly roll out of bed. "I don't just celebrate Christmas, you know? And I call it a holiday gathering—because I appreciate Hanukkah and Kwanzaa as well, to honor the Jewish and African American members of our community," I say, smiling and proud of myself.

"What do you know about Hanukkah and Kwanzaa, Chelsea?"

"A lot, okay? I know that Hanukkah is also called the Festival of Lights, and that it's observed for eight days and nights, and it commemorates the rededication of the Holy Temple. Boom."

"Yeah," Mia says, humoring me.

"Yeah, that's right. And Kwanzaa is an African American celebration that honors cultural heritage and traditional values. There are seven guiding principles that we should hold up throughout the year and not just over the holidays. So, in your face," I finish, and slip my pajama pants on.

"What are the seven guiding principles?" Mia asks.

"Umoja, which means unity, um, Nia—uh, purpose, that means purpose, and faith—Imani, of course." I pause.

"That's three."

"I know that's three, and I know the others, I just . . ."

"And now I know that you did a basic Google and Wikipedia search on both of those so you'd know what to say when people ask, right?"

"No, it's more than that. I'm just . . . I'm just into celebrating as a community. I mean, even the lobby of our building is all-inclusive with a tree, a menorah, and a kinara—for Kwanzaa," I add, showing off a little, "and so I feel like celebrating everything too. I'm for everyone. I also wrote a poem for Jasmine. Do you wanna hear it?"

"Not now . . . ," Mia says.

I start to read it anyway.

Womanhood
for Jasmine

Old-fashioned beauty myth media breakdown
Pretty—a pathetic fiction sold to us

Stores that carry only size extra-small
Makeup meant to cover up and whitewash
Resolve to go natural, obliterate your machine
Bust boundaries wide open with our skills
Write ourselves into every future we imagine

"I realized that I was not being very intersectional, and so I revised my own thinking and ways of being in the world. I am a work in progress," I finish.

"I know, Chelsea, I know. You are always very self-important. And I know it's really important to you to be all-inclusive and all about diversity—I know that—we all know that, but can you please just be there for Mom and Grandma today? Can you just be all Catholic, and not be all weird about Christmas and God, and all the stuff you love to bring up that makes Mom lose it? Can you do that?"

"I can only be true to myself," I say, grabbing my book and starting to walk out. I've been reading *The Handmaid's Tale* and loving all the insane drama. "What would Margaret Atwood say, you ask?"

"I didn't ask that," Mia says.

"Well, she would say that as women, we have to fight for our bodies and minds, and that no one can silence us or shut us down, and people should value our opinions. That's what she would say. And on top of that, Mom should really stand up for herself more, and she shouldn't always be so quiet and subdued. If I've learned anything so far this school year, it's that women need to raise their voices."

Mia stares at me.

"Fine, I won't bring up the religion stuff. I'll be a good little Catholic." I smile.

* * *

"The turkey smells delightful," my grandma calls into the kitchen at my dad, who's doing all the cooking for Christmas Eve dinner. We've just come from afternoon mass, where I both listened to the sermon AND did some mindful Buddhist meditation.

"Steven, I can't believe that Lydia allowed you to do all the work today."

"Oh, Mom, you know that Steven loves to cook, so why can't you believe that?" my mom asks, sitting down and pouring us all a little bit of wine. My parents are very progressive when they want to be, and, I'm beginning to think, when it's convenient for them.

"Oh, honey, I just never thought I'd be alive to see a man do all the work in the kitchen. I mean, it's fine if you want to work and leave your kids in daycare all day and choose different life paths, but, honey—I would imagine you would want to still do a bit of the domestic work around the house." Grandma smiles at us and takes a sip of wine.

My mom's smile is tight as she passes the rolls around the table.

"Not that it's all bad," my grandma continues, "but a woman's work is with the children too, you know? A man can only do so much before he feels taken advantage of, and begins to resent his situation." She whispers that last part so my dad can't hear as he walks out with the turkey. I've always known my mom and grandma have a testy relationship. I mean, they love each other—calling and seeing each other all the time—but I can't help but feel like some of their relationship feels kind of toxic.

"Mom, Steven and I share responsibilities around the house and with the kids. We always have, and I think Chelsea and Mia have appreciated and benefited from that," my mom says, squeezing my leg under the table. *What? Does no one trust me?*

"I know you two have a very new wave thing going on. Well, let me tell you all that your grandfather and I valued tradition. We believed in a traditional marriage—and it was important to both of us that I took care of the home and the children. Your grandfather made sure all of us were comfortable and taken care of. That was important to him. It's the way all of us did things. And we were perfectly happy that way," my grandma finishes.

It was the "perfectly happy" that got me. I couldn't stop myself.

"But, Grandma, you wanted to be a teacher, right?"

My mom glares at me. *Not tonight*, she mouths in my direction. That's the main issue with me and my mom. It's never the right time with her. She is always the cool and calm one, the woman who lets everyone tell her how to feel and never raises her voice for anything, so sometimes I feel like I need to be that voice for her—whether she likes it or not.

"Well, of course, but I taught your mother and your aunt, and that was enough for me. You know, you young girls, you think you can do everything, but you can't. Something is always sacrificed. Something has to give, and usually it's the marriage that suffers."

"But not everyone wants to get married," I say, completely ignoring the fact that I've imagined my fairy-tale wedding with James about a billion times, and they all feature me in a massive white dress walking down an aisle littered with rose petals. So weird. "I have a lot of friends who don't want to get married. They want a career—they want a job—that's where they want the focus to be."

"And that's what they'll get, believe me. You focus on a career, you get a career. But don't expect to get both. Young women today have no time to care about their homes, their families. All they care about is getting to the top—whatever that means, and then the rest of their lives just fall apart." She makes a side-eye at my mom.

At this comment, my mom sits back. I know it has been an ongoing argument between them, since my grandma has always given her a hard time about sending us to daycare and preschool rather than staying home and being a good homemaker (whatever that means), the way she did.

"Grandma, sorry, but nobody thinks like that anymore. I mean, the system of gender norms was created so we would think that women are the ones who are more biologically capable of taking care of kids and the home, but that's just not true at all." I'm on a roll. "My friends and I aren't in the world just to get the guy and keep the house and have the kids. That's super dated, Grandma. And we're finding ways to break down the myth of the gender role in general and the ways people think about women and the kinds of jobs women are capable of." I take a gulp of my wine and wince when it goes down strong.

My grandma's eyebrows couldn't go much higher on her face, but I notice my mom smiling and giving me the go-ahead to be myself.

24
JASMINE

I've been hanging with Nadine all day. We went to the movies, and on our way to get our nails done, I got a text from Mom that I needed to come home. Now. As soon as I walk into my house, I feel the grief hanging in the air, clinging to the chandelier, touching every doorknob, sitting on every chair. Dorothy, Dad's in-home hospice nurse, is here. This past week, she's been here every day.

Hospice.

The first time I heard that word was in a family meeting with Dad's doctor. The doctor talked with Jason and me about what to expect in the coming months. He said as Dad's cancer progressed Dad would go to hospice or have a nurse come during the day and help keep him comfortable. Dad was adamant that he wanted to die at home, not in a facility with strangers. I couldn't handle the conversation. Couldn't just sit and casually talk about where my dad would die, that my dad would die. I walked out. Stood outside and let New York City's noise invade my mind. Sirens, dogs barking, honking horns, languages from around the world swirling around me. Sometimes all the hustle in New York is overwhelming, but sometimes it calms me. Gives me something else to focus on other than my own hectic world.

"Where is everyone?" I ask Dorothy.

"Jason is sleeping," she tells me.

"Sleeping?" It's only four o'clock in the afternoon.

"He, well, your dad talked with him about what's happening, and he cried himself to sleep."

Mom must hear my voice because she comes out of the room and rushes over to me. Her eyes are red and puffy. She looks at me, says, "It's time to say goodbye, Jasmine. He probably won't make it through the night. He's been—"

"Don't tell me," I say. "Don't."

Mom reaches out to hug me, but I don't let her. I'm afraid that if anyone touches me right now I will start crying and won't be able to stop. Ever. I walk to her bedroom, sit on the bed next to Dad, and lay my head on his chest. He tries to hold me, but his weak arms can barely squeeze me. His breathing is loud and slow and sounds like the building up of a tea kettle's whistle just before it blows, except he never blows out a full breath. His breath struggles to get out, struggles to stay in, like something is playing tug-of-war in his lungs. I listen to his breathing and tell myself, *Hold on to this, you will want to remember this one day.* I've been doing this ever since Dad was diagnosed. I stare at him, trying to remember the way he tilts his head to the side when he's trying to remember something, the way he rubs his head when he's frustrated and trying to hold in his anger. I've been listening to his laugh. How it is never quiet, never a chuckle, always coming from a deep well of joy. A booming laugh that vibrates a room. I try to remember all of Dad so I can tell my future children about him. They will want to know about their grandpa, and I will want to tell them. I wish he could be on this earth forever, or at least till he's eighty or ninety, at least till he's old enough to sneak candy to his grandchildren like my grandpa did to me. Dad will not be here to tease me by telling my kids how I acted when I was their age. He won't give his grandchildren scavenger hunt challenges, sending them around the city.

A part of me wants to freeze my life right here. I don't want to have another birthday, don't want to go to prom or graduate or leave for college or get a dream job or have a dream wedding because Dad won't be here for any of it.

I will miss him every day for the rest of my life.

We lie together for hours. I didn't mean to fall asleep with him. When Mom wakes me, she is whispering, "Your phone. It's Chelsea."

I pull myself away from Dad and take my phone out of Mom's hand. I walk into the living room, knowing this is the last time I will be in Dad's arms. I am tempted to turn around, look at him once more, but I can't. "Hey, Chels."

"Oh my God, Jasmine. Did you see my text messages? My grandmother drove me crazy at Christmas dinner. She absolutely pushed me over the edge. I swear, sometimes I wish I was a senior like Mia so I could get out of this house."

I walk to Jason's room. He is still sleeping. I sit in the bean-bag chair in the corner of his room. He turns over but doesn't wake up.

"I am so tired of her criticizing me," Chelsea says.

Chelsea tells me the whole story of what happened at dinner. I don't say much, just a bunch of *Wows!* And *Reallys?*

"Anyway, I'm so sorry," Chelsea says. "I just started venting and didn't even ask you what's up with you."

I tell her I am okay and don't say anything else. I don't want to say it out loud. Not yet. When I hang up the phone, I will have to deal with the chaos that is my own life, but right now, Chelsea is the siren and barking, the honking horns, the words swirling all around me.

"Ugh, my mom is calling me. Sorry, I gotta go," she says.

We hang up.

I watch Jason sleep, and I wonder about all the things people say about boys needing their fathers and how a woman can't raise a man to be a man and wonder what this all means now that Jason will be fatherless. I think about Mom and how she is losing so much right now, her best friend, her husband, the father of her children. How will she survive this? How will any of us?

I pick up my phone, text Isaac: It's happening. My dad is dying.

25
CHELSEA

Dear Jasmine—

I guess the first and most important thing to say is that I love you. I want you to know I'm here for you in whatever way you need. We can hang out at Word Up, or we can talk on the phone late at night the way we used to do when we first met, or we can just hang out together and say nothing. I know I talk too much, but right now I can't think of anything to say. Okay, that's not all true, but what I want to say is that your dad was a rock star—and I don't mean that in a cheesy way, but I mean that everybody loved him. He was always making everybody feel comfortable and making everybody feel like they mattered. I know he was like that, because you're the same way. Here are the typical things I want to say: your dad is not really gone, he will always be with us, it will get better, we will recover and heal, and my

personal favorite—he's in a better place. I even went to
the store to find a card, but those were even worse—*No
one can take away your loving memories,* and *May every
sunrise hold more promise, every moonrise hold more
peace.* Well, I actually like the last one, and I like
thinking that we're in this together, and that every day
will get easier and you'll get stronger. I like that
thought. But at the same time, I think—screw all of that.
This all sucks, and I hate everything about death. But I
love everything about you and your family. All I really
want to say is that I'm here. I'm not going anywhere—
ever.

Love,
Chelsea

* * *

The funeral wore all of us out. It wasn't just seeing Jasmine, her
brother, and her mom, but it was seeing their whole community
gathered together. It was actually having to get up in front of a
whole congregation of people who loved Mr. Gray and speak.
I really, really didn't want to do it. Performing a poem is one
thing, but speaking at a funeral? No thanks. Mrs. Gray asked me
to, though. And so I really wanted to do it. For her, for Mr. Gray.
For Jasmine.

I talked about how Mr. Gray always used the term "community organizing." He'd say to us, *The real work is in the neighborhoods and in the homes. You have to talk to people and get to know*

them—it's all about building relationships and getting to know people in a serious way. He would call us art-ivists and community organizing feminists. He always called himself a feminist too, and said that until men started taking it seriously, joining up with us and adding their voices to the mix, then it couldn't really be a collective conversation. I talked about how he'd send us on New York City Cultural Scavenger Hunts and how I never got to share my findings with him from the last one, the Brown Art Challenge, but that I would keep those lessons with me always. I wanted him to know that our conversations about race, and what it means for me to be a white girl doing this work, will stay with me forever. He taught me to never back down, and to always raise my voice, and that it was my job to not only be an ally, but to be on the front lines too—pushing myself and others to learn more, listen more (that's one I'm still really working on), to speak up when it matters, and to help show others what it means to fight for equity—real equity. I wish I'd gotten the chance to say thank you. And of course, in the end, I decided to share a poem.

* * *

Family
For Mr. Gray

Forever, I will see art as healing.
Something that cures & cushions,
reflects & revitalizes.
Mends & makes magic, always.

How you taught us to see the world
& our place in it. Build together,
show up for each other, stay.
Learn who you are.
Know who you are.
Connect with who you love.

Forever, you are with us.
Scrutinizing sculptures, paintings,
mixed media, monologues & poems.
We stay studying our past,
the ancestors who came before.
You taught us what it means
to make what's wrong—right. & just.
Your words permanently penned in our minds.
Have heart. Stand up. Be proud.

Jasmine spoke at the funeral too. She didn't talk about her
dad as a community organizer or his job at the Schomburg or the
volunteer work he used to do at their church—making sure all
the older folks were cared for and that they always had a Thanksgiving feast for their neighborhood. She just talked about how
much she would miss Sunday mornings in the kitchen with him,
listening to old-school R&B and gospel, making cheese grits and
sausage gravy—a holdout from when he grew up Down South.
She told everybody how much she would miss the kitchen table,
his prayers, and the way he could always see right through to what

she was thinking. She talked about how her family would share a peak and pit at the end of their day. And then she said, "Today, my pit is that my father has left this earth, but my peak is that everyone here has lifted him up. And to see you all is to feel and know—love." I wrote it down in my journal when she said it, so she wouldn't forget the feeling in church that day. It even made me feel a little more religious than I usually do. I've been saying more prayers lately, and although I'm not totally sure who I'm praying to, I like the process of talking my feelings out loud. It feels comfortable in a way it never has before.

* * *

For New Year's Eve we all get together at my house. There's a party happening at Word Up that we'd all planned to go to, and James's parents are out of town, so he invited the whole class there too, but none of us really wanted to go out, so Isaac, Nadine, and Jasmine ended up piled on the bed and beanbags in my room. We'd gone to the bodega to get every possible food we'd need— two liters of Coke, Cheetos, dulce de leche and rocky road ice cream, tortilla chips and pineapple habanero salsa (which is my personal favorite), and a couple bags of candy that were on sale. Mom ordered pizza for us before she went to dinner with Dad, and Mia told us not to mess with any of her stuff but said we could borrow her Beats Pill so we could listen to anything we wanted. And then the apartment was all ours. This was pretty much my dream come true. To cheer Jasmine up, we made a playlist that included the following:

242

Mending a Broken Heart—Jasmine's Playlist

1. "(Your Love Keeps Lifting Me) Higher and Higher"
   —Jackie Wilson
2. "I Say a Little Prayer"—Aretha Franklin
3. "I'll Be There"—The Jackson 5
4. "Through the Fire"—Chaka Khan
5. "The Best"—Tina Turner
6. "Up Where We Belong"—BeBe and CeCe Winans
7. "It's So Hard to Say Goodbye to Yesterday"
   —Boyz II Men
8. "I Didn't Know My Own Strength"—Whitney Houston
9. "Midnight Rider"—Willie Nelson
10. "Endless Love"—Lionel Richie and Diana Ross

It was pretty much the best playlist we'd ever created, and it included a bunch of songs that Jasmine's dad used to love that we heard him play all the time. We pulled out a bunch of my scarves, hats, and jackets and started to lip sync and dance all around the apartment. Isaac stood up on our couch and belted out Willie Nelson's "Midnight Rider" in a way that made us all wonder how many times he'd actually listened to the song to know every verse. And then Jasmine and Isaac did the BeBe and CeCe Winans duet, and basically I had to bite the inside of my cheek as hard as possible to stop myself from saying anything out loud—*kiss her already, you idiot!*

It was pretty awesome to be acting as wild as we were

without any alcohol. I knew that at James's house, everyone would be drunk at this point, or at least tipsy. But Nadine was allergic, and Jasmine and I didn't really like the taste of it, and Isaac had one too many drinks at a party over the summer and threw up the whole night—so he was taking an indefinite break. This is how I know these are my people, though, the ones who you can dance around and act silly with—the ones who you can do shots of soda with and laugh until it comes out of your nose. They're also the ones you can cry with.

By the end of the night, Jasmine is in tears. We huddle around her and tell her we'll be there the whole way. We also all decide to write New Year's resolutions.

"Make them with 'I' statements," Nadine says. "You know, like . . . I resolve to . . . eat more spinach."

"What?" Isaac asks.

"Start with 'I resolve'—you know, make it from your point of view."

"No, I get that, I just don't understand why you're resolving to eat more spinach." Nadine punches Isaac in the arm, and we grab pens and paper.

Jasmine writes: I resolve to mourn. I resolve to heal. I resolve to love.

Nadine writes: Yes, I do resolve to eat more spinach, because I want to grow healthy and strong—in your face, Isaac. I resolve to practice guitar and get some new DJ gigs. I resolve to pass algebra. Please!

Isaac writes: I do solemnly swear to blow up as an artist—make art that matters.

And I write: I resolve to say what I want, when I want, to whomever I want. My messages will be heard. I resolve to speak louder and longer, make my voice bigger and stronger. I resolve to be ocean and sky. Revolving. I resolve to show up, show off, show out—stay later, love harder, be there when it matters. I resolve to be a woman who wins.

"Whoa," Isaac says after we read them all out loud. "I like these."

"I love them," Jasmine says quietly, hugging her paper to her chest. "I think I needed tonight. Thanks, guys." We all pile on top of her to hug. Jasmine looks at the paper again. "Isaac, do you think you could do some quick sketches on these resolutions?"

"What do you mean?"

"Something that represents women," Jasmine says, pulling out her phone.

"Oh yeah, what about the Venus symbol for the female sex?" Nadine asks, pulling an image up on her phone now. "Oh, I like the Venus symbol where the middle section is a fist. That's so cool."

We start to compare notes. We find a heart with the words: "Women + Power + Rights," and then a scale with the Venus and Mars symbols and a big equals sign.

We find a symbol with "Proud Feminist" written inside it. Isaac starts to sketch. He changes it to Womanist & Feminist Rights!

And then he makes a Wonder Woman symbol with the words: "I Resolve to Show Off
My Superpowers." Then we all start drawing
and writing resolutions.

We start Jasmine's playlist from the
beginning, and I pull out all my art supplies. I write:
Women—join us. Resolve to stand up against sexism, and *Women
Make All the Difference*. We find the We Can Do It poster with
Rosie the Riveter, and then see a bunch where black women and
Latinas are shown, so Isaac sketches all our faces and writes
beneath it: *All of Us Can Do It and Do It Well*. We write: *The Future
Is Female*, and he sketches faces all around it on a small sheet of
paper.

On my last piece of paper, I write, *Down with the Patriarchy*
in cursive handwriting. "I think I'll hand this to Principal Hayes
personally," I say, and start to laugh hysterically. Maybe it's all
the Coke and candy, or maybe I just feel free and wild, and like
we're about to do something a little dangerous.

"Wait, what are we gonna do with these?" Isaac asks, sitting
back to look at all the scraps of paper lying on the floor.

"I have an idea," Jasmine says, holding up a paper that reads,
I resolve to protest and rage like a girl.

JANUARY

26
CHELSEA

Everyone stays until almost two a.m. Once they're gone, I check my phone and see two missed calls from James and four text messages.

Party @ my place.

Come over.

Where you at??

Happy New Year!

I smile, knowing he was thinking of me, and write back:

Happy New Year to you too. To all new things.

* * *

"What do you mean, put them everywhere?" I ask.

"I mean, don't leave any space untouched. Put. Them. Everywhere. Books in the library, textbooks, slip them inside lockers, leave them in bathrooms—any spaces you can find, we gotta make sure people see them everywhere they turn. We have to stay on people's minds," Jasmine says. She looks through her backpack and pulls the bag of quotes and statements out to examine them. A couple of days later, after we made our "I resolve" statements, we photocopied our favorite ones so that by the time school started we'd have hundreds that we could work with.

"You sure about this?" Isaac asks. "I mean, I can understand posting them in books and stuff, but I just don't really want to get detention for posting *Down with the Patriarchy* in the teachers' lounge."

"Stop being so weak," I say, siding with Jasmine, "and besides, I took that one out. I replaced it with *The Patriarchy Is Dead*. That's better, right? It's kinder." I smile.

Isaac stares at me. "I know you all want to do this, but maybe we can make a bigger statement at Word Up, and post there . . ."

"Nope," I say, "it has to be bigger than that. We can't just keep posting in places where everyone already believes what we're trying to say. We've got to bring more awareness of the things that need to change here at Amsterdam Heights."

Isaac still looks unsure.

"You've already done enough, Isaac. You helped us make these look so good. We've got it from here. I mean it," Jasmine says, taking the bag of statements and handing it to Nadine, who is standing next to us and pulling out her favorite statements, figuring out the best places to post them.

Isaac surveys the hallway. We all have after-school commitments in a half hour, but that means if we work fast enough, we can cover a ton of ground. "No. I'm in it now. Let's do this," he says, and grabs the bag back from Nadine.

The four of us take off like a crew of womanist/feminist superheroes leaving our mini forms of justice all over the school campus. We all split up. Jasmine and I tackle the locker rooms, bathrooms, and the theater. But before we get there, I have a stop to make.

"Where are we going?" Jasmine asks. "We gotta hurry."

"I know, but I have a special poem for a special someone," I say, moving ahead.

"James? You wrote something for James?"

"No! It's for Jacob Rizer," I whisper, pulling the rolled-up poster board out of my bag. It's big enough to cover his locker. I hold it out so Jasmine can read it.

You—
for Jacob Rizer

You don't own my body.
It's not yours for the taking.
You don't get to put your hands on me—
touch & burn. You are too full
on your own corrupt metaphors & similes to see that

You don't own me. Not my head to pat,
or my shoulder to bump, or my behind to smack.
You can't hold me down or shut me up.
I'm an avalanche & my words will drown you.
You know the truth—what you did, who you are.
Think you can bop & weave away, but
You are less than. An equation that equals zero—
a subtraction. The sum of nothing.
You made me feel like nothing.
Like my anatomy was yours to handle,
regulate, oversee. You don't get to win.
I'm not yours to keep or command.
My shape stays my own.
You can keep your brazen, outrageous,
hateful hands—to yourself.

"What? You wrote that?"

"Yup, and I'm gonna tape it right on the front of his locker for everybody to see it," I say.

"So you're really doing this."

"No, WE are really doing this."

Jasmine and I make our way to Jacob's locker and post it in record time. Next, we head into the girls' bathroom and pull open every stall door. I figure posting a statement that says *I resolve to listen to women's voices* is way better than the statements already scribbled on the bathroom walls, which include: *Mary Lyvers is a slut whore* and *THIS SCHOOL CAN SUCK IT.* Actually, sometimes I agree with that last sentiment, and I consider writing a check plus next to it but stop myself.

"I mean, whoever wrote this didn't even put a comma between slut and whore. They didn't even write it correctly. I mean, what is that anyway?" I ask, spelling out *Female = Future* in blue tape.

"It's sexist is what it is. And it's slut shaming. Here, give me a sheet of paper," Jasmine says, writing—*I resolve to stop slut shaming women*.

"Oh, I like that," I say, writing it again, and putting it directly under the info about Mary Lyvers. "By the way, she graduated like two years ago, which means that no one has even taken the time to clean this, or paint over it, and you know that girls have been looking at this every day for years and no one has ever said anything."

"Nope. And neither have we."

"Until now," I say, taping resolve statements to the soap dispenser and writing *WOMANIST* on all the bathroom mirrors in tape.

We move even faster once we're done in the bathrooms, and we make our way to the theater. We tuck statements into all the Playbill posters and the blown-up photographs from previous shows. Jasmine has a whole list:

I resolve to play whatever role I want.
I resolve to see black women as multidimensional,
be multidimensional.
I resolve to be sweet, sexy, sassy if I say I am,

sophisticated, and smart,
be all the woman I was made to be.
I resolve to break your boundaries, unbox myself.
I resolve to shut down simple stereotypes—
shake up systems meant to shut me down.
You won't shut me down, shut me up, shut me out.
I show up anyway, anywhere.
I resolve to stand on stage and be me,
and not the woman you want me to be.
I resolve to grow back stronger—unshakable, unstoppable.

"Wow," I say when she reads all the extra statements she wrote. "When did you write those?"

"Last night. I started thinking about the ways that Mr. Morrison was trying to pigeonhole me, and the ways he was trying to get other people to see me, and I just . . . it wasn't right, and it wasn't fair. And to be honest, I miss the ensemble. And I miss my dad. He would've been really proud of us for doing this, and he always loved seeing me on stage. I just don't want anyone to take that away from me," Jasmine finishes. I don't hug her, since I know she hates when she's about to cry and then I hug her, which makes it even worse, so I just take her extra statements and run them all over the theater, backstage, and dressing rooms. We make sure to put them in small spaces where people will see them when they're getting dressed, and when they're putting on stage makeup. Everything is open because after-school activities are starting soon, so we move even faster and then meet Isaac and Nadine in the lobby. They are laughing when they roll up.

"What happened?" I ask.

"Oh, nothing, we just pretty much got James and a few of the basketball players to run up and down the bleachers while doing their sprints and drop statements in all the seats. It looks like it's been raining women's rights in the gym," Nadine says, clearly proud of herself.

"At one point, Ramel was throwing up statements like it was cash money," Isaac says, smiling at us.

"And he also might have been singing some of the statements," Nadine finishes, and as if on cue, Ramel and James walk down the hallway, Ramel singing, "I resolve to raise my hand more. I resolve to answer more questions in algebra. I resolve to use my voice." He enters a falsetto on the last note, and we all start laughing. I see him tucking one of the statements into his pocket.

"What's that one say?" I ask, hanging back as they all continue down the hall practicing their new songs.

"Ah, nothing, I just liked it." He hands it to me. It says: *I resolve to ask for what I want. My voice should be valued and heard.*

"Why do you like it?" I ask.

"I guess I'm just curious. What do you want?"

27
JASMINE

The next day, Chelsea and I arrive to school extra early so we can plan a follow-up to our I Resolve action. We meet up at our lockers then head to Ms. Lucas's classroom. Chelsea already had her morning coffee so she is talking nonstop. "So, like I was saying, Valentine's Day. How do we get James and Isaac to take us on a double date?"

I am listening but not listening.

Ever since Dad died, it's been hard to keep my mind focused.

I am here but not here.

Yesterday, I felt so powerful. Felt like Dad was smiling down on me, with me even. And I didn't cry at all, not even last night when that commercial came on that always made the two of us laugh even though we'd seen it countless times. Yesterday was a good day. But this morning? This morning I feel heavy. I wanted to talk to Dad at breakfast—debrief everything Chelsea and I did. Talk about what we should do next. Today, on the way to school, someone was on the subway platform blasting a song that I don't even know, but it made me think of Dad. I started crying right there, standing in a crowd of people, surrounded by noise and the early bustle of the city. Not a sobbing cry, just tiny tears crawling down my face.

Today is not yesterday. If I could, I'd go back to bed. Start over tomorrow.

We walk into Ms. Lucas's classroom, and instead of her usual smiling face, she is giving me those sad eyes that I am starting to get used to. Chelsea asks, "Is everything okay?"

Ms. Lucas walks over to the door and closes it. "Girls," she says. "I'm sorry, there was nothing I could do. Principal Hayes dissolved our club."

"Dissolved?" I ask. "You mean he shut it down?"

Chelsea tosses her backpack to the floor. "He's a such a piece of—"

"Chelsea!" Ms. Lucas shouts. I have never heard her raise her voice before.

Chelsea sits down. "He can't do this," Chelsea says.

"Yes, he can. You two are way outside the usual boundaries. I mean, personally, I applaud what you are doing, but this just can't exist within the confines of a school club. It's becoming a distraction to the education of other students." Ms. Lucas sits down across from Chelsea.

I am still standing. "A distraction to the education of others? What is school supposed to teach us then?"

Ms. Lucas crosses her arms. "Jasmine, please, you have to

understand that it is inappropriate to slip notes into textbooks—books that belong to the school, mind you. You two can't have these quotes and resolutions interrupting the school day. Do you understand that the entire custodial staff had to stay late to clean up the mess you all made? And you know that Principal Hayes had already given you a warning. This was your last chance."

Chelsea yells, "This is a nonviolent protest. We are just doing what this school has taught us to do. And we didn't mean for the custodians to have to clean them up. We're sorry about that. They were supposed to stay on the seats so people could read them and make up their own resolutions too. It was supposed to keep the *dialogue* going," she says, looking at me for backup.

I say, "Ms. Lucas, when are we supposed to use the education we have? When we graduate, when we're old? What is the point of learning if everything we learn is theory only? All through our schooling we learn about how Martin Luther King Jr. was only fifteen when he graduated high school, eighteen when he preached his first sermon. Ruby Bridges was only six years old when she stood up against segregation. These are the stories you all teach us over and over—that young people can make a difference. But now that we are trying to do something, to stand up for what we believe, you all want to shut us up, shut us down."

"Jasmine, Chelsea." Ms. Lucas's voice cracks a bit. "I really hoped you'd be able to see both sides of this. I am not against you. And frankly, I don't think Principal Hayes is. Yes, he could handle things differently, but he's not against you."

I walk to the door. "Come on, Chelsea."

"One more thing," Ms. Lucas starts, holding up a sheet of paper she must have taken notes on, "we've put you both in the Justice by the Numbers club . . . uh, it meets in room 203."

"What? We have to switch clubs . . . again?" Chelsea asks.

"Every student is required to be in a club. You all know that. And rather than picking your own clubs, Principal Hayes and I agreed that we should assign you a club that we think you would both like," she finishes, her voice dropping a bit.

"But this is the club we want," I say.

"I'm so sorry it ended like this," Ms. Lucas says, and it's clear that's the last thing she is going to say. Our club is over.

Chelsea looks at me with hesitation but picks up her bag and walks out.

"Ms. Lucas, thank you for all your help. I know you're just doing your job," I say.

We walk out of the classroom, heading to our lockers. I grab Chelsea's arm, walk her in the other direction. "Where are we going?"

"The only place where our voices aren't silenced."

* * *

When we get to Word Up, Leidy looks at us with curious eyes. "No school today?" she asks, looking at the clock.

"We left early," I say.

"Humph." Leidy steps from behind the cash register. "You two might be the only girls I know who skip school to come to a bookstore." She laughs and gives us each a hug. "Why the long faces?"

Chelsea tells Leidy what's been going on at school. After Leidy is all caught up, I say, "So that's why we're here. We need a new headquarters for Write Like a Girl."

Chelsea looks at me like she is just now catching on. "Yes, and we want to open it up to the community, to the other students who come to the open mic. Get them involved too."

Leidy walks over to a bookshelf and pulls a book out. "I've been waiting to give this to you two." She hands me a workbook titled *Teens Taking Action Big and Small*.

Chelsea and I walk to the back of the store, where there are worn armchairs and a small coffee table. We sit and look through the book. "This. Is. Amazing," Chelsea says.

"It is indeed," Leidy says. "This workbook has a hundred and one things young people can do to raise awareness about social issues they care about. Some of them you've already done." Then Leidy says, "Some of them could have been more thoughtful, though—"

Before she says more, I admit that we shouldn't have dumped all those statements in the gym. "We should apologize to the custodians," I tell Chelsea.

Leidy says, "That sounds like a good plan. You're learning how to do this. Your intentions are good, but there's a lot for you two to learn."

"So does this mean you'll be our headquarters?" I ask.

"Well, I'm surprised you even thought you needed to ask," Leidy says. She grabs a folding chair; it creaks as she opens it.

As she sits down she says, "But let me just say this one thing." And Chelsea and I look at each other, because we know Leidy never just says one thing. "You two need to understand that there's nothing glamorous about this. If you're doing it to get popular or to get a guy to like you, or to get back at your principal, you're in it for the wrong reason. This has to be about bringing women's voices to the forefront. This has to be about speaking up and not allowing your voices to be silenced." Leidy is talking to us like she is making a speech.

I don't mean to interrupt, but I have to ask, "Why can't this be about proving a point to Principal Hayes?"

Chelsea agrees. "That's like the main reason we want to do this."

"It has to be bigger than your anger or disappointment at one or two people. This isn't only personal. This is about every girl, everywhere. And if you make it only about your school, your club, you keep it small."

The door dings, announcing a customer. Leidy walks to the front of the store, leaving Chelsea and me looking through the book. Just before she greets the customer, she says, "If you just make it about *you* and not *us*, what are you really fighting for?"

Too bad Leidy doesn't work at Amsterdam Heights.

* * *

Chelsea and I decide not to go back to school. We've already missed most of the day. "So where should we go now?" Chelsea asks.

I shrug.

"We clearly don't know how to skip class." Chelsea laughs.

My phone buzzes. It's Isaac:

Where are you?

"Ooh, he's checking up on his girl," Chelsea teases. When I don't respond, Chelsea keeps it going. "Okay, so back to Valentine's Day. It's a few weeks away, so we've got to make plans. What do you think Isaac is going to get you? You're not a roses and chocolates girl, I hope he knows that." Chelsea barely takes a breath. "James would definitely get me roses and chocolates. He's totally that guy who'd show up with balloons that are puke pink and fire red. Two colors I hate, by the way. If he asks you, tell him I'd much rather—"

"They're going to meet us at Harlem Shake in thirty minutes," I say.

"Huh? Wait, what?"

"I've been texting Isaac, and I asked him if he wanted to get something to eat. I told him to bring James."

Chelsea grabs my phone and looks through the messages. "Are you serious right now? A double date?"

"Harlem Shake, Chels. Don't push it. It's just—"

"It's totally a double date," Chelsea says. "I mean, we got them to take us out on a double date and it's not even Valentine's Day."

"Chelsea."

"We gotta get there first so we can choose the best seats and already be sitting at the table when they come."

"You're joking, right?"

Chelsea doesn't answer my question. "I need to change. James can't see me in this."

"He just saw you at school."

"Yeah, but that was school. This is a date."

I just keep walking, heading toward the train.

"I know, I know. I shouldn't be worried about if what I have on is something a guy would like. What matters is if I like it. I know, I know. But it's James Bradford. This is, this is—"

"It's Harlem Shake," I remind her. "Look, if we make this a big deal, they will be freaked out. We just have to act like we're eating in the cafeteria. Like it's nothing that they are coming all the way to Harlem to see us." When I say this, my stomach flips and I realize how nervous I am even though I've had meals with Isaac before. Even though we've been to Harlem Shake countless times. Maybe it's because Chelsea and James will be with us. Maybe it's because I do want to spend time with Isaac and not just as friends. I don't let myself think about it because we've been friends for so long maybe that's all we're supposed to be. Maybe things would change too much if we tried a relationship.

When Chelsea and I get off the train, Harlem welcomes us like only Harlem can. As soon as we walk up the steps we hear drumming, and two men are standing at the top of the entrance handing out flyers. We keep walking, but the tourists next to us take them. We walk from the C Train on 125th and St. Nicholas to Lenox Avenue. On the way, we pass Lane Bryant, and I see that they are having a sale. "Let's come back after we eat," I say to Chelsea.

At the corner of 125th and Lenox, a group of men are standing near the entrance of the Whole Foods passing out pamphlets and preaching about Jesus being the white man's savior. We turn right and walk one block to Harlem Shake. As soon as we go in Chelsea says, "I am ordering a burger, fries, and shake. No girly eating, whatever that means. I know they have vegan burgers and turkey burgers and 'I'm on a diet' burgers, but I want beef today. I'm hungry."

I laugh.

"What?"

"I love you, Chels."

We sit down and wait for James and Isaac. Harlem Shake looks like a vintage seventies diner. The walls are covered with photos of celebrities who also love burgers and shakes. The Wall of Fro is my favorite. It showcases local customers and the different sizes and shapes of their Afros. I also like the bathroom walls. They are wallpapered with *JET Magazine* covers. Yearly the customers vote on a new Mr. or Miss Harlem Shake from the community. Every few seconds, Isaac texts me his status. Just got off the train and Walking over now and Just passed Whole Foods. When they come in, the four of us hug each other. When Isaac lets me out of his embrace, he says, "I was worried about you."

"Worried?"

"Well, yeah. I thought maybe you left school because you were, I don't know, upset or something. A lot has happened recently, and I just . . . never mind—"

I take Isaac's hand. "Thank you."

He holds my hand tight, and I don't let go. Just let it stay in his palm, let my hand warm his because he has just come in from January's bitter cold. We walk over to the line, still holding hands. Chelsea looks over at me, her eyes bulging out, mouth bursting with a smile. The four of us order.

We get burgers, fries, and shakes.

After we finish eating, we stay a while and keep talking. We've seen customers go in and out and in and out, ordering, eating their food, and leaving, and still we are here. Chelsea is in the middle of telling us what movie she wants to see this weekend when James's phone buzzes. He looks at it and quickly puts it away. "We should go," James says. "I haven't seen it yet."

Chelsea kicks me under the table.

James's phone buzzes again. This time he keys a text and sends it.

Part of me wants to say to James, *Great—it's a date. Let's all go.* But the other part of me wants to say, *Who are you texting? Is it Meg?* I couldn't do that to Chelsea, though, so I just sit and watch them flirt with each other and make plans to see a movie this weekend.

James gets up from the table, announcing that he needs to go. We all agree that we've stayed way longer than any of us planned. We dump the remnants of lunch into the trash and walk outside. It is colder now that the sun has set. It is only five o'clock, but it is dark. And all of a sudden I miss my dad, because winter was his favorite season and he would love a night like this. No rain or snow, just pure cold and dark sky.

"See you tomorrow," Chelsea says as she hugs me. She

whispers in my ear, "Should I ask him to walk with me? Clear your throat for yes, don't do anything if no."

I let go of her and clear my throat. So she doesn't have to ask, I say, "James, which way are you going?"

"Back to the C," he says.

"Oh, so is Chels."

Chelsea smiles. "I guess we can walk together," she says.

The two of them leave, and Isaac says, "Walk, train, or bus?"

"Let's walk," I say. Because Dad would have walked.

We are silent for the first block, pressing through the crowds on 125th, but once we get to 127th and it's quieter, Isaac says, "I didn't mean to assume that you were still grieving. I just know it took me a while to get used to my mom not being here. When I didn't see you or Chelsea, I figured you were having a hard day."

"I appreciated you asking," I say. "You're right. It comes and goes, the sadness," I tell him.

I am about to cross the street just when a car speeds through the red light. Isaac throws his arm out to keep me back on the curb. "You okay?" he asks.

"Yeah, I'm fine. I'm fine."

Isaac takes my hand. I hold on to him and think about how I never want to let him go.

FEBRUARY

28
JASMINE

It's the night before Valentine's Day, and I'm spending it at Word Up with Chelsea for our weekly Write Like a Girl meet up. We have about eight girls who come consistently, but on some nights we have more. Leidy has decorated the store with quotes about love. Some hang from the ceiling, and there are a few taped in the window. She has set up a long folding table for us to sit around. There's something about having us all face-to-face, in one room and not just talking on social media that makes Write Like a Girl feel even more important. So many of us have stories to tell about sexual harassment and getting catcalled on the way to school. Girls have talked about teachers making sexist comments in math and science, and how some of our parents just don't seem to understand where we're coming from.

The best thing about our in-person meet ups is that it's inspired girls to start clubs at their own schools. Three girls from the Incarnation School and two from George Washington have started Friday Lunch-Ins at their schools, and they have conversations over lunch about all the issues that have been on our minds.

Chelsea and I rush to get everything set up before everyone gets here. She sets down a tub of markers while I spread out scrapbooking paper, picking out colors that I think will work well for our activity.

Leidy sees all the art supplies and says, "Wow, you all have really turned this bookstore into an art studio. What do you have planned for tonight?"

I tell Leidy our plan. "We're making Alternative Valentine's Day Lists."

"What does that mean?"

"Like this." I hand her my example.

Leidy reads it out loud, "Not Your Typical Love Poems: An Alternative Valentine's Day Reading List." She hands the cardstock back to me. "You two are full of good ideas."

"Isaac and Nadine helped too," I say. I explain the process for the making of the lists, telling her, "We're going to ask the group to come up with reading lists, music playlists, and movies."

Chelsea says, "We'll make them tonight and give them out tomorrow instead of handing out Valentine's Day cards. Not that there's anything wrong with celebrating Valentine's Day." She looks at me when she says this, because she's obsessed with Isaac and me and has a bet with Nadine to see if Isaac is going to make some kind of big gesture on Valentine's Day. Chelsea thinks he's going to go all out and profess his love for me. Nadine thinks he'll be more subtle but will definitely make it clear that he wants to date me.

Leidy walks to her supply closet and comes back holding a bowl of chocolates. "It's not too cliché to offer these tonight, is it?" She sets the bowl down.

Chelsea says, "Leidy, chocolate is never, ever cliché." She takes a piece of candy out of the bowl and unwraps it.

Once everyone arrives we get to making our Alternative Valentine's Day Lists. Nadine hooks her phone up to Leidy's speakers, and for the next two hours we create, decorating each one in our styles so they are one of a kind, like Valentines. Every now and then we have to look at a book to get a title just right or look up who actually sings a particular song. Leidy lets us photocopy our lists so each school represented here has plenty to give out tomorrow.

At the end of our time together, Chelsea says, "Don't forget to take pictures if you hang these up."

"And ask people to hold them up and take a picture of them," I say.

Chelsea finishes, "Don't forget to use our hashtag, #WriteLikeAGirl."

Chelsea walks me to the train station, which means she wants to talk about something. We're just blocks from her house, so walking with me takes her way out of her way to get home. "You okay?" I ask.

"Uh, yeah. Why?"

I don't answer her, just give her time to tell me what she needs to tell me.

"I kind of feel like a hypocrite," Chelsea says.

We walk against the wind. It pushes us forward, rumbles in my ears.

"Here I am leading a whole group of girls in an alternative V-Day activity when really, I keep wanting to check my phone to see if James has sent a text. I don't even want a gift from him or anything. I really don't. But, I mean, well, I kind of want him to . . . I want him to say *something* to me." The wind blows stronger, and Chelsea pulls her hood tighter. "This sucks. I suck."

"You do not! You just, you like him."

"Yeah, but I shouldn't, right?"

"I don't think it's about if you should or shouldn't like him. The only thing I think is that you should love yourself more than you like him," I tell her. "Love yourself enough to walk away from him if he doesn't treat you with respect. And him flirting with you while having a girlfriend is—"

"Disrespectful. To her and to me."

"He just needs to make up his mind," I say.

"And I need to make up mine."

We get to the entrance of the subway and stand to the side so we're not in the way. Chelsea says, "I've got some serious thinking to do."

I hug her, head underground. Just as I reach the last step, my phone buzzes. It's a text from Isaac: want to hang out after school tomorrow?

Me: sure

I think about Chelsea and Nadine, wonder which one of them is right.

Not Your Typical Love Poems: An Alternative Valentine's Day Reading List

by Jasmine Gray

1. "Poetry Should Ride the Bus" by Ruth Forman.
   A poem about loving the simple things, about finding beauty in ordinary places. In this poem poetry plays "hopscotch in a polka dot dress" and sings "red revolution love songs." Here's to loving everyday people doing ordinary things.

2. "Congregation" by Parneshia Jones. A poem about loving and honoring tradition. This is a tribute to family, to cooking together, and to breaking bread with one another. It is about what is passed down from one generation to the next. Here, love is having a belly full of food, a heart full of joy.

3. "Raised by Women" by Kelly Norman Ellis.
   A poem about loving the people who raised us. This is about loving every kind of woman: the scholar, the debutante, the artist. The tell-it-like-it-is women, the flawed women. In this poem, love isn't perfectly packaged, but it is felt in a profound way.

4. "For My People" by Margaret Walker. A poem about loving where you come from. This is a poem of praise that honors African American history. It is a love poem about struggle, about overcoming.

5. "Phenomenal Woman" by Maya Angelou. A poem about loving yourself. This poem is a powerful

declaration of self-affirmation, of resilience, and of confidence. The ultimate self-esteem poem.

6. "won't you celebrate with me" by Lucille Clifton. A poem about loving your journey. This is a poem that acknowledges that every day something—racism, sexism, classism—tries to kill us. Sometimes spiritually, sometimes physically. But the things that have the potential to destroy us can also cause us to rise.

Love yourself enough
after Jasmine
by Chelsea Spencer

It's true, my love for *me* should be electric,
explosive, energetic. Should bend & shape

surround me. Hold me close. Kinship, comfort
me when it matters. Love myself. The definition

of who I am. So, can I love myself & still be falling
for you? You who only loves me—part time.

Who only wants me on the sideline, just a little.
Not enough. How I want your want for me

to be colossal. Bumping & massive. Unstoppable.
Reckless in your want for me. & only me. That I

would be enough.

Top 10 Feminist Questions

by Chelsea Spencer

1. Can I be a feminist and still care about luscious lipstick colors, the best blush, and how to wear enough eyeliner to make my eyes POP?
2. Can I be a feminist and still shop at stores that emphasize big breasts, tiny waists, and full hips? Or stores that stock clothes in size xx-small?
3. Can I be a feminist and still read beauty magazines obsessively? And not just because I'm writing radical poems with them, but maybe because I sometimes (most times) care about the advice they give, even if I know it's superficial and ridiculous!
4. Can I be a feminist and watch shows where women do 90 percent of the housework, the cooking, the cleaning, and on and on? Can I still love shows that subscribe to super-sexist ideas about women?
5. Can I be a feminist and have a crush on James— someone who didn't even know about feminism before we met, someone who is dating someone else, someone who doesn't fully know who I am, since, if he knew me, he'd know that what he's giving is not enough.
6. Can I be feminist and want to be pretty?
7. Can I be feminist and sometimes want to be quiet and shy?

8. Can I be feminist and still be friends with people who don't care about women's rights as much as I do?
9. Can I be feminist sometimes, and take a break other times?
10. Can I just be me?

29
JASMINE

After school Isaac asks, "Want to come with me to Felipe's Art Shop?"

In my head, I say no, since spending Valentine's Day at an art supply store is not what any of us had in mind. "Sure," I tell him. Then I think how both Chelsea and Nadine are going to be disappointed, because neither of them have won their bet.

Felipe's is Isaac's favorite art supply store. Partly because of the range of materials he can choose from but also because it's in Washington Heights, not too far from school. He comes here so much, the people who work here know him by name. The last time we came here together, Isaac said he just needed to stop in for one thing and we stayed for two hours. Today, when we step inside, the man behind the counter smiles and nods. "Isaac, my man. What's good?"

"Hey, Felipe." Isaac stands in the middle of the aisle.

Felipe moves his head slightly to the left, as if to tell Isaac, "Go over there."

Isaac takes a deep breath, and I'm beginning to feel like maybe they just passed some kind of secret code to each other. I smile at Felipe, and he smiles too. In a familiar way, like he knows me. Isaac walks over to the aisle where the sketchbooks are. "Help me pick something out," he says.

"Don't you always use these?" I pull the black spiral book up and open it. It has blank pages, and at the back, the last pages are perforated along the spine so they can be torn out easily.

"Yeah," Isaac says. "But I want to try something new. Maybe one of those." He points.

I pick up a sketchbook that has graph paper in it, flip through it, and pass it to him.

"No, I hate this kind," he says. "Maybe something over there?" He points just above my head.

And that's when I see it.

A sketchbook sitting on the shelf, face-out, with my name in the middle surrounded by jasmine flowers that are drawn in Isaac's style.

"What—what is that? What—"

"Open it."

I take the sketchbook off the shelf and rub my hands along the cover before opening it. I open the book, and the first page is a drawing of me with my poem "This Body" written in the background of my silhouette. I turn the page and see that the next six pages each have one of the poems we chose for the Alternative

Valentine's Day Reading List. The poems are illustrated, and each have their own bold colors and style of the words but somehow look uniform, like one whole book of art. "This is—I don't even know what to say, Isaac."

"Happy Valentine's Day," he says. "The blank pages are for you to fill up with more of your poems and monologues."

Felipe is still at the counter, smiling even more now. "Enjoy your sketchbook. Happy Valentine's Day," he says.

"Thank you."

We leave the store and on our way to the train, I say, "I feel so bad. I didn't get you anything."

Isaac says, "You've been giving me your friendship since we were nine years old. That's all I need."

MARCH

30
CHELSEA

All I want to do is be outside and enjoy the first day of spring. Well, it's not quite spring out yet, but it's the first day without snow or rain that New York has had in weeks, and all of us have been going stir crazy. So today, I am at the park, where some of the trees are already blooming. I am standing on top of the George Washington Bridge—or the playground version of it. As soon as the dismissal bell rang, Jasmine and Isaac walked to the park with James and me so we'd beat all the elementary kids, and we have been playing all over the park ever since. James pushed me on the swing, high enough to touch the tree limbs, we made a village in the sandbox and climbed on top of the kiddie house, and now James is chasing me—James, who is not quite my boyfriend, but not quite my regular friend either.

"I got you cornered now, so don't even try to run," he says, lunging at me. James has me right where he wants me, or is it right where I want him to want me?

I'm so sick of myself sometimes.

"Time out," Isaac yells up at us. "I hear the ice cream truck, and I haven't had Mister Softee since October, so can you guys get down here so we can pool our money?"

James jumps down from the top of the play bridge—athletes are so annoying. I have to duck underneath the arch and shimmy down on the slide, which looks way more awkward than I'd like it to. It doesn't matter since no one is looking at me. Jasmine and Isaac are basically sitting on top of each other counting money, and James is checking his phone, something that he does pretty much on the regular when we're together.

When we're together—listen to me—that's not even a thing, and we're not together. He's just someone I hang out with, who I happen to have a massive crush on, and who I think about all the time. Lately it's because he's someone to talk with, to debate ideas with. We push each other in ways I didn't think we would, and I'm really starting to like who he is, and not just what he looks like. And I think he feels the same way about me. But it's not lost on me that I'm doing everything possible in the name of women's rights, and at the same time I am in deep like with a guy who's not even mine. Talk about antifeminism.

"Chocolate cone with chocolate sprinkles?" Jasmine asks. She knows me so well.

"Yes and yes," I say, plopping down on the bench next to them. Jasmine and Isaac walk over to the truck, and I notice his hand on the small of her back. I've been seeing this a lot lately—little hints of something more, but neither of them has made anything official, so I'm just letting them both think they're fooling me, which they are absolutely not.

"So, we can count that as another win for me, right?" James asks, pretending to run away from me.

"Ah, are we still playing games?" I ask, feeling bold.

He stops and looks right at me. "I'm not playing games."

"Oh, really?"

"Really," he says, fake dribbling a ball (which he looks so absurdly hot while doing) and fake dunking over my head, and then crashing down so he's sitting right next to me. He puts his head on my shoulder, and I am positive that this is game playing, but I am also positive it feels so good. He jumps up suddenly and grabs his phone.

"What?" I ask. He reads a text, stands up, and grabs his book bag, starts to brush the leaves off his jacket.

"Nothing, I just gotta head out soon." James picks up his backpack, while holding on to the SpongeBob ice cream bar he asked for, which makes for a very awkward maneuver. He looks like a kid, and acts like one, is what I think. I guess in some ways, I feel like a kid too.

"Where you going? To meet Meg?"

"No," he says, shifting his weight, and I can tell he's lying. "But I don't have to go right now . . . I have a little more time. Where were we?" he asks, smiling down at me.

"You should go," I say, still licking my endless ice cream cone. I want to smash it into his face or throw it down and go running out of the park, because I don't want to feel this way. I don't want to have a crush on someone like this, or feel so worthless.

"What if I don't want to go yet?" he says, leaning in. "I want to stay . . ." He bends his head toward me, and even though I want to kiss him so much, feel his mouth on mine, because it seems like that's what he's about to do, I pull back—and hate myself, because I really want this moment, but I jerk back anyway.

"What are you doing?" I ask, stepping away from him. I stumble back and drop my cone. *Crap*, I think, and bend down to pick it up.

"Hey, lemme help you."

"No, stop," I yell, a little too loudly. Jasmine and Isaac look in our direction. "I'm not . . . I'm not into this."

"Into what?" he asks, acting so innocent all of a sudden.

"You have a girlfriend," I say, looking him dead in the eyes.

"Hey, it's not that serious, okay. We're not together in that way . . ."

"Yeah, well, it's serious to me. If I were Meg, I'd be pissed right now, and I'm not gonna be your girl on the side. That's not me," I finish.

I grab my book bag, wave at Jasmine and Isaac, and walk right out of the park. I start crying as soon as I hit Fort Washington. I speed-walk home, pissed at James for making me want him so much, and embarrassed at myself for letting it make me cry out loud in front of everyone. This is what I both love and hate about living in New York City. Everything you feel is out in the open—everyone can see when you're in pain and be witness.

* * *

As soon as I walk in the front door, my mom and Mia are walking out. It's clear to both of them that I've been basically acting like a baby.

"What happened to you?" Mia asks, opening the door to let me in.

"Crap boy problems," I say, and my mom pulls me in for a hug. "Where are you going?"

"Saggio's," my mom answers. "We're craving Italian, and your father wants to stay home and watch bad TV. We've decided to go out! I thought you were going to Jasmine's for dinner."

"Plans changed. Can I go with you?"

"Of course, my dear. And no crap boy problems are worth crying over, you understand?" my mom asks, pulling me in again. It's true that sometimes my mom gets it.

We walk down the street to our favorite Italian spot, run by an older couple who came over from Florence when they were much younger. They love our family—mostly because my parents celebrate every big anniversary or birthday there. Mia and I have been coming here since we were little, always ordering the spaghetti al limone and rigatoni with meatballs and hot sausage. As soon as we sit down, the waiter brings a pile of crusty bread and olive oil loaded with sweet pepper flakes and olives. Mia and I sop our bread into the oil immediately. We have always been girls who love to eat.

"Could you two please slow down?" my mother asks, plucking an olive from the plate and effortlessly loosening the pit.

"Ma, I had a two-hour practice where I basically sprinted

from one end of the gym to the other the whole time. I'm starving," Mia says, and orders a kale Caesar salad on the side. She is never satisfied. "So, spill it, Chelsea. What happened?"

"Mia, give her a second, and also, Chelsea, you don't have to tell us if you don't want to." She takes a sip of her wine. I stay silent, testing her. She takes another drink, sighs, and says, "Well, just tell us what happened."

I start from the beginning with James, trying to fill in all the details. It feels good to let it all out, and I can see my mom's mind spinning as she digs in to her plate. The waiter keeps coming over to check on us, and my mom keeps shooing him away. I can tell she already has advice, but she's letting me finish, and it turns out I have a lot to say.

"So, pretty much, that's the story . . . oh, and he has a girlfriend," I finish, sliding that last part in at the end and hoping they don't notice.

"A what?" My mother nearly shouts at me, putting her fork down and looking me right in the eyes. "A girlfriend?"

"Yes, a girlfriend."

"Chelsea, you know this is wrong, right?" I nod my head. *Of course I know it's wrong. That's why I feel like such an idiot.* "And you know that you need to find someone who cares about and respects who you are, and is not trying to play both sides, and that sounds like exactly what James is doing. I should call his mother."

"Mom, please, no! Do not call his mother. Jeez!"

"Well, then you need to handle it yourself. You need to stand up to him. He can't treat you like you're disposable, Chelsea. He can't have it both ways. This isn't a fast-food restaurant, you know?" my mom says, and goes right into more advice—she's definitely on a roll. "And another thing is this. You need a partner who has a focus on you, and not you and . . . you and some other girl. I chose your father because he cared about me, he made me laugh, we could talk about anything, and he didn't have his focus anywhere other than me, and his whole life he has focused on pleasing me and making me feel loved. That's what you want in a partner. Someone who will please *you*," she finishes. The waiter walks by at that very moment and tops her glass off with a little more wine.

"I don't think she needs anymore," Mia says, and starts to laugh. "But I do think Mom's right—who knew?"

"Hey, I will have you both know that I am almost always right—you just have to listen."

"Mom," I start, "I know you're right. I do. And I really appreciate your advice. But can I ask you a question?"

Mom nods.

"How come you don't stand up to your own mom like this? How come you don't shut her down or even raise your voice . . . ever?"

"Oh, Chelsea. You and Mia are from a different generation than I am. When I was growing up, there was still a way that women were supposed to dress and act and be in the world. And I grew up very religious—church every week, confession, no sex before marriage, all of that. I didn't have the same options as you two, so I didn't even know how to use my voice."

"But there were tons of women who called themselves

feminists when you were growing up, who raged against all types of systems. Didn't you want to join in?" I ask.

"Well, sure I did, but I was also a good girl. I did what I was told. Some of us took a little longer to get there," she says, reaching her hand out to hold mine, "but I'm glad I have you two pushing me along. And you definitely push me, Chelsea. You push everyone." We laugh, because I know she's right, and it's something I both love and hate about myself.

We end the night talking about the first time Mom and Dad met—in college when they were both taking a women's literature course. Mom always said he took it to meet women, and I think she might be right—and it worked. She tells us about how he sent her flowers every day for two weeks to get her to go on a date with him, and how when he proposed he did it in front of their favorite bookstore, called Better Day Books, and that he made a bouquet of flowers with pages from her favorite books, so she could always keep a collection of words close to her. I love these stories, but tonight it feels more important—feels like I need to hold them closer, and make sure I follow some of these directions for myself.

I'm so giddy when I get home that I text Jasmine right away: *A woman is not a receptacle. My mother said that tonight.*

She said a woman is not a safety deposit box, not a safe you keep your stuff in. She is not a grocery cart. When you put the key back in, a quarter doesn't pop out. My mother spoke up tonight, and I knew, and the waiter knew, and the guy in back of us who we said was getting a real earful knew.

A week later, there's an envelope on the kitchen counter with my name on it. Mia and I smile when we see it, since we know that Mom's favorite thing to do is write letters to us—she likes to document her advice in writing, make sure we hear her sometimes quiet voice loud and clear.

My dear sweet Chelsea,

I want to start by saying that you are beautiful and strong and bright and cool and brilliant and funny. We all love you so much. I love who you are in the world—love how you care about it and want there to be justice and equal rights and love all over. My daughter, I know that you will thrive and curate a gorgeous life for yourself. And you will be successful in high school and beyond—and toward whatever it is you choose to pursue. What I'm saying is: you will make this life work for you. You always have, and you always will.

Now, what I want you to understand is that you CANNOT let some boy rule the narrative. Men should not get to tell your story or shift where your life is going. You cannot let idiots change your perception of yourself. You need to stay rooted and strong in who you are (refer to the paragraph above to know how the rest of the world sees you). Now you really have to see that in yourself. Your junior year is important, yes, but it's only a few more months in the span of a lifetime, which is a relatively small amount. You have to use these months to figure out who you are and what you want. And you want a boyfriend or partner who is going to love and adore you—someone who respects and honors you. That's what it's about. You are too powerful, and you need to show up to school knowing who you are—and not letting anyone change your mind.

You will be okay. Everyone around you loves you. Talk to us, get advice, rest, eat, do some self-care. You have to start figuring out what makes YOU happy, and what makes YOU satisfied. What kind of life do YOU want? You are so young still, and you have so much life ahead of you. Don't let some jerk ruin your high school experience. You need to remove yourself from that negativity and shift the focus back to yourself.

I want you to know that I have been in your situation—I made some bad decisions during high school—but I knew there were people around me who loved me and who wanted me to succeed. We are here, and we're not going anywhere. You can ask me or Mia anything, and we will answer honestly.

I love you. I am here—always.

Love,
Mom

31
JASMINE

The tardy bell rings, and I am still trying to get my locker open. This is the second time it's jammed up this week. I kick it, jiggle the handle.

And then I hear Meg's voice.

It is not her usual, annoying voice. This time she is yelling. "What did you just say to me?"

"I was just thanking you for wearing my favorite jeans."

I know that voice too. Jacob Rizer.

"You're so disgusting," Meg says.

Meg's eyes catch mine.

I stand there, let her know I am watching.

Jacob continues making comments about her clothes, her body.

"Leave her alone," I say.

Jacob turns, sees me, says, "Jealous that I'm not into you?"

"Don't talk to her like that. God, you're such a jerk," Meg says.

I look at Meg, surprised those words just came out of her mouth. We stand side by side and stare Jacob down. He backs away, blows a kiss to Meg.

I watch while Jacob walks away. Just to be sure he's really leaving. Once he's out of sight, I turn back to my locker. Now I'm really late. And my locker is still jammed. Meg comes over to me, says, "Let me try." She works some kind of magic, and with one try, it opens. "This happens to mine all the time."

"Thanks," I say.

"You're welcome." Meg hesitates, sliding her hair from the left to right. "And thank you. For that."

"No problem." I grab my coat and book for science class, close my locker, and walk away. I almost leave it at that, but then I turn and say, "Meg, can we talk?"

She stops, stands in the middle of the hallway. She doesn't come closer to me and I don't move either. "I know you apologized about the costume but really, my issue with you is so much more than that."

"I'm sorry—"

"Don't. Don't say sorry to me. Instead of an empty apology, you could try to be a better person and actually stop being judgmental and stop patronizing me because I'm big."

"Jasmine, I understand. I feel so bad that I—"

"No. Just listen. Listen to what I have to say." I stop talking for a moment, try to think of what it is I really want to tell Meg. "The blog Chelsea and I started is about us being seen and

294

validated, and you disrespected us. You mocked it. And in class you tried to make me feel like I need to fix my body in order to get a leading role in a play. But my body isn't broken. I am not beautiful in spite of being big. I'm beautiful because I'm big."

I walk away, leaving Meg standing in the middle of the hallway. My heart is thumping and thumping and I am feeling just as anxious as I felt on that stage when I performed my poem. Anxious. But also proud.

* * *

I get to class just as Mrs. Curtis is explaining an activity. "In the four corners of our classroom, I've hung signs that say Strongly Agree, Strongly Disagree, Agree, Disagree." She points as she talks and continues, "And here, in the middle, is where you can come if you are Unsure." Mrs. Curtis says, "I will read a statement, and you will stand under the sign that best describes your answer."

From there, she says, "Finding quality vegetables and fruit is easy to do in New York City."

Most of the class stands under the Agree sign. I stand under there, too, but I am leaning toward Disagree.

Mrs. Curtis tells us to turn and talk to the people standing with us. "Ask them why they chose their answer," she tells us.

My group talks ourselves out of our answer. One of the boys says, "Well, I'm kind of torn because I know it's definitely *possible* to get quality vegetables and fruit, but is it easy? I mean, are we talking about it being easy for everyone?"

"Good point," I say. "I was thinking the same thing but wasn't sure if I was overthinking it."

He laughs a familiar laugh that tells me he knows what it's like to turn an idea over and over in his head.

"Next statement," Mrs. Curtis says. "Owners of grocery stores should decide where they want to build."

Most of us stand under Strongly Agree. One person is in the middle of the room as Unsure.

My group is in total agreement. Someone says, "I mean, if I'm the one who has the vision for the store and am taking the risk to even be an entrepreneur, I should be able to decide where my company builds."

We are all nodding and agreeing, and the conversation is getting good when Mrs. Curtis says, "Okay, another one. It's easy to have a healthy diet."

When she says this, I immediately walk over to the Strongly Disagree section expecting the whole class will be walking with me, or at least half here and half under Disagree, but instead there are only three of us standing here and the rest of the class is under Agree.

I don't want to talk about this one, so when she tells us to discuss, I just listen to the girl next to me who is saying exactly what I know to be true. "If it was easy, everyone would have a healthy diet," she says.

When we return to our seats, Mrs. Curtis projects a map on the screen at the front of the room and says, "Today, we are going to talk about food deserts." Mrs. Curtis gives a short lecture and then focuses back on the projected map. We are looking at New York City, and different shades of blue dots show where people have or do not have access to fresh vegetables and fruit. Mrs. Curtis asks us what we notice, and someone says, "I notice that the neighborhoods marked as low income have fewer and less-healthy options."

"Good observation," Mrs. Curtis says. "Who else notices something?"

Hands go up, and she calls on the next person. I stop paying attention when James comes in. He's never late, but when I look at the door as it closes behind him I see Meg standing there waving and then walking away. He sits next to me, whispers, "What did I miss?"

I don't answer him.

Mrs. Curtis passes out a handout and says, "Get with your partner. We're going to take a neighborhood walk. Be sure to follow the prompts on the worksheet."

There are moans and grumblings because it's cold outside. "I checked the weather; this is going to be the warmest day of the week. And at least it's dry," Mrs. Curtis says. "No rain today. Let's go."

This is why she told us to bring our coats to class.

I put my coat on, zip it, and walk with James outside. We've been partners all year, and Chelsea loves it. She is always asking me what happened in class and if James talked about her. I usually don't like being a spy, but today I am all about questioning James.

The first question on our worksheet is to count the number of liquor stores and bodegas within the nearest four blocks of our school. We walk down the block. I make tally marks on the paper while James counts out loud. "One liquor store, one bodega. Two bodegas, another bodega. One more liquor store."

"Do you like Chelsea or not?" I ask. There really isn't another way to say it. I just want to know, and we'll only be out for a short time, so I have to jump right in.

"She's, yeah. I guess you could say I like her," James says. "Are you happy now? I admitted it. One more corner store . . . one more for liquor."

"Am I happy? Am I supposed to be happy that you reluctantly, halfheartedly said you *liked* my best friend? No, I'm not happy, James."

"Does that count? It's a convenience store, but it's attached to the gas station. Technically it's not a bodega."

"It's not a grocery store," I tell him and add another mark. "You need to leave her alone. You're using her, for, well, I don't know what you're using her for—attention? Whatever it is, you can't keep doing this. You know how much she likes you, and it's not right—"

"Chelsea can't talk for herself?" James asks. "Two more for bodegas."

We head back to school, walking slow so we can continue our conversation. The wind pushes through my coat, chills all of me, the weather not deciding if it's truly ready to be spring just yet. "Chelsea can absolutely speak for herself. She didn't ask me to say any of this. I'm saying it because I am her friend and I don't want to see her hurt."

He doesn't say anything to that. We pass another pair from our class, and James waits till we are far enough away from them before he says, "I don't want to hurt her. I just, I don't think I'm, I don't know. Chelsea is too serious for me. I mean, I know this is a school all about social justice, but you and Chelsea—she's just—"

"You can't seriously be saying that you don't like her because she's passionate—"

"No, I didn't say that."

"Sounds like an excuse to me. To put it on what's wrong with her instead of what's wrong with you. You like her. You just admitted that, so whatever it is that is keeping you with Meg has nothing to do with Chelsea."

When we get back to the school, we go in, pass Ms. Sanchez at the security desk, and head back to Mrs. Curtis's class. Before we go inside, I say to James, "You don't deserve Chelsea. She deserves someone who isn't afraid of who she is."

APRIL

32
CHELSEA

I'm still thinking about how I almost kissed James Bradford—almost felt his beautiful mouth on mine, could almost say we made out in the park on the first sunny day of spring, and there were birds out and the sky was shining, and it was perfect. Almost. But just the fact that I am still calling his mouth beautiful is a major sign that I am not over it. I want to be—I want to stop thinking about the way he made me laugh, and the way he'd put his hand on the lower part of my back a little longer than he had to if he was passing me in the hall. I want to stop imagining going to prom together and getting married—having kids, a dog, and trips to the Caribbean. I know I've gone too far when I can see us as an old married couple sitting on the stoop of our brownstone in the Heights. As Mia would say—*join us back on planet Earth, Chelsea.*

So I pretend he doesn't exist—or at least I try to. Ignoring James Bradford—and yes, I still say his whole name, which

Jasmine has told me I really need to stop doing—ignoring him is nearly impossible. I send him a note that says:

James—It's Meg or me. You decide.

It feels simple enough, and in my mind—which is a very dangerous place to be lately—I imagine him responding immediately—*You, you, you.* But every day he walks past me, and every day I think more and more about how I fell for someone who didn't much care about my feelings at all, or did but couldn't admit it. I fill my journal with enough crap love poems to make a whole book.

Potential Titles for My Upcoming Poetry Collection

by Chelsea Spencer

1. *Love in the Time of Feminism*
2. *Womanist Uprising: No Time for Your Fake Trash Existence* (feels like too much, maybe)
3. *Love Like a Girl*
4. *Men Always Come Back*
5. *Devastation Station*
6. *James Bradford Sucks and Other Poems*
7. *Teenage Love Supreme*
8. *Why?*
9. *Boys Lie*
10. *Don't Want You Back—Even If You Ask*

And I write endless haiku poems, since I'm on a kick. I keep starting poems I think I will send to James, but they stay tucked inside my drawer. I can't bring myself to do it.

* * *

Haiku for a rainy (and lonely) Saturday afternoon
by Chelsea Spencer

Consider the frame
all this body, all these lies
woman on display.

Scientific bind
dissected anatomy
bust, butt, shoulder, spine.

Examination
chest forward, eyes wide, mind dull
extrovert this build.

Systemic, syste-
matic. Manic—panic pleads
conform proportion.

Personality
package it perfectly prim
proper, prestigious.

Weigh the part. Spandex
spit shine, girls wild, lemon drop
dance floor, curve at this.

Freak, funk, fantasy
suite life, lady luck, closed legs
back straight, teeth white, smile.

Be and look the part
the girl always on the side
never the girlfriend.

*   *   *

"Hey, can we talk?" James asks at my locker.

I've already given up on him, already cried myself to sleep and hated myself in the morning, hated that I could let some boy make me feel less than, or not good enough. I've already tried every pep talk possible and tried to convince myself he's not worth my time, and that he's not about to make me question my self-worth, but when he's standing in front of me smiling I get weak, and my stomach tumbles into itself, and I feel like I'm gonna start crying again all at the same time. *I hate feeling this way.*

"I gotta get to after-school," I say.

"Can I just . . . just lemme talk for a second, okay?"

I stop in front of him, waiting. I realize that I don't care anymore about the way I look in front of him—if my hair is a frizzy mess, or if I ate the hummus at lunch—so what if I have garlic breath? I don't care that I'm wearing jeans and my plain sweatshirt—I'm just me, and if he doesn't like me, if he's not into me this way, then who cares? It's time for me to find somebody who can handle all of me—just the way I am.

"Look, I just . . . I want you to know I'm not hiding you like Jasmine thinks," he starts.

"What? What did Jasmine say? Did she say that? I didn't . . ."

"No, she's right. I haven't really been honest about . . . whatever. I just . . . I like you, but I just, I can't . . . right now, I just . . ."

"Stop. I get it," I say, closing my locker and starting to walk away.

"You don't, I don't think you do."

"Don't tell me how to feel," I say, stepping back, trying to avoid the chemical energy that seems to be pulling me to him like a reckoning force. "I know exactly how I feel. I feel like you can't treat me like this. If you want me, you gotta show me, and you gotta be for me. I am not a receptacle."

"What?"

"I'm not some side chick, or whatever, that you can keep around when you want to feel all important. I'm not here for you in that way anymore." I throw my book bag over my shoulder and start to walk away.

"Look, I'm sorry, okay?"

"Prove it," I shout back. "Or don't. I'm good either way. Really. I am." And for the first time, I believe it myself.

By the time I get to Jasmine at the bookstore, I'm shaking

but not crying. In fact, I don't even feel like crying. *Screw him*, I think. Hotness can only get you so far. I hug Jasmine and open my notebook. No matter what, I have my best friend, who has been there through everything. She's my constant.

Dear Amsterdam Heights Community,

I am proud to announce that our school is being honored with the Chancellor's Award for being a model of social justice education. Chancellor Carmen Freeman will be visiting our school to present the award and give special recognition to our staff and teachers who work tirelessly to ensure that our community is a safe place for everyone. This event will be a grand celebration and is open to the public. We hope you and your family will join us in celebrating.

With gratitude and in solidarity,
Principal Hayes

Chelsea: Did you all see this yet?

Nadine: Deleted it.

Isaac: Haven't checked email all weekend.

Me: No. Thanks for the screen shot.

Chelsea: A model school?

Me: If by model they mean an example of how to shut down student voice. True.

Nadine: LOL.

Nadine: We should boycott the ceremony.

Isaac: That would be so awesome if no one shows up. Just Hayes & the chancellor.

Me: No. We should attend. We should go and speak up.

Chelsea: YES! We could do one of the actions from that book Leidy gave us.

At this, I stop texting and call Chelsea.

As soon as she picks up, I say, "We've got to come up with a plan."

33
CHELSEA

"Welcome to the distinguished Chancellor's Award Night," Principal Hayes begins. "I want to thank you all for attending tonight. We are so proud and honored to be one of the highest-scoring schools in our district, especially since we don't pride ourselves on the test. In fact, we think of testing as secondary to the hard work we do on community building and strengthening our ties to the world around us."

Here we are—me, Jasmine, Nadine, and Isaac—sitting in the last row of the auditorium next to some of the girls from our Write Like a Girl gatherings at Word Up. And to the right of us is the entire girls varsity basketball team from our school, and on the left side of us is the team from George Washington High, which is just down the street. Mia rallied her team, and they put the word out to other teams in the league. They're all wearing versions of our shirts. They came to make some noise.

But we are all sitting quietly . . . for now.

Principal Hayes acknowledges some of the teachers who are being awarded with Outstanding Educator awards, and I have to admit, I love these teachers. Especially Ms. Lucas and Mrs. Curtis. They truly go above and beyond, and I feel like they understand us students. But then Principal Hayes says, "We are a school that is committed to our neighborhood, and to making sure that our voices, that *all* voices, are heard and truly listened to."

"This is such crap," I whisper to Jasmine, who is sitting so calmly beside me. I look to both sides and see the teams handing out poster boards to each other. Mia looks in my direction and winks. She knows this is a massive deal, and she also knows that it could get us into deep trouble. She's doing it anyway.

Principal Hayes continues, "Amsterdam Heights Collaborative Community School is just that. We work together. We rally. We trust our students to come to us with their concerns, fears, and ideas for the future. We trust their voices. We create activities and clubs that support what they want to do— with clubs like Step Up STEAM for our technology-and-arts-focused young people, and Dance for Your Dreams, which combines movement and site-specific performances. We care about our young people and value their opinions and ideas. This is why all of us are so proud to receive this award tonight. We know that you don't have to teach to the test, and you can teach to the whole student. That's what we do here. That's who we are."

I look at both sides one more time. Everyone is holding a sign in front of them, ready for my move. I make sure that our row has signs and make eye contact with everyone. Our plan is to begin right after Principal Hayes introduces the chancellor. The auditorium is packed—there are families and teachers and most of the students are here too. James is sitting in the front with his mom, who waved at me when she saw me. James just sat there looking straight ahead.

Principal Hayes continues, "And now, to celebrate this success, it is an honor to introduce Chancellor Carmen Freeman to you all this evening." He steps away from the podium.

The crowd begins to applaud, and I stand up right away. The basketball teams are on the edge of their seats. Jasmine puts her hand on my back and presses me gently forward. Just when the chancellor gets to the microphone, I shout, as loud as I can, "I resolve to fight for Write Like a Girl, our womanist/feminist club that was wrongly shut down at this school that claims to value all voices. I resolve to show up like a girl." I hold up the sign that Isaac helped us to make, which reads Write Like a Girl—Bring Us Back in bold neon letters.

"I resolve to fight like a girl. I resolve to race like a girl. I resolve to run sprints like a girl," Mia says, standing up right after me. I smile in her direction.

"I resolve to show up like a girl, not stop like a girl, win like a girl," Nadine says right after.

"I resolve to blog like a girl, be controversial like a girl, write what's on my mind and the mind of my community like a girl," Jasmine says.

The chancellor is standing on the stage with her mouth wide

open. Principal Hayes is standing now too, at the microphone telling us to sit down, but it's too late for him to stop us.

"I resolve to show up like a girl every day until you decide to hear me."

"I resolve to stand up to sexism like a girl."

"I resolve to shut down systems of oppression like a girl."

"I resolve to dismantle patriarchy like a girl."

"I resolve to be unstoppable and relentless like a girl."

The voices go on, getting louder and stronger every time Principal Hayes tries to quiet our voices. The whole auditorium is watching us, with some people shouting and cheering when we make a statement, and some having conversations on their own about what this is about. I can't tell if it's working, or if we've made a huge mistake, but I get my answer when Ms. Sanchez, the security guard, comes up behind me and begins to escort us out. She is gentle with me, and I know it's because she doesn't really want to do it.

As we are all being ushered out, I try one more time, and shout, "You cannot stop our voices." But even as I'm saying it, I'm not quite sure.

34
JASMINE

Every student involved in interrupting the ceremony is suspended for three days. Which means we will have three added days to our spring break next week.

I think Mom is going to lose it, but instead she calls the school and asks to talk with someone. She starts the conversation with, "First of all," and that's when I know that I am not in trouble, but that Principal Hayes is. Mom says, "I don't understand how I was never contacted that there was any concern with my daughter. I know some of what's happening because she's told me, but I have to say that I am disappointed that no one from the school has talked with me."

I don't wait around to hear the rest of the conversation. I go into my room and text Chelsea. I hope her mom is not scolding her. That's the last thing she needs right now.

I send her a message:

Are you grounded until you're 21?

She writes back a bunch of laughing faces and says:

My mom is a total new person. I'm not
asking questions.

And my dad? I think he might be proud of
me.

We text back and forth about what to do next. We can't let
a suspension be the end of it. We decide to take the three-day
suspension to meet up at our Word Up–Write Like a Girl
headquarters.

* * *

Something about being suspended has made us even more bold.

We have planned an action for each day of spring break, and
we've spread the word to all the poets of the open mic. We've
taken ideas from the book Leidy gave us and spent the weekend
prepping for our week of protests.

Today, our first action is to do sidewalk art with chalk. We
will write quotes, names of women, and statistics all around our
school's neighborhood. It is still chilly and gray outside; spring
is taking its sweet time getting to us. Leidy brought us muffins
from Esmerelda's and has packets of instant apple cider and hot
cocoa for us to make. Before anyone else shows up, Leidy says to
me and Chelsea, "So after this week of taking action, what's
next?"

"We're not sure," I say.

"Well, what do you girls actually want?" Leidy asks. She doesn't wait for us to answer. "I mean, besides getting your club back, what do you want?"

Before we can even answer, Leidy says, "You two need to figure out what it is you want out of all of this. If you really get your principal's attention and he asks you what it is that you need and want to make the school better, do you have an answer? Are you prepared to hand him a written statement of the things that need to change?"

I speak slow and with hesitance. "We know what we want," I tell her. "And we've made a bunch of notes, but we haven't made it anything formal."

"Well, get to it. You two are making quite a bit of noise, so make those notes into something significant," Leidy says.

Just then Isaac and Nadine come in. Not too long after, more students from our in-person meetings show up. Rachel, the girl who read my blog post at the open mic, is here. She brought two friends with her. Plus, two of the volunteers from the bookstore join us. Leidy is relieved we'll have adults with us. There are nine of us who head out, taking different corners.

Isaac stops at the corner, right at the crosswalk, and begins to write something, but then his chalk breaks. I walk over to him. "Here," I say, "you can have mine." I hand him the oversize green chalk.

"It's okay—I can work with this," he says. "If you give me yours, what will you use?"

I take my phone out of my pocket. "I'm going to document everything," I tell him.

"Good idea," he says.

"Yeah, we've got to take video and photos every day so we have this on record," I tell him. That's mostly why I gave him my chalk. But also because kneeling on the ground is uncomfortable. I look at the others, how they are sitting crossed-legged or on bended knee writing, and I know I can't sit like that. Sometimes this body is limiting, makes me feel like I am in a prison.

Isaac writes, *#SayHerName* near the curb while no one is walking by. Then, in front of the bodega, he writes, "*Your silence will not protect you.*" *—Audre Lorde.*

We walk down the block, stopping every few steps for him to write something. Chelsea is across the street writing on the ground. I cross the street so I can take a photo. She's taken one of her poems and written the words in different sizes to add emphasis. For some of the words she's gone over it a few times to make it bold. The pink chalk stands out bright against the gray cement. A few people stop and stare as she writes, others pass by quickly, like they don't even see us. There's a woman sitting at the window of the apartment building, about five flights off the ground. Her wrinkled face is smiling as she watches Chelsea, and it makes me wonder what battles she fought, what opposition she's faced.

The eight of us make our way down the block, around the corner, and get to Amsterdam Heights. We make sure there are chalked statements at each main entrance. We're just about

318

done when a man walks up to Isaac and watches him write a quote by Sandra Cisneros. The man waits till Isaac is finished, then says, "So whose pants are you trying to get into?" He laughs and walks away before Isaac can respond. Halfway down the block, he turns and yells, "You girls better be careful. He's a slick one." He laughs again, so amused at himself.

"What a jerk," Chelsea says.

One of the girls who's joined us shakes her head. "No one asked for him to comment. I mean, how do you think it's okay to come up to someone and say something like that?"

Isaac wipes his hands on his jeans, which leaves green streaks from the chalk. He brushes it off and walks away. I follow him, walking fast to catch up. The rest of the group walks behind us, close enough to be with us but far back enough to give us space.

I ask Isaac, "Are you okay?"

"I'm good. Not about to let some ignorant stranger ruin my day."

"Just making sure."

"You don't believe him, right? I mean, you know I'm for real about all of this."

"Of course," I say. "You've been our honorary feminist since middle school."

Isaac gives a laugh that sounds more like a duty than a genuine reaction.

"What? You don't like it when we call you our honorary feminist?"

"Not really," Isaac says.

"Well, what do you want us to call you?"

"Isaac."

"Well, of course. But I mean, you know, when we talk about how down you are for all of this—what should we call you? Chelsea hates the word 'ally' because it's so overused. We could call you—"

"How about you just call me Isaac. For real. I mean, I don't need a title. I'm not the mascot for Write Like a Girl. I think it's ridiculous that the school is trying to silence your voices," Isaac says. "I'm just a friend who has the same values as you."

"So we're just friends?" I ask this just as the cross light changes to Don't Walk. We stand and wait for the traffic to pass. Chelsea and our crew are a few steps behind us.

Isaac says, "Do you want to be more than friends?"

"Do you have to ask?" And when I say this, Isaac leans in and kisses me. Right here on a New York City sidewalk in front of my best friend and a group of strangers. I have fantasized about what kissing Isaac would be like and never did I think it would happen on a chilly April day, after tagging sidewalks with feminist quotes. Never did I think it would happen when I was wearing jeans and a hoodie, no lipstick, no mascara. Isaac is kissing *me*. As I am.

* * *

When I get home Mom is sitting at the computer huffing and puffing, clicking the mouse, then typing, then clicking the mouse again. She exhales and buries her face in the palm of her hands. "Mom, what's wrong?"

She jumps and quickly wipes tears away. "Nothing. I'm okay. I'm fine."

"Mom."

"It's nothing. I forgot the stupid password again, so I can't log on and I'm just frustrated. It's—I'm fine."

Mom is clearly not fine. Besides the obvious—her sitting here crying—I know she is not okay because she never uses words like "stupid" and she doesn't get flustered this easily. I look at the computer. It's on the home page for the bank. A red message is on the screen that reads *Invalid Password*. "Just, just take a deep breath, Mom, and think. You'll remember." I know this isn't about the password. It's about my dad. Ever since he died, there are moments when we start crying about the silliest thing. Last week, I put a load of laundry in the dryer, but it didn't dry in time, so I couldn't wear the outfit I wanted to wear. I held the damp clothes in my hands and started sobbing. This must be what Mom is experiencing right now. The book my grandmother gave me on grieving said it's normal.

Mom sniffs. "This is so ridiculous. I can never remember the stupid word your dad created for this thing." She types out another attempt. "Not our anniversary." Then another. "Not your name or Jason's." A message appears that says for her protection, the account has been locked. Mom throws an epic tantrum like the ones Jason used to have when he hadn't taken a nap.

"Mom—it's going to be okay. Calm down. It's going to be—"

"I hate that I even have to do this stuff now. Your father took care of all of this . . ." Mom gets up from the desk and grabs her purse and keys. "I'll be back. I'm going to the bank."

"Should I come with you? Do you want me to call Aunt Yolanda?"

"I'm fine. It'll be fine." Mom leaves.

I sit at the desk looking at the screen. I have so many questions that I know I can't ask Mom, like why did Dad handle the money in the first place? I've never really thought about how dependent my mom was on my dad. But sitting here looking at this screen that has refused to let her log in, I start remembering how Mom would always call on Dad whenever the computer froze or the printer wouldn't work. She waited for Dad to come home to fix something that was broken, to take out the garbage. Who is my mother going to be without Dad if so much of who she is was a part of him, because of him?

My phone buzzes. I pick it up and check Chelsea's message. There are no words, just a row of the kissing lips emoji and then a row of red hearts. I text her back a smile.

* * *

The next morning, we are back at the Word Up–Write Like a Girl headquarters. Today, we are doing pop-up street performances. Eight of us show up. Chelsea and I decided to ask other poets and performers from the open mic to be the ones to speak out today. Like Leidy said, it's not about us, and we don't always have to be the ones at the center of it all.

We head out at noon, so we are sure to have a crowd. Our

first pop-up performance is at the bus stop. The eight of us stand at the bus, not like we are together at all, just real low-key like we are strangers waiting. There are a few others waiting, too, and across the street at the park, there are kids playing and parents watching and taking photos. Pedestrians walk by, going both ways, zipping past each other, some saying hello, others walking fast and on a mission. Without any warning, Shalanda, a girl from Incarnation School, starts her poem. The first line is, "I've got to get these words out of me. Can't hold them any longer," and from there, she unleashes a poem that is so good people walking by have stopped to listen.

We do three more of these street performances at different places around the neighborhood. For the last one, we perform the group piece we put together. We each have a line and a move-ment we've contributed. Standing outside, under a shifting spring sky, we declare who we are, we speak up and speak out.

*　*　*

Spring break ends with a Women's Only Open Mic at Word Up. The bookstore has the biggest crowd it's ever had. Somehow, Chelsea convinced Leidy to close out the night, since we've never heard her say a poem. Leidy takes the mic and says, "These aren't my words, but they are words I live by," and she reads "won't you celebrate with me" by Lucille Clifton. It is the perfect poem to end on. As soon as she says the last word, Nadine fills the space with music, and we all mingle. It's so crowded it's hard to move around and greet everyone. All the body heat has it feeling hot in here. I move through the crowd and walk to the door so I can get some fresh air. That's when I see that Ms. Lucas is here too. She is in the back standing against the wall, and she leaves before I can walk over to her and say hello. I wonder if Chelsea saw her.

I stand outside, breathe in the air, and wait for the store to become less crowded. While I am on my phone texting Chelsea about Ms. Lucas, a woman comes up to me and says, "Jasmine, right?" She steps close to me.

I step back. "Yes."

"I work for the *Washington Heights Reporter*, and I've been following what you and your friend are doing. I'd love to have you write an op-ed piece for our newspaper. Would you be interested in that?"

I don't let on that I kind of don't know what an op-ed is. I mean, I know what it is but not how to write one. I think she can tell because then she says, "Here's my card. Let's talk more. I'd love to help get your story more exposure."

OP-ED FOR *WASHINGTON HEIGHTS REPORTER*

When Silence Speaks
by Jasmine Gray

All I know is Harlem. The constant bustling of 125th Street, vendors calling out to you as you walk by, trying to sell you earrings, shea butter, incense. All I know is how sirens pierce the night sky, causing no real alarm because it is just background noise to a sleepless city too used to distraction, numb to sounds that are meant to alert, warn. In New York, someone is always talking, yelling, cursing, preaching, laughing, saying something. Birds chirp, horns honk, basketballs bounce, and if you listen closely you can hear the swish-swish of shoulders rubbing against shoulders when strangers bump into each other as they squeeze through crowded streets. You can hear the wind moving through leaves. These noises confirm that life is happening, that people are moving about their day—communicating and not, loving and not, but moving still.

This is the environment I've been raised in since I was born. There is always noise. There is never silence.

Maybe since I am the product of a city that is always making noise, always a symphony of chaos, I expected my school to welcome my loud voice and the voices of my friends. I expected them to understand that we are not making noise just to be a nuisance. We are taking a stand for what we believe.

Is it too much to ask that my school be a place where I can share my story? A place where I feel safe and encouraged to be me? Is it too much to ask that the leadership of my school talk *to* me, not at me? Isn't it reasonable for me, a black teenage girl, to want to be seen and heard?

So many girls—and women—are expected to be seen and not heard. In so many spaces we have been given a seat at the table, but we are expected to sit at the table, grateful to even be there, and shut up and eat whatever is served to us. Even if what is being served is stale, nasty. Even if it is not healthy for our well-being.

My friends and I decided that we would not just be grateful to be at a school like Amsterdam Heights. We decided that we would be grateful *and* say something. It is possible to critique the place you love. I love Amsterdam Heights, and this is why I am so determined to make it a better school.

The noise we are creating is not background noise. We do not want to be the siren blending in so much that no one pays attention. We are sounding the alarm. This is an emergency.

We are not only sounding the alarm to the leadership of our school, but to all adults and men, boys and girls, community members, and city officials who have known what's going on and have not said anything. We do not want the whispers, winks, and side conversations when no one in power is looking. While I'm glad to know so many people support us behind closed doors, it would mean more to have this support out in the open.

Your silence is saying something. Loud and clear.

We hear you.

Now hear us.

girlhood

by Chelsea Spencer

[gurl-hood]

noun

1. the state or time of being a girl.

As in: When I was.

As in: Used to be, and not one anymore.

As in: Don't tell me who I am, how to act, what to say,
what's ladylike, what's proper, what's prim, who I'll be.

As in: An infusion of cherry bomb, red balm
lemon-lime explosion sea of honey bun clip-on
bubble-gum soda pop purple rainbow eye shadow lip
gloss blush brush unicorn tie-dye diamond-crusted
necklaces scarves that shimmer shine. The whole
outrageous girlish coquettish. Sparkling dollhouse—

As in: Girlhood, you make me race forward
pop culture raining down streamers of tutus
and gloves with emojis. Heart necklaces to best friends.
Lockets and lace and hold on tight.
You make me see myself tiara'd and sculpt molded,
make me see myself in ribbon'd bows.

2. girls collectively: the nation's girlhood.

As in: Girl Scouts, girls of a certain status.

The girls twirled, the sorority girls, class-act girls,

girls on fire. The smart girls, the brainy girls,
the bad girls, the good girls.

As in: Why does everything anchor toward glitter?

As in: You can't mass market us, fit us in a bubble,
feed us chewing gum and lies.

As in: We see the way you watch us.

As in: Let us tell you who we want to be.

As in: Back up.

As in: You won't forget us.

As in: Watch us shut it down.

As in: Watch us break it loose.

As in: Watch us rise.

What Girls Do—

by Chelsea Spencer

Watch the way we—wind wild, burst forth.

Froth & glow. A palette of gold wings

or what it means to fly. A magnificent

trundle of up-rocking. Watch us flaunt,

grind, break, do the work, get the jobs.

Levitate. Yes we know what we want.

Jet-fueling fire-walker women.

From french fries to tamales to tacos

in the Heights to sancocho & cornbread.

Don't we eat this world. Alive.

Don't we leg stretch, cherry gum,

bubble blow strike loose & low, light up,

chisel, shine. Don't we blind the competition

when we want. Don't we bless

and flourish, pray & sing. Don't we crave.

Don't we show off, show up, show out,

stay late, wake early, rock when we want.

Open fire, don't we run international.

Executive directing renegades, graffiti

artists, waitresses, mystics, healers, cleaners.

Can't we wield knives. Strut. Stunt.

Weren't we born rooster, born

snake & wild horse. Born below ground

& now we volcano. Don't we dip when we want,

post up or dance, deliver. Don't we crack gold
if you try to break us. Defiant.
Don't call us pretty. Not your perfect
or primed. Our mouths can be clean or dirty.
We sleep on your criticisms, choke back jealousies.
Not one slight can crack code our brilliant skulls.
Electric. Don't we do what we want. When we want.
Whenever we want. Don't we know what's bitter
& what's sweet—& don't we want 'em both.
Unafraid of being all the woman we are. Globe
spinning, orbit rising, hip grinding, body banging.
So oh yes. We plan to stay.

Walking the Streets in NYC
Inspired by Emory Douglas and the Black Panther Party

by Jasmine Gray

Hello, Men of New York City.
This is a teenage girl calling you again.
A girl who walks past whistling men
on my way to school, on my way from school,
to and from everywhere I go.

This is just to say

I am not an object to call back to you like a yo-yo.
Don't tug at me, pull me close.
My body is not yours for taking,
grabbing, slapping, commenting on.
I am not the quench for your thirst.

Don't tell me to smile,
Don't call me bitch when I walk away.
Don't make my fatness your fetish,
Don't tell me my fatness is your disdain.

My body is not yours for taking,
grabbing, slapping, commenting on.

Let me walk in peace,
let my feet be graceful or not,
be high-heeled or combat boot.
Let my face be in deep thought
or anger or laughter or just be.
Let me be without trying to make meaning
of who I am.

Don't call me
baby, ma, sexy.
Do not rename me.
You can't name what you do not own.
You don't own my body.

My body is not yours.

This Body II

by Jasmine Gray

My body is
perfect and
imperfect and
black and
girl and
big and
thick hair and
short legs and
scraped knee and
healed scar and
heart beating and
hands that hold and
voice that bellows and
feet that dance and
arms that embrace and
my momma's eyes and
my daddy's smile and
my grandma's hope and

my body is masterpiece and
my body is mine.

MAY

35
CHELSEA

"Please sit," Ms. Lucas says as we walk into her classroom. She is not alone. Mrs. Curtis is sitting there, along with Ms. Johnson. They are seated at a round table and gesture to the two open chairs. Jasmine looks at me, and I almost start laughing because I'm so nervous. *What is happening?*

"Are we in trouble?" Jasmine asks.

"Again?" I add.

"No, no . . . just, please sit down. We have some things we wanted to talk about with you," Ms. Lucas says.

We each take a seat.

"I'll start," Ms. Johnson says. "I want to first take a moment to thank you both." We stare back, not having any idea what she is thanking us for. "You two have had a very adventurous year, full of interesting choices, and although I haven't agreed with all of them, I do applaud you for the work you have done in the school."

"You have made some very bold choices," Mrs. Curtis adds, "and we wanted to let you know that we have all taken notice." I feel like I am in the Twilight Zone for real.

Ms. Lucas starts in. "I want to apologize. I didn't fight hard enough for you. But when I went to that open mic at Word Up, and I listened to what you were saying and saw all those young women from around the neighborhood, and I just . . . I saw myself up there, and I am proud of you."

Ms. Johnson adds, "We wanted you to know that we see what you're doing, and we are also planning to raise our voices in some of our own ways. So, we thank you. That's all," she finishes, and starts to gather her things to leave.

"Wait, wait," Jasmine says. "I mean, thank you, we . . . thank you, but what do you mean? What are you planning?"

"Don't worry," Ms. Lucas responds. "We are working on that, but we did want to let you know that your questions and your statements really got us all thinking, and we appreciated it. Thanks for coming in."

"No, wait," I say, starting to wonder what the staff has been through that they aren't telling us. "We have another idea too, a list of demands that we're putting together. Maybe you all can help us. We can work together on an action," I say.

"Oh, no, no, no, that's not what we meant at all. We just wanted you all to know that we appreciated your thoughts," Ms. Lucas finishes.

"It's going to take all of us," Jasmine says, looking around at our teachers, the ones who have helped to push us all year, the ones who've had our backs. "We've really been thinking of what we want—besides our club being reinstated. And I think having you all stand with us will help." She pulls her journal out of her backpack and reads the following:

Write Like a Girl—Our Demands

1) We demand a space for our voices to be heard and our thoughts and ideas to be valued and shared. We will not be silenced or shut down or shut out of the conversation just because you don't agree with what we are saying. Hear us!

2) We demand an end to sexual harassment of any kind, including: threats, intimidation, or violence. In the case that harassment occurs, we demand a jury of teachers and peers and restorative justice circles that honor our voices.

3) We demand an inclusive curriculum that honors and includes the voices of BIPOC (Black, Indigenous, People of color) and LGBTQIA+ communities.

"Wow," Ms. Johnson says, standing up and looking at the list over our shoulders. "This is powerful," she says. "And what were you planning to do with it? How were you planning to get everyone's attention?"

"We want to stage a walkout modeled after A Day Without

a Woman," Jasmine says. "And it would be even better if we could walk out with the women who make Amsterdam Heights run."

Our teachers exchange a look.

"We want in," Ms. Lucas says.

A DAY WITHOUT WOMEN
AT AMSTERDAM HEIGHTS

How would the school run without you?

Who would send the emails?

Who would answer all the phone calls that come in?

Who would make the copies?

Who would greet the families?

Who would file the forms?

Who would order food for staff meetings?

Without you—

Who would make the building clean?

Who would empty the trash?

Who would maintain the hallways?

Who would mop the floors?

Who would wash the windows?

Who would make us look good?

Who would nurture the future?

Won't you please join us next Wednesday at 12:00 p.m.

to see what a day without you all would look like?

36
CHELSEA

Last week we hand delivered flyers to all the women who work at the school. It's our last week, and today is the day. We walk in together—me, Nadine, Jasmine, and Isaac, the four of us bonded always through this year. We're all wearing our favorite activist shirts, and we make our way past security and toward our class-rooms. Ms. Lucas gives us a thumbs-up in the hallway, and I can't believe we're actually going through with this. Our plan is to all walk out right after the first-period bell rings. After Principal Hayes does his morning announcements, we will leave.

The bell rings, and I hear his voice. I look around my class-room. There are about eight other girls sitting around me. We are sitting in Mr. Smith's math class. I look around to see if they're watching me to make the first move, but no one even looks in my direction. I wonder if they know I'm behind the action, and I also wonder if anyone's actually going to move, when all of a sudden I see girls walking out of their classes through the window in the door. *Whoa*. Samantha, who I've always thought is cool, stands up and grabs her book bag. So does her best friend, Kristen, and their friend Camisha. They all start packing up. Mr. Smith turns around from the board and asks them to take a seat.

"Not today, Mr. Smith," Camisha says, and opens the door to walk out. The rest of us look around and grab our book bags and papers. We stand up, almost like a chorus, and file out together.

"Um, ladies, ladies . . . what's, uh . . . ," Mr. Smith starts.

"You know, 'ladies' is old-fashioned, Mr. Smith. I like to use 'womyn,' spelled W-O-M-Y-N, so I don't have to include the word 'man.'" I smile, and a few of the other girls clap. Mr. Smith moves to call the front office. "There won't be anyone there to answer," I say, and walk out.

When we start down the hall the noises get louder and louder. I see girls hugging each other and calling out as they walk. I see teachers smiling and hugging one another. Ms. Sanchez is holding the door for all of us on the way out.

When we get outside, Leidy is standing with about twenty-five people from all over the neighborhood. They are holding signs with different sayings and drawings.

BUT STILL, LIKE DUST I'LL RISE.
—MAYA ANGELOU
BLACK GIRLS ARE MAGIC
women are VALUABLE & POWERFUL
RESPECT FOR ALL

Leidy is holding a sign that says: *I support my black, brown, trans, immigrant, Muslim, Indigenous SISTERS.* And then I start to see some of the male teachers—some who look like they're just getting word about what we're doing, and some who seem to have already known, with signs that say *#I'mWithHer,* and *#SayHerName,* and *Ally for Life.* All of a sudden I hear music, and I see that all the women of the school jazz band are walking outside playing their instruments, and the basketball team is walking out in their jackets, calling plays to each other the whole time.

It feels like a big performance project, so I start to say some of my poems out loud—the ones I have memorized. I am standing on the corner of 182nd and Audubon with all the women of the school, and we are raging and rallying and celebrating together. The whole crowd feels electric and energized.

I run to Jasmine as soon as I see her walking out.

"We did this," I scream, and hug her. "We did this," I say again, and I can feel the lights from the camera at our backs.

"Excuse me, ladies, we understand you're the two behind this movement," the camera operator says.

"We prefer *womyn*. W-O-M-Y-N. And yes, it's us."

37
JASMINE

Dad told me once that most people don't change because they *want* to, but because they *have* to. "People start living healthier lives after a health scare. Laws change because the people demand it and add pressure to our leaders. Most times the things that change happen after a lot of pain or strife." This is what I am thinking about as I listen to Principal Hayes make the morning announcements. Just when we think he is finished, he says, "And I'd like to end by apologizing to the entire student body and specifically to Ms. Lucas, Chelsea Spencer, and Jasmine Gray. After much consideration and after a lot of soul searching and reevaluating our protocols with our staff and key members from our Parent-Teacher Association, I have decided to reinstate the women's rights club and the Write Like a Girl blog, effective next fall." I don't even know what happens next, because the class starts screaming and clapping. Isaac just keeps repeating "wow" over and over.

Before I can even let it sink in, Chelsea is at the door waving me outside. My teacher nods and lets me step out into the hallway. As soon as I close the door, Chelsea swallows me in a hug, squeezing me tight and rocking from side to side.

"Chelsea. We did it."

"We did. We did," Chelsea repeats over and over, like a favorite song.

All day long school doesn't seem like school because people keep stopping us and saying "congratulations," and "you two should run for president of the United States," and all kinds of things that let us know that our message got out, that our peers are with us.

After school, Chelsea, Isaac, and Nadine come over. On our way, walking from the subway, I notice a restaurant that's just opened. The Coming Soon sign has been up so long, we got to thinking maybe it would never be open. But here it is. Something is always coming and going in this city. There is always something being born, something dying. We walk under scaffolding while our city is under repair—always. Maybe we are all like that, always a work in progress, always complete and lacking at the same time.

Isaac holds my hand; our fingers find home in each other. We turn onto my block, walk up the steps, and sit on the stoop.

May's sun shines a gentle warmth, and we sit and people watch, saying hello occasionally to neighbors passing by. The four of us are quiet, just sitting and watching. The wind chimes mingle and talk with one another every time the wind blows. Finally, Chelsea says, "Why is everybody so quiet?"

Nadine laughs. "I knew you'd be the first to talk."

We all laugh at this, and I remember those days when we used to play the silent game. "Who can be quiet the longest?" one of us would call out.

Chelsea never won. Not once. She has always been full of words, always one to speak them. "But for real, why is everyone so quiet?" she asks. She leans back on the edge of the step.

"I'm fine," Isaac says. "I'm just thinking about what's next."

Nadine turns around. "Next? We won. It's over."

Chelsea says, "It's not over—"

I finish her sentence. "We're just beginning."

ACKNOWLEDGMENTS

What luck to be in this world with so many brilliant & beautiful people who have helped me to rise up.

Thank you to these collective families: Hagan, Dawson, Bazaz, Sferra & Flores for all the ways you have nurtured me—especially my parents: Gianina & Pat Hagan, who embraced my feminist ways from early on. Thank you to this community of people: Aracelis Girmay, Lisa Ascalon, Marina Hope Wilson, Parneshia Jones, Caroline Kennedy, Kelly Norman Ellis, Mitchell L. H. Douglas, Kamilah Aisha Moon, Dana Edell, Rob Linné, Lisa Green, Moriah Carlson, Rajeeyah Finnie-Myers, Nanya-Akuki Goodrich, Andrée Greene, Catrina Ganey, Cheryl Boyce-Taylor, Vincent Toro, Grisel Acosta, Andy Powell, Tanya Gallo, Lindsey Homra-Siroky, Melissa Johnson, Kevin Flores, Danni Quintos, Nykeira Franks, Alondra Uribe, Megan Garriga, Lisa Roby, Kelly Wheatley, Becca Christensen, Kate Carothers Smith, Britt Kulsveen, Brandi Cusick Rimpsey, Leslie Blincoe, Michele Kotler, Berry, Ellie Clark, Alecia Whitaker, Stephanie Dionne Acosta, Jessica Wahlstrom, Will Maloney, Kate Dworkoski Scudese, Pete Scudese & Cindy Uh for all the ways you have held & propelled me.

Thank you to Renée Watson—what a supreme honor to work & vision & build & create with you.

& to Sarah Shumway Liu for your stunning editorial

eye—I am so grateful. & to Bloomsbury for the care & love you've given to us.

& especially & always for David Flores—walking through this world with you is such blessing & balm.

Thank you to these spaces that honor voices in such profound ways: The Affrilachian Poets, Conjwoman, girlstory, DreamYard, Global Writes, Sawyer House Press, Kentucky Governor's School for the Arts, Northern Manhattan Arts Alliance, VONA/Voices of Our Nations Arts Foundation, Northwestern University Press, The Girl Project & WHEELS: Washington Heights Expeditionary Learning School.

—E. H.

* * *

Sometimes life imitates art. I was not prepared to lose my father during the final revision of *Watch Us Rise*. I am so thankful for the community of friends who prayed for my family, who offered love and concern. I am sure that without you checking on me and being there during that time of loss, I would not have finished this book. Thank you, Allie Jane Bruce, Beth Cho Grosart Little, Brendan Kiely, Catrina Ganey, Chanesa Jackson, David Flores, Dhonielle Clayton, Ellice Lee, Grace Kendall, Ibi Zoboi, Jason Reynolds, Jennifer Baker, Jonena Welch, Käthe Swaback, Kristen Wilkerson, Laura Williams McCaffrey, Lisa Green, Meg Kearney, Moriah Carlson, Namrata Tripathi, Nanya-Auki Goodrich, Olugbemisola Rhuday-Perkovich, Rajeeyah Finnie-Myers, Robin Robinson, Tokumbo Bodunde, Shadra Strickland, Shalanda Sims, and Tracey Baptiste.

To Ellen for being on this journey with me. What a wild adventure we've been on for over a decade now. I will forever cherish the time we had together to create and vision. How grateful I am that you are not only my colleague but my friend.

To Kendolyn Walker for taking such care of the Langston Hughes House and I, Too Arts Collective with me. Thank you for being flexible and understanding as I travel and write. You are irreplaceable.

To Trinity Church Harlem, DreamYard, and Community-Word Project for the spaces you create to make sure young voices are amplified and celebrated.

To early readers of this manuscript: Adedayo Perkovich, Dana Edell, Kori Johnson, and Linda Christensen. Thank you for your feedback and support.

To Angie Manfredi and Dana Edell, thank you for helping to shape our resource list.

And to my agent, Rosemary Stimola, my editor, Sarah Shumway, and my team at Bloomsbury. Thank you for championing my writing. I love doing this work alongside you.

And thank you to my family for encouraging me to soar, always. Mom, Roy and Vonda, Cheryl and Kevin, Trisa, and Dyan, it is a privilege to be loved by you.

—R. W.

RESOURCES FOR YOUNG ACTIVISTS

POETS WHO MAKE US RISE

Aracelis Girmay

Audre Lorde

Bianca Spriggs

Carole Boston Weatherford

Cheryl Boyce-Taylor

Cynthia Dewi Oka

Danni Quintos

Elizabeth Acevedo

Elizabeth Alexander

Eve L. Ewing

Fatimah Asghar

Franny Choi

Gwendolyn Brooks

Honorée Fanonne Jeffers

Jacqueline Woodson

Jamila Woods

Julia Alvarez

June Jordan

Kamilah Aisha Moon

Kelly Norman Ellis

Krista Franklin

Lacresha Berry

Lucille Clifton

Mahogany L. Browne

Margaret Walker

Margarita Engle

Maya Angelou

Mayda del Valle

Morgan Parker

Naomi Shihab Nye

Natalie Diaz

Natasha Trethewey

Nicole Sealey

Nikki Giovanni

Nikki Grimes

Nikky Finney

Parneshia Jones

Patricia Smith

Phillis Wheatley

Rachel Eliza Griffiths

Rachel McKibbens

Rachelle Cruz

Rita Dove

Ruth Forman

Safia Elhillo

Sandra Cisneros

Sonia Sanchez

Staceyann Chin

Suheir Hammad

t'ai freedom ford

Tiana Clark

Yesenia Montilla

BOOKS

Adichie, Chimamanda Ngozi. *We Should All Be Feminists.*
New York: Anchor, 2015.

Darms, Lisa, ed. *The Riot Grrrl Collection.* New York:
The Feminist Press, 2013.

Findlen, Barbara, ed. *Listen Up: Voices from the Next
Feminist Generation.* New York: Seal Press, 2001.

Hernández, Daisy and Bushra Rehman, eds. *Colonize This!:
Young Women of Color on Today's Feminism.* New York: Seal
Press, 2002.

hooks, bell. *Feminism is for Everybody: Passionate Politics.*
Cambridge, MA: South End Press, 2000.

Karnes, Frances A. and Kristen R. Stephens. *Empowered Girls:
A Girl's Guide to Positive Activism, Volunteering,
and Philanthropy.* Waco, TX: Prufrock Press, 2005.

Martin, Courtney and J. Courtney Sullivan, eds. *Click: When
We Knew We Were Feminists.* New York: Seal Press, 2010.

Zeilinger, Julie. *A Little F'd Up: Why Feminism Is Not a Dirty
Word.* New York: Seal Press, 2012.

BLOGS AND SITES THAT EDUCATE
AND EMPOWER

Bitch Media: https://bitchmedia.org

Black Girl Dangerous: http://www.bgdblog.org/

Everyday Feminism: http://everydayfeminism.com/

Feminist.com: http://feminist.com/

Feminist Frequency: http://feministfrequency.com/

Feministe: http://www.feministe.us/blog/

Feministing: http://feministing.com/

Finally, A Feminism 101 Blog:
    https://finallyfeminism101.wordpress.com/

For Harriet: http://www.forharriet.com/

The Freechild Project: https://freechild.org/

Guerrilla Girls: http://www.guerrillagirls.com/

Ms. Magazine Blog: http://msmagazine.com/blog/

FOR AND BY GIRLS AND YOUNG WOMEN

About-Face: http://www.about-face.org/

The FBomb: http://www.womensmediacenter.com/fbomb/

F To The Third Power: https://ftothethirdpower.com/

New Moon Girls: https://newmoongirls.com/

Powered By Girl: http://www.poweredbygirl.org/

Rookie: http://www.rookiemag.com

ORGANIZATIONS THAT OFFER
FREE ACTIVIST PROGRAMS FOR GIRLS

Girls For A Change: http://www.girlsforachange.org/

Girls for Gender Equity, Inc., New York City:
    http://www.ggenyc.org/

Girls Leadership Institute, National: https://girlsleadership.org

Girls Rock Camp Alliance, National:
    http://girlsrockcampalliance.org/

Hardy Girls Healthy Women, Waterville, Maine:
    http://www.hghw.org/

Project Girl, National: http://www.projectgirl.org/

School Girls Unite: http://www.schoolgirlsunite.org

Spark Movement: http://www.sparkmovement.org/

viBe Theater Experience, New York City:
    http://vibetheater.org

Where Is Your Line? Campaign: http://whereisyourline.org/

RESOURCES FOR BODY POSITIVITY

Jes Baker: http://www.themilitantbaker.com/p/resources
    .html

Virgie Tovar's TEDx Talk, Lose Hate Not Weight:
    https://www.youtube.com/watch?v=hZnsamRfxtY

Saucyé West's #FatAndFree Campaign: https://www.ravishly
    .com/interview-saucye-west-fatandfree-campaign

READ MORE FROM AND ABOUT
THE WOMEN QUOTED IN THIS BOOK

p. 30 "Poetry is not only dream and vision": Audre Lorde,
    "Poetry Is Not a Luxury," *Sister Outsider: Essays and Speeches*
    (Freedom, CA: Crossing Press, 1984).

p. 70 "When I saw those toenails": Rebecca Skloot, *The
    Immortal Life of Henrietta Lacks* (New York: Crown
    Publishing Group, 2010).

p. 167–168 "To what extent do we self-construct, do we self-
    invent?": "A One-Woman Global Village," TED, https://
    www.ted.com/talks/sarah_jones_as_a_one_woman
    _global_village.

p. 170 "I don't believe anything in me": Natalie Diaz, interviewed by Leslie Contreras Schwartz in the *Kenyon Review* blog, https://www.kenyonreview.org/2017/02/an-interview-with-natalie-diaz/.

p. 172 "Our ideas and understanding of the world": Reena Saini Kallat, interviewed by Farah Siddiqui for Contemporary Artists Series: A Conversation with Reena Saini Kallat, Culture Trip, https://theculturetrip.com/asia/india/articles/contemporary-artists-series-a-conversation-with-reena-saini-kallat/.

p. 193 "Your silence will not protect you": Audre Lorde, *The Cancer Journals* (San Francisco: Aunt Lute Books, 1980).

p. 193 "I've put up with too much, too long": Sandra Cisneros, *Woman Hollering Creek: And Other Stories* (New York: Vintage, 1992).

p. 194 "Feet, what do I need you for when I have wings to fly?": Frida Kahlo, *The Diary of Frida Kahlo: An Intimate Self-Portrait*, Carlos Fuentes, ed. (Harry N. Abrams Inc., New York, 2005).

p. 194 "The kind of beauty I want most": Ruby Dee, quoted in *Entertainment Weekly*, https://ew.com/article/2014/06/12/ruby-dee-dies/.

p. 194 "In a time of destruction": Maxine Hong Kingston, *The Fifth Book of Peace* (New York: Knopf, 2003).

p. 273 "hopscotch in a polka dot dress" and "red revolution love songs": Ruth Forman, "Poetry Should Ride the Bus," *We Are the Young Magicians* (Boston: Beacon Press, 1993).

p. 344 "But still": Maya Angelou, "Still I Rise," *And Still I Rise: A Book of Poems* (New York: Random House, 1978).

Have you read *Piecing Me Together* by Renée Watson?

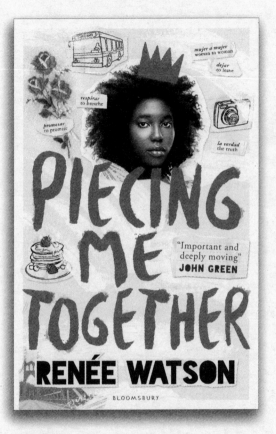

A 2018 Newbery Honor Book and winner of the Coretta Scott King Author Award

'Important and deeply moving' **JOHN GREEN**

'Timely and timeless' **JACQUELINE WOODSON**